I0822452

K.J.HERITAGE

THE LADY IN THE GLASS

VOLUME ONE:
12 TALES OF DEATH & DYING

Copyright © K.J.Heritage 2023
The Lady In The Glass

Published 2023 by *Sygasm Publishing*
All rights reserved.

Cover design: *K.J.Heritage*

No parts of this publication may be reproduced, stored in retrieval systems, beamed via black hole to other dimensions, copied in any form or by any means, electronic, mechanical, photocopying, recording or otherwise transmitted without written permission from the publisher except for the use of brief quotations in a book review. You must not circulate this book in any format.

Travelling back in time to publish this book before its official publication date is strictly prohibited.

All characters in this publication are fictitious and any resemblance to persons, living, dead, undead, existing in parallel dimensions or those having reached a higher plane to exist as intelligent corporeal gases, smells or colours, is purely coincidental.

Sygasm Publishing
http://sygasm.com

ISBN: 978-1-915927-09-5

CONTENTS:

PROLOGUE:

THE LADY IN THE GLASS

THE RIVER sings, babblin' and gurglin' around the smashed concrete, turnin' the blackash into enchantin' shapes.

I dunno why I luv this place. The twisted metal and the black, smelly mud where no grass grows, but where dragonflies hum and strum.

The Father forbade me from comin' here, but he saw the evils everywhere. He's gone now and so I can returns whenever I wants, to sit upon my favourite seat—a black rock *Melted By The Great Lights*, or so the Father tolded it to me.

I luv to rub my hands over it. Strokin' and feelin' it.

Sometimes, the many storms bring rusted fings from the river, or melted glass, or burned bony heads that stare at me from the waters. Best of all... are the secret treasures. Strange fings. Shiny, wonderful, strange fings.

The Father told me they belonged to the *Ainshunts,* who were wicked and full of evils—and that I must put 'em back into the mud. But I said *no* to him. *They're mine!* I told him. *I cherish 'em!*

At night, high on the hill in my little shack, where the Mother and Son hang on the rusty metal walls, I sometimes spy out of my one window to look down at my special place on the valley floor. The glow is enchantin'—shinin' even when Mistress Moon swallows up the sky. The warm light fills me with feelins of safety and belongin'.

I luv my special place!

The Father can't stop me comin', here. *Not now!* The Sick curled his legs into angry knots and strangled in his throat. I giggled when all his teeth and hair falled out. But soon his gaspin' and sobbin' stopped and he was gone. *Dead and departed.* That was many moons ago. I was glad. I put him into the Blackash and spat on him.

The Father brung me to his shack after I was Reborn, after I found *The Light Of The Jesus.* After he showed me *The Error Of My Ways.* But only when the Father was gone, did it become my proper home. I'm thankful for its roof and walls—they protect me from the storms and winds and the hot sweaty days.

It's different without the Father, but how cans I be lonesome when I have my very, very special friend… *The Lady In The Glass?*

At first, when the waters showed me the Lady, I thought she was a sister of *The Jesus*, for she smiled at me. But when I gave her another looksee, I knew she was also *Devil*, for she comes from the Blackash and was broken.

Her flesh is white, stuck inside twisted glass that bends and curls—one arm reachin' out to me, the other at her side, her fingers clenched into an angry fist. Thick, curly-curly hair circles her face—trapped by the glass like the halo of light around *The Jesus.*

Beautiful and red.

Nothin' like my poor, sore-covered head. Her chin is dented, noble—touched by *The Jesus.* The mark of his finger…

But her eyes?

They are two horrible holes. Sometimes I sees *Devil* in 'em, givin' me a looksee. Watchin' me.

I don't like *Devil.*

I often feeled *Devil* in the Father's sweaty hands. In all his touchin' and squeezin' and… the other stuff he did to me—even tho he promised his luv came from *The Jesus.*

But when I got bigger. Big enough to tell him *never, ever again!* The Father became angry, makin' me pray for the sins of selfishness and disobedience. He beat me day and night, so he did.

But the Father was evil.

Devil was in him. I told him that before he died. I told him many times and laffed at his sobbin'.

But now I have *The Lady In The Glass.* My only friend.

And, on special days, she calls to me. Wantin' me to come listen to her words. She speaks to me, tellin' me stories, of dark, doomy worlds, of peoples and places, and of shadows where horrors lurk. Stories that play out in front of me.

For when she whispers, I see fings. Twistin, turnin fings.

Her tales are always full of sufferin'. But like the Father, she is good and bad, cruel and kind—and sometimes I am rewarded with a story of pure joy.

The Lady is *Devil*, but *The Jesus* has touched her. *Devil* and *The Jesus* fight for her words, so they do.

She called to me again today. Softly and sweet. She has more stories to tell!

And, crawlin' off my metal bed, I crept down to the river. To my special place. To sit on my seat of black, shiny stone.

I knew *The Jesus* was worried for me, but I dint look at him. All I cares about are the stories. The Lady's stories and tales. Wonderin' what she will show me.

Hark! Her lips begins to dance! Serpents that whisper and hiss. Words that spin and curl, twistin' and swirlin' and I can do nothin' but watch, watch, watch…

ONE:

WHITE NIGHT

ALONE, LOST and abandoned, Anisha stood on the white plain that straddled the planetary equator and sighed.

Wrapped in the shiny black of SurvivalSkin™, she cut a stark, aberrant figure—a line of precisely spaced footsteps diminishing to the horizon behind her. Harsh sunlight splattered against the unremitting snow like an insult.

Anisha wanted to scream at the unfairness of it all. Instead, she stood and shivered, silently spitting the odd obscenity into her ice-encrusted helmet.

The scenery was featureless, the planet a cold, eternally lit ball of snow hanging in the empty blackness of space. Anisha hated every inch of this place. And in her heart of hearts, she feared her destiny was to tread every one of those inches, over and over again until this planet fell into doom.

"We must continue, Anisha. Safety awaits!" SurvivalSkin™ said to her. The years had done nothing to dull its inane, yet insistent optimism. "When we find a Haven, you may wish to relax your c-cares away," it stuttered, before listing a whole range of products and services whose application were nothing more than vague memory.

Anisha's life had been one fuck-up after another.

Why do I attract so much bad luck?

She knew the answer.

I'm a loser.

There was no other rational explanation, and her present predicament was the extra fecal icing on the cake of shit she'd been forced to eat all her life.

Sure, she'd fought back. She'd taken her fill of all those positive thinking, life-affirming courses, was in touch with her 'inner child', had been sensory readjusted, re-birthed, and had even changed her name and physical appearance.

All to no avail.

Some people were just born unlucky. Pointless trying to fight it.

Only someone truly unfortunate could have ended up in this predicament—the lone survivor of the normally reliable Econ^SHIP^

that had destroyed itself and everyone on board high in orbit around this goddamn frozen world.

How many years ago was that?

Anisha had no real idea. That was the curse of this place, of this planet. Time stood still here. She was trapped inside an ever-present whiteness—an eternal winter's day from which there was no escape.

Her SurvivalSkin™ was a basic model—hence the constant advertising. The annoying walking billboard was the only thing that stood between her and a quick, freezing death.

It was also malfunctioning, keeping her on the edge of an unending chill that filled her bones and joints. Warmth was a long-forgotten thing, and so was a full stomach. Nutrition came in the form of reclaimed calories and proteins infused into a brackish trickle from a tube hooked into her mouth.

Enough to keep her alive, but nothing more.

She had tried to chew it off, but it was made of the same resilient material as the rest of SurvivalSkin™.

Suicide wasn't an option. SurvivalSkin™ made sure of it.

Anisha had a wonderful, dreamy recollection of lying on a beach. Warm sand underneath her, the sound of lapping waves, a gentle cooling spray on her feet and a glorious hot yellow sun. A vacation in a time when people actually had holidays. And she'd been blissfully happy.

How I'd love to return there, to be able to end this walking, frozen, nightmare.

But that was not to be. It was just a dream. A memory chafing at her sensibilities. "Please, let me lie down," she whispered.

"SurvivalSkin™ cannot do that, Anisha. Our sponsors have put vast amounts of energy and work into ensuring your comfort in this survival s-situation."

"Just for a short while."

"You can rest when we find a Shelter."

"Shut up, you walking coffin! I hate you!"

"Please remain positive. I am SurvivalSkin™—a superior AmalgamatedSpace^TRADE product designed for exactly this set of conditions. SurvivalSkin™ knows what must be done to ensure your survival. You may be disorientated by your ordeal. Delirious even. The sooner we find corporate hospitality, the better."

"But I'm so tired. I just need to rest."

"You *are* resting," the suit insisted. "You are supported by SurvivalSkin™'s body-hugging exoskeleton incorporating a wide range of muscle enhancing and massaging technologies, keeping you fit, healthy and ready for anything the modern survival s-situation might throw at you. Shelter awaits!"

Anisha knew SurvivalSkin™ wouldn't let her lie down—the request was rote, a masochistic mantra she'd performed thousands of times whenever the skin stopped to adjust its bearings. It was on a damn mission to rescue her, looking for a MacHaven^INC.^, or a ColaHut™ or one of the other automated Coffee or Subs or Chicken Nugget-themed survival pods launched when a ship was in danger.

The trouble was that the Econ^SHIP^ hadn't successfully launched any. When it had tried, the procedure triggered an explosion that destroyed the already crippled carrier.

Anisha hadn't been in her pod when the disaster happened. She was the token human chosen at random and raised from Hyposleep to spend a lonely six months monitoring the fully automatic systems.

She hadn't complained. Anisha was used to this kind of thing.

In another lifetime, she could've had a lucrative career as a 'Casino Cooler'—the pathetic sap employed to prowl the gambling floor—a walking, talking breath of bad fortune.

If only I could have died with everyone else…

The ship exploded, breaking apart in high orbit. The skin saved her, rushing her out of the smashed ship into cold, lonely space where she passed out from pure terror. She'd awoken in this God-forsaken place.

Since then, she'd gone through all the stages. Elation, hope, anger, suicidal depression and finally calm, if not annoyed, acceptance. Her life had become an unremitting vista of black and white. Even her dreams were etched with these two stark hues.

Colours were long forgotten things.

"What if you're more damaged than you realise?" Anisha said.

"That is not possible. My automated Self-Repairo™ system takes care of an extensive range of damage or wear situations. I am f-functioning well within acceptable par—par—parameters."

The stutter was a new development, giving her a sort of dark hope. *If the skin breaks down, I can maybe find peace from this mess of a life.* She didn't want to freeze to death alone and lost, but that was all she had left to live for.

"Listen, you stupid machine, they are no Havens. I saw them all destroyed in the disaster."

"Finding a Haven and a hot, nutritious meal, balanced to your body's unique dietary, emotional and marketing requirements, is my over-riding directive, Anisha. Soon, you will eat in the highest of luxury at any one of our kind sponsor's survival shacks. From your arrival to rescue, all your buys, treatments and entertainments will be available at special discount prices. Remember… your credit goes further with SurvivalSkin™."

Credits were the last thing she cared about. "So just where are all these survival huts?"

"The net is temporarily down, Anisha. But do not worry, once contact is again established, SurvivalSkin™ will whisk you to cor-cor-corporate paradise."

"But there is no net—don't you realise that? Everything was destroyed in orbit. Your clock has malfunctioned and you're lost. Please… just let me lie down."

"Time is not your concern. Not with SurvivalSkin™. Relax while my fully automated systems ensure your survival is a stress-free and enjoyable experience. My p-power networks are all in the green. You will be safe and happy with SurvivalSkin™."

Anisha groaned. The skin had its own fusion generator. It could practically function forever. "I want to die."

"SurvivalSkin™ will not let you die, Anisha. You are uninjured, but showing signs of delirium."

"What if I expire before we find one of your Havens? What

happens then?"

"My directive is to find shelter, Anisha."

"You'll turn me into a working corpse, I know it."

"SurvivalSkin™ is the complete survival package, easy to use and totally self-regulating. SurvivalSkin™ protected you in the vacuum of space, SurvivalSkin™ kept you cool from the heat of atmospheric entry. And SurvivalSkin™ will now take you immediately to one of many survival Havens generously donated by our range of sponsors. You will await rescue in the height of comfort."

Anisha had had this conversation thousands of times. She'd tried to vary her responses, but the machine heard only what it wanted to hear. She couldn't blame it. Despite its redundancy-protected systems, it wasn't designed for this situation.

She drew breath to speak again, a range of extreme expletives designed to fuck with the skin's inbuilt nanny system, when she saw something glint against the perfect line of the horizon.

"What is that?"

If the suit hadn't been carrying her, she would've staggered backwards in shock. She raised her arm and pointed.

"*What is what?* I am detecting no Haven in that direction, Anisha."

"I saw something… there it is again!"

"I am sensing a significant rise in your heartbeat and blood pressure. Brain activity is also—"

"Zoom in!"

"But there is nothing there, Anisha. Please calm down."

"Just indulge me, okay? Please."

"Yes, Anisha. Your visor is kindly provided by FastGlass^INC^ incorporating the latest in nano-focus technology. *Your world… but closer and in Hyper-Def-Real.*"

The glass in the visor changed subtly and the horizon zoomed into tight focus.

Shaking, Anisha stared at a tall, blackened spire jutting out of the ice. The thing was obviously unnatural. Alien.

She had no idea what it might be—and for the first time since she'd found herself marooned on this goddamn death-world, she experienced a surge of hope.

"You've got to take me there. You just have to!"

"I cannot take you there, Anisha," the suit replied in its depressing 'know-it-all' tone. "That is no Haven. Where is its corporate ident?"

"Listen for once, will you? We've been walking this planet for years trying to find something that doesn't exist. You don't realise that because your time sensors are all shot to pieces. The planet is empty. This is the only thing we have ever found here. We have to investigate. We just have to!"

"We can investigate after we have found shelter, Anisha."

"Listen to me!" Anisha tried to jump up and down but the skin held her perfectly still. "Just listen to me and for once do what you're goddamn told!"

"Cussing will not be tolerated, Anisha. Not in any form. You have been charged five credits for the use of Potty-Mouth, bringing your present Potty-Mouth balance to a debit of twenty-seven-thousand, four-hundred and thirty-five credits. Remember—SurvivalSkin™ is here to help you. If this help is not respected, SurvivalSkin™ has the power to sedate you."

"No, no—don't do that. Not now! I apologise, okay? I'm sorry. Very sorry."

A long pause, no doubt designed to make Anisha think again about her use of 'expletives'.

If I ever get the chance, I'll take great pleasure in burning this stupid fucking machine alive and laugh while it pleaded. But I have far more important concerns.

"Okay, Anisha. But remember, cussing can only be tolerated in the most extreme of pain situations."

Anisha took a deep breath, consciously trying to reduce her heartbeat that thumped in her ears. "I have something very important to tell you. I'm invoking a Special Request, okay?"

A special request was the only way Anisha could force the skin to shut up and listen. Not that it ever did. But if ever she needed the thing to stop what it was doing and concentrate on her words it was now.

"SurvivalSkin™ is more than happy to converse with you on a wide range of services and products," the suit replied.

"Your backpack thruster is no longer functioning, correct?"

"That is correct. The Fly-In-Style™ Additional—*All your emergency flying needs covered in our easily worn deliverable' –*was unfortunately jettisoned after its energy reserves became depleted under article 6098124.0235.09.03 of agreement—"

"Yes, yes, yes. I know what happened to the backpack. You don't have to tell me again. But… if it was still operational, you would be conducting your search for a Haven from the air, yes?"

"Yes, Anisha. Under article 6098124.0235.09.03 the Fly-In-Style™ Additional can be jettisoned under the following conditions. One: Fuel reserve depletion. Two: Unexpected environmental—"

"Right. And that thing—that spire—must be at least a hundred metres high. If we climbed to the top, it'd give you a greater range to scan for a Haven. Wouldn't that significantly shorten your search of this area?"

The skin stopped walking. "There is logic in your argument Anisha. My over-riding directive is to find a Haven. We shall go."

Anisha swooned within the skin. Its intractability was the one constant of her existence on this planet. She'd never convinced it to do anything. Ever. Hers was an unheard voice pitted against the unremitting purpose of this damn machine.

For the first time since this nightmare began, she felt the return of hope—a new lust for life that had been bleached out of her by the depressing monotone of this place. Her heart thudded in her chest. She felt dizzy and excited.

"Is everything all right, Anisha?" the skin asked. "I am becoming concerned for your well-being."

"I feel good, Skin. I feel very good," she answered though trembling lips.

"I am detecting heightened levels of adrenaline in your bloodstream. You need to rest, Anisha."

"No!"

"My systems are showing many accelerated readings. Sleep will be beneficial. I will awake you shortly."

"Don't you dare, not now!" Anisha could feel her sensibilities blurring as the skin sent her into unconsciousness. "You bastard," she whispered, slipping away.

Anisha awoke at what passed for sunset on this planet. Night was a fleeting moment between the setting and rising of twin suns. The present sun hung low on the horizon. The enormous black spire stood before her, limned by light shining almost horizontally across the plain. Anisha blinked.

They were here…

The jaggedly etched shape stuck upwards out of the snow, its vitreous surface pocked and almost evil-looking. This was no work of nature. It was a beautiful, yet disturbing object crafted by some form of intelligence—that much she was sure of.

"What is it?" she gasped into the icy cold of her mask.

"It is something long old and dead," SurvivalSkin™ said dispassionately.

"But it's a ship… it must be!"

"But no Haven, Anisha."

"Forget the Havens! Don't you understand? There aren't any, you stupid machine. They were all destroyed in orbit."

"That cannot be true, Anisha. The Havens must exist otherwise I would not be programmed to find them."

"Don't you get it? Can't you understand what we have found?"

"It is an interesting anomaly. That is all."

"An anomaly?"

"It is detectable on visual wavelengths only."

"Then it must have a power source of some kind, maybe a shield."

SurvivalSkin™ will investigate.

A short pause.

"We have to go Anisha. SurvivalSkin™ is computing a small but significant radioactive signature. We must move away."

"No! I'm begging you. This is our—my—only chance to get

out of this. You've failed. There are no Havens, no rescue!"

"SurvivalSkin™ will not fail," said the skin, moving her away.

"No!"

"Do not despair, Anisha. Shelter awaits!"

Shrinking inside the skin, Anisha sobbed.

"Please remain positive. I am SurvivalSkin™—a superior AmalgamatedSpace^{TRADE} product designed for exactly this set of conditions. SurvivalSkin™ knows what must be done to ensure your survival. You may be disorientated by your ordeal, delirious even. The sooner we find corporate hospitality, the better."

"Shut up!"

"We must c-c-c-continue Anisha, safety awaits! When we find a Haven, you may wish to relax your c-c-c-cares away,"

They padded into the sudden dusk and SurvivalSkin™ flipped the visor to rear view. Anisha stared at the peculiar spire standing between the nearly simultaneous sinking and rising of the two suns.

As she watched, wracked with loss, the object caught the light that came from low on the twin horizons and reflected it back twice as bright.

A blaze of rainbow colours flashed across the surrounding bleakness. Light shone all around the tower. Glinting. Picked into silvery beams by mist that hung in the air. Twin, eerie shadows caressed the compacted snow—contrasting against the light that glittered all around.

It was the most fantastic display Anisha had ever seen. She had forgotten what colour was. The shadows began to shorten as the two suns moved away from each other, quickly carried by their own opposite motion.

The moment passed, and the spire returned to black against the ever-present white.

She watched the spire recede for as long as she could and all too soon, it disappeared from view.

It was many hours before Anisha fell again into sleep. But this time and forever, all her dreams were etched in colour.

TWO:

QUICK-KILL JANE

1

I SQUEEZE the laser and, with a crackle and hiss, a beam of fiery light slams into the shoulder of the escaping mark.

I let him run just for the fun of it, tracking him as he criss-crosses the dusty alleyway between the old buildings of the abandoned spaceport, followed by pools of harsh white light courtesy of my few remaining drones.

With the power outages this far out of town, the area is as dark as a tomb—an excellent location for villains of all types to hang out.

The mark is Rollo Barla, a low-life high-tek data-cracker. A rotund ball of quivering fat in his late fifties. By the look of him, he'd drop dead from a heart attack if I let him run any further—red-faced and sweating with the effort of trying to stay alive. But killing is my profession… and I love my job. The beam spins Rollo around, slamming him face down into the dust. He struggles onto his back, screaming in pain. But we both know it's over for him.

I take off my hat and let my long auburn hair spill. Classy but nuthin more than a wig. Quick-Kill Jane ain't the type to leave her DNA lying around. A swift touch up of crimson lipstick and I'm ready for Rollo's big moment.

Things need to go quick this evening. Later on, I'm all set to go meet my latest squeeze, a cute little cityblok-chick called Angie. We've been going at it for a few weeks. A business agreement. After tonight, she says, I don't need to pay no more. She wants us to be legit—when I settle her rent and her bills, she's all mine. No other johns.

Nice.

Rollo kicks at the drones, pushing his immense bulk up onto his feet with his one useful arm. A quick glance over his shoulder and I wave the laser at him, smiling. Other killers become bored but I always get a thrill from seeing desperation shining in doomed eyes. The realisation that *time has been called.*

He runs again, holding his injured shoulder, his other arm

useless—flapping around like a wet stocking on a windy tenement washing line. The fat of his belly also flaps and I can't help a sneer of disgust. But Rollo is typical of the losers trapped on this backwater planet. The low-grav allows them to carry a lot more weight. And there ain't much else to do here other than eat, screw and defecate. And, by the look of him, Rollo had no interest in sticking his dick where it wasn't wanted, unless it was in someone else's pie.

I'm not so much an inventor as an *enhancer*. The laser was originally a mining tool, industrial, and too heavy for me to handle—even in this low grav. I'm petite, standing just over five foot—not that I'm any less dangerous than a man twice my size—*or any man.* A few modifications here and there, shrinking the laser's size and augmenting the different functions and—using a sturdy but discreet exoskeleton worn under my clothing—I'm a walking one-woman laser turret.

A quick flick on the control butt to alter the beam and I fire again. The widened heat-ray setting of my own design hits Rollo in the legs. His stretch-corduroy trousers catch alight and he screams but carries on running.

I walk forward, watching him stumble, flames licking towards his face. He finally falls to the dusty alley floor, desperately rolling around, extinguishing the fire only to lie motionless and smouldering in defeat.

The drones converge on him, their machine guns cocked and ready, focussing lights onto his face.

"Rollo Barla," I say, all business-like standing over him, toying with my red hair and pursing my ruby-red lips.

It's always nice to let the mark know it's a woman who is gonna do them in. A bit of icing on the cake.

"Why'd you run off like a frightened cat?" I ask. "You know Quick-Kill Jane ain't never failed to deliver. You somehow think you could beat my hundred percent record?"

"Don't do it," Rollo splutters from a red and sweaty face. "I got kids and family. I was only looking out for them. I can pay you double."

Angie is waiting for me and I don't wanna be late. I already wasted time letting this mark think he had a chance of getting away. "You've been a naughty boy," I say, the words rolling easily off my tongue. "Judging by the amount of money on your head, you must've pissed off some very bad people."

"I ain't done nuthin," he blurts. "I've kept my head down, kept schtum like always. This ain't fair."

"I can tell you all about unfairness," I reply. "Don't pretend you don't beat your wife in front of your kids every night. You're a bully, Rollo. A nasty piece of scum. If anything, I'm doing your family a favour." I alter the setting of my gun, and stand back.

"Bitch!" he spits from a screwed-up face. A sudden, sharp pain behind my eyes makes me blink for a second. I raise the laser and let him have it.

Rollo explodes in a conflagration of blue flame. The laser's beam intensifies and engulfs him. Fat and skin boils, catches fire and is turned to quick ash. The ash glows white and becomes a molten slurry into which his bones crumble and disappear, leaving only a charred stain in the red dust of the alley. No body, no DNA… just ash fused into glass. When you hire Quick-Kill Jane, you get the full service.

I replace the laser in its holder—the heatsink warm against my thigh. The sensation of a job well done.

I'm a professional and take pride in my work. Sure, being a dame used to put some clients off but they soon learned that gender ain't no bar to the art of murder. More than anything, I've a rep for know-how and getting the job done. That matters in this town. As for Rollo? He's gone to wherever people go to when I off them.

Just another day and another mark.

I straighten my hat and command the drones to return to the Loft using my enhanced cerebral wafer—a top of the range illicit job with all the latest tek. Brain augmentation ain't new. I was dubious about the procedure—and the thing cost me plenty of hard-earned bucks—but the result? Hey, I'm now a walking library with a perfect memory. I can also patch into my augmented phone or access the net. Cool. Sure, the wafer's illegal but Quick-Kill Jane ain't the most law-abiding of gals.

I flick open my phone and patch through to my contact. A guy called Tewis who set up tonight's little date with Rollo, although I doubt Tewis is his real name—but who am I to quibble about using a pseudonym? "Hello Tewis."

"Is it done?"

"Yeah, no problems. I'm expecting your transfer asap."

"Did Rollo say anything… before he died?"

I snorted. "Just the same old regular bleating of a john who realises his time is finally up."

"Tell me exactly what he said."

I shrug. "Everything is recorded by drone. Minus my little part in the show, of course. I ain't stupid. I'll patch the vids over to you now."

"Yes you will, just as it states in the contract. But I also want you to tell me."

This ain't the normal procedure for a post-kill chat, yet I ain't too bothered. So what if Tewis is a little uptight?

"Sure," I reply, "I'll even mimic his damn whine for you. He said, *Don't kill me. I got kids and family. I can pay you double.* That was it. Apart from calling me a bitch."

"Rollo didn't attempt any other deal? Offer you anything?"

"Like I said—take a look at the vids. And if you want, I'll send you a copy from my own personal wafer. But that'll cost you more."

"A wafer?"

"Yeah. Top of the range and highly illegal. Is that a problem?"

Tewis is quiet for a few seconds and I've wasted enough time on this conversation already. "You gonna make the payment, yes or no?" I smile at the edge of threat in my voice. Everyone understands you pay assassins their dues, anything else would be stupid.

A few clicks and whirs. "Payment made." The connection ends.

The conversation was odd but in my profession, you get to

deal with odd every other day.

I make my way to my transport—to all intents and purposes a '69 Dodge Charger ...*custom*. A five-hundred-year old design but she still makes heads turn. She's electric, not that pollution is a problem on the backwater planet of Plenty—the most unfortunately-named world there ever was. The oil reserves didn't pan out as they were expected to, otherwise this baby would roar like a monster. Petrol is a luxury even I can't afford.

I slip inside, start the engine and head for town.

2

THE SPACEPORT lies a good thirty miles from the city. Back in the day, the port was a bustling town of arrivals and take-offs, of trade and barter.

Now? Ships are few and far between.

Since planetary living has become unfashionable, it's mostly empty apart from the low-lives who hang out there. Rollo Barla for one.

I did my homework on the mark. Rollo was a safe-cracker. One of the best. He possessed an advanced cerebral augmentation similar to my own wafer patched into some impressive hack-based software of his own design. An artist, by all accounts. But despite all that extra cerebral power, he was too dumb to take his profits and get off this rock. And, to be fair, the chump was so overweight he would've never survived take-off.

But escaping is my plan. If you wanna do anything in life you gotta think big. Rollo Barla was a small-time criminal and he died a small-time death. That won't happen to me. Not to Quick-Kill Jane. As for my real name—you know what? I never even had one. But growing up on the streets alone, with no family and no one looking out for me, that name just started to follow me around. I was quite the ace with the catapult and then with a gun. But Quick-Kill Jane didn't come from my skill with all types of weapon but from how effectively I used them. In the end, I took the name as my own. Why not? It instilled fear and respect. And despite Angie, or any of the other girls, I'm a one-woman operation. And once my pot of bucks hits a certain size, I'm taking the first available rocket out of here. It'll be goodbye Plenty and hello Good Times.

I push my foot down hard on the pedal and the Dodge picks up speed. No auto-drive for me. I like to be in charge of my own destiny. Besides, auto-drive puts you on the system. The cops may turn a blind eye but you never know when that might change. When I drive anywhere, I drive anonymously.

Amsterdam City is ahead, silhouetted against the dark night sky and lit up like an electric red thistle. The lower gravity means that it boasts some of the tallest high-rises and skyscrapers in this forgotten solar system. But the money has long-gone, leaving decades ago to invest itself in the 'next big thing'—which happened to be space habitats.

Amsterdam is Plenty's first and only city, its buildings mimicking the red of the surrounding landscape. The conurbation was once considered a marvel. But now? It's nothin more than a crumbling prison, home to thirty or so million people wishing they were someplace else. No towns, no resorts… *nuthin*. Just a few outlying industrial farms and the spaceport. The locals—who I do not count myself a member of—call it the *Forgotten City*. And I can't wait to put it out of my memory.

I enter via the ring road, taking the turnoff that brings me close to Angie's apartment. At this time of night there's little traffic.

I park outside, amongst the other transports. I open the boot, take out the tarp and drape it over the Charger. It serves a double purpose—keeping out the red dust and hiding it from prying eyes.

Sure, a Dodge is gonna generate attention, which, considering my occupation, is counter-productive. But hey, what's life if you can't indulge yourself once in a while?

Talking of indulgences, I cast my eyes up to Angie's windows. The lights are off and alarm bells start ringing. She should be waiting for me, all dolled up and a meal prepared. A celebration. Tonight, of all nights, she'd be there with the lights on. And she ain't the type to throw a surprise party. Besides, she's like me when it comes to friends… she can't see the point. That's why we get on so well. That, and our disinclination towards men.

The foyer is an oasis of light on the dark street. Just inside I spot Joe, the robo-doorman. He's seen better days. His once colourful costume is faded, as is his absurd top hat. I push open the doors and head for the elevator.

The metallic face inclines towards me. The eyes sunken and slightly sad. "Are you here to see Miss Angie?" he asks in servile bass tones.

I see the gun in his hand long before he can raise it against me.

I snap out my laser and play the beam over his face which collapses in on itself. The cooked bio-circuitry smells like a pie in the oven. Which reminds me… I'm hungry. Whoever's upstairs waiting for me hoped Joe would to do their work for them.

Mistake.

I flick the laser's beam over the rest of Joe's twitching artificial body. He collapses into nuthin more than a few whirring, metal cogs and smoking servitor modules. I never did like the condescending creep. Good riddance. If I had my way, I'd melt all these robotic half-breeds to glass and laugh while I did it.

My next action is easy. I get in the elevator and arrive on Angie's floor a few seconds later. I step out, make my way to her apartment and knock. I shout, "Honey, I'm home!" and sidestep a hail of bullets that turn the door into plastic shreds.

I power up the laser again and play it at head-height across the wall. It punches through the extruded pseudo-cement like, well, like a high-powered industrial laser through a cheaply-manufactured living module. I know Angie is in there, I'm just hoping she's sitting down.

I flash the laser across the wall a second time and the whole thing collapses. I look into the smoking ruins of the room and it's as I guessed. Angie is tied up in a chair, her hair singed from where the laser caught it. Good girl, she'll survive. Shame about her apartment. I guess I won't be eating anytime soon.

For my attacker, it's another story. He lies on the floor, his head a burnt mess.

Nice.

I make eye-contact with Angie. *Anymore goons?*

She shakes her head and, as I push through the rubble, Angie's binds suddenly fall away and she fires a pistol at me.

I take the shots in my midriff, twisting away from the bullets, swinging the barrel of the laser at her head. Metal meets flesh with a clunk and she falls forward, her neck broken. The exo is a useful tool but a little heavy-handed.

Damn, and I thought me and Angie were a match made in heaven.

I grab the pistol from Angie's still twitching fingers and fling it aside.

Under my clothing is pretty much the most expensive and lightest armour a gal can buy, incorporating a one-molecule thick nano-mesh. At the close-range I was shot, I'm still gonna bruise. But I'm alive and, in my game, that's all that counts.

I go over to the dead guy and rifle through his pockets. A hired goon. And there's the first mistake. The whole thing with Robo Joe and this now dead wannabe wise-guy is one fatal misstep. If you want rid of an assassin, you employ another assassin, not someone like this joker. There may be honour amongst thieves but assassins will take anyone out for the right amount of cash.

Tewis is behind this. He must be. Something to do with Rollo Barla. This whole ambush stinks of last-minute thinking, which means my kill didn't go to plan. I don't get it—I took out Rollo with no fuss. A straightforward job. Something must've gone wrong… but what? I'm gonna go find Tewis and ask him, before I make him eat his own giblets that is.

I take one final look at Angie. She was a real honey. My guess is that she was offered more money than she was able to say no to. Angie took her chance to get out of this hole but the dice didn't roll her way. Shame. Yet she tried—and I respect that. A real stand up gal. I'll miss her… and her cooking.

I walk back onto the landing to be met by worried faces poking out from the other rooms on this floor. Losers, the lot of them. Trapped in a decaying tenement on a dead-end planet with no exit plan.

"Nothing to see here," I say. "And remember that, because if any one of you blabs, I'll be coming back. You understand?"

The doors close with a chorus of bangs and clicking locks and bolts. Like I said… *losers.*

I exit via the stairs, jumping over the bannister and dropping down the twelve or so floors to the ground. The exo absorbs the shock. The artificial outer-skeleton is not just a powered cage giving me the strength of many, it's also a means of transportation and escape. I'll never match a man for bulk or weight but why should I need to when my brain is by far the bigger muscle? And besides, wearing my exo, I could pull them all apart and dance on the pieces.

A few seconds later, I'm running through the back door and into the side-streets.

I can't return to the Loft—my rooms on the top floor of the Heinrich Hotel—a modest apartment where I eat, sleep and tinker with stuff. If Tewis knew about Angie, it's a good bet he knows where I live.

As to how? I'm gonna have to pump Tewis for that information. But first… I'll need back-up.

I patch a signal from my wafer into the phone and silently call my drones. I increase the power to my exo and jump onto a low roofed building, and then hop to the next, making my exit via rooftop, putting quick distance between myself and Angie's destroyed apartment.

This is no blind run. I may be Quick-Kill Jane, I may drive a Dodge Charger and spend a little bit too much on the show of it all but that doesn't mean I don't plan for contingencies. Sure, I love my Dodge and all my gadgets but should I ever need to, I can disappear in a puff of smoke—or so it would seem to anyone who came looking.

I keep to the shadows using alleyways and shaded rooftops, heading for a bolthole. I have various hideouts around town and tonight is all about 'Just in case'.

I need to lie low and think this through… before I go after Tewis. He must know that if he doesn't get me, I'll get him. That's gonna make him desperate and desperate guys make mistakes.

The almost silent whir of rotors—a sound that only I would recognise—and my flying helpers arrive. All three of them. But something is wrong. The drones are lit up like Christmas trees and, as they close in on me, I hear the click and snap of their machine guns, readying themselves for firing.

I dive behind a roof dumpster, almost deafened by the cacophony of bullets slamming into its metal sides.

I can't afford to be angry but I'm certainly irked. These are my machines.

No one touches my stuff and gets away with it!

To be honest, since I created the laser, I've used the drones as threat only. A way to round up a mark who wouldn't give in to the inevitable. Luckily, they work on the principle of point and shoot. There's nuthin intuitive about their programming. Whoever is controlling them has not keyed in a stop command.

I wait till the barrage comes to an end, the magazines clicking and whirring as they reload, and jump out of my hiding place.

The laser makes a quick job of their props and they come crashing down.

I have no time to waste. I grab their data-links and throw the remains in the dumpster.

Below me I hear the sound of approaching vehicles. But I refuse to be trapped. I drop down the opposite side of the rooftop into a darkened alley. I run to a nearby drain cover and disappear into the sewers.

A click of my exo's beams and I'm soon racing down the circular tunnel, scaring rats and splashing through shit and piss.

3

TWENTY MINUTES later, I'm in one of my boltholes and I ain't happy. Far from it. It's one of many lock-ups in the industrial end of town nestling beneath the arches of a long-abandoned railway.

To any intruder or perp, it's a room full of junk. The kind of stuff cheap motels throw away every day. Beds, mattresses, tables, chairs, wardrobes, bits of service-robos and other worthless rubbish. All stacked up and covered in crap.

At the back, there's a hidden door to one of my hideouts.

The room has everything I need in an emergency.

First things first, I heat up a food pack. This is a lot more than a simple set of cardboard-like plastimeat and nutrients. I had time to set up these places and made sure I stocked them with the best money could buy. Pretty soon, I'm sitting back eating a plate of sliced beef, potatoes and vegetables covered in thick gravy and sipping from a hot mug of milky tea.

I don't do booze. In my job, I need to keep my wits about me.

By now I should've been cuddled up with Angie. Something else I can blame Tewis for.

Time to find out what all the fuss is about. Tewis had been worried about what Rolo said before he died. *Why?* I power up the digiscreens that fill one wall and patch-in one of the data-sinks scavenged from my damaged drones.

White noise and flickering replaced by the scene from the spaceport alleyway.

I observe myself holding up the laser. I sure am a fine figure of a woman. My exo is invisible, following the curves of my body seamlessly.

Angie made a bad choice. Loyalty goes a long way with Quick-Kill Jane. Hell, I might've even taken her off planet with me but the offer of real money can turn a gal's head.

I turn my attention back to the screen. A flash of the laser and Rollo goes down. A second flash and he's on fire. The drones now close in on him.

I turn up the volume.

He says his last words just as I remember, except for one glitch. I replay the vid. But there can be no mistake. After Rollo calls me a *bitch,* the vid feed crackles and drops out for a briefest of moments.

The data-sink captured all three drones' cameras. I replay the other two angles and get the same result. Rollo died. I don't doubt that. The laser turning him into a quick stain of blackened glass but he did something to me…

I remember the brief stab of pain from behind my eyes. Shit! A flash-dump to my wafer.

My interface is back at the Loft. I can't perform a diagnostic but I can still bring up the directory files. The screen blinks and there it is. An extra folder, tetraquads in size.

But how?

My wafer was supposed to be hack-proof. Having said that, Rollo was just about the best file-smasher on the planet—a very small insignificant planet with one city but impressive all the same.

What did that bastard do to me?

I try to open the file but it's security locked. Copying and deleting gets the same result. For now, the file is stuck in my head—the last place I need it to be.

For Rollo to flash me that file before his fiery end means it's damn important. Tewis wanted Rollo dead, and these files destroyed with him. That's why the contract was to leave no trace behind. Yet the mark did something unexpected.

Still, Tewis can't be sure I have the file, he can only suspect. But I went and told him I have a wafer didn't I? Showing off again. I damn well knew that one day it'd get me into trouble. Tewis won't rest until I'm dead and also disintegrated.

I take another long drink of tea and shuffle my options.

One. I stay here and lie low. I've enough rations to last me many weeks. But I'm not the sitting around type.

Two. I go find someone who can get this file out of my head, or maybe get me access to it. Knowing what I'm dealing with may give me a bargaining option.

Three. I further investigate Rollo Barla, his associates and his family. See what they know. But Rollo was a career criminal who always worked alone, it's unlikely that avenue would throw up any information.

Four. Go find that bastard Tewis, and ask him direct.

I finish the tea and stand up, resting my weight on the exo.

I'm going to make Tewis pay, there is no doubt about that but a bargaining chip—such as downloading the file and saving it elsewhere—will get me close to the bastard without him shooting on sight.

One and three are no-goers. Four, although my favourite, is too dangerous. I decide on option two—*find someone who can get this file out of my head.*

Like Rollo Barla, I work alone but I have associates. People who I go to for expertise. People who can be trusted. Like the guy who augmented my wafer…

I replace my clothes with a disguise I've worn many times. A quick augmentation of the exo widens my shoulders and thickens my arms and legs.

I look at my reflection in a full-length mirror and if not for my hair and make-up, I'd be easily mistaken for a man.

A hasty wash of my face, a new short-haired wig, my cheeks padded out with an injection of gel and I complete the look.

The exo even gives me a few more inches. I ain't ashamed of my height. If anything, it makes me a damn sight cuter than other chicks… and more dangerous.

I pick up a hat and a raincoat and fasten the belt. I finish the tea and slam the mug down on the table. It shatters but I'm not concerned. Adrenaline is still pumping through me, and the exo is an extension of that. But it gives me an idea.

I locate a rack of stims and place them in my pockets. Like I said, I prefer to remain in control but stimming myself to the eyeballs may be an option I will need later on.

I pull the hat down over my face and exit into the night.

I close the graffiti-covered metal shutter, fasten the lock and make my way to the steps leading into the local station and catch a tube-train to Amsterdam Central. Here, I dummy out to the West-End and take an autocab south-westwards to the mainly run-down area of Heim.

I find a suitable bar. It has a roof area and three other exits in case I need to escape in a hurry. I find a booth giving me an eye on all three exits and the stairs, sit down, order a tea, and wait. Watching for anything out of the ordinary. Anything off-key. *Anything odd.*

My phone ain't your bog-standard model. Yeah, I enhanced it a little. Put my mark on it and made it my own. For a start, it possesses stealth tek. I checked it back in the hideout and got the same result—there's a constant sweep looking for my phone's ident. *Looking for me.* But the signal is too broad and bouncing off too many towers, for me to track it backwards.

The handheld has another special feature—a short-range weapons detector. I got it from a police contact. One of the few chicks who's allowed to wear a badge and she's cute with it. A piece of hush-hush software that only law-enforcement is supposed to know about. It can't identify a gun but it can sure detect their presence up to two-hundred feet. A series of red dots on an electronic map. Something to do with the ambient signals from gun-specific circuitry present in all modern weapons. Damn effective, and the reason why I switched to my trusty laser.

Guns are commonplace in New Amsterdam, used for 'home-protection' as the saying goes. But carrying a gun outside the home without a license is against the law.

My phone will alert me if any weapons are close by. So far, it's showing nada.

I access the net to check out the news and, via an earpiece, to eavesdrop on the supposedly secure police channel. Both bring up nuthin of interest.

I wait another ten minutes. I order my second cup of tea and speak a single word into my phone: *Dynamo*. It's a stupid name, sure, but who am I to judge?

"Jane?" says a surprised voice at the other end.

"I'm data-patching you my location. Come see me. And make sure you're not followed." I hang-up and sit back. If anyone can help me, Dynamo can.

He arrives in the bar twenty minutes later.

Dynamo is a tall, skinny, stretched rubber-band of a kid, his almost white hair sticking up in the style of any regular twenty-something tek-boy. I wave him over.

Sure, I've taken the piss out of his name. Lots of times. Dynamo comes from the Greek word 'dynamis' meaning 'power'. The kid is the antithesis of command—all nervous, twitching limbs and mumbled half-words. But I get it. Wafers have been around a long time now. His expertise is in boosting their capacity whilst keeping power demands low. Anything that is charged by the electrical-chemical balance of the brain ain't gonna receive much in the way of current, not unless Dynamo is on the case.

He stares around, confused.

I hold up my cup of tea and, smiling in realisation, he comes over and squeezes into the booth. A long-legged spider folding into its hole.

"Why the public place and the neat guise?" he says, staring into my eyes.

I glance at my phone. No red dots. "I needed to make sure you weren't followed. Assassin one-oh-one—don't walk into an ambush."

"An ambush?" Dynamo's manic blue eyes dart around the bar like a cat following a blob of light. "What the hell is this, Jane?"

"Mention my name again, and I'll kill where you sit. Understand?"

Dynamo's head nods on a long neck, his Adam's apple bobbing up and down. "Yeah, sure. Sorry," he replies—a scolded puppy.

I give him a precis of recent events. "Things are shit-serious right now, okay?"

"Sure. I get it. Serious shit." The head nods again, eyebrows furrowing in exaggerated apology. "So you got me here. What do you need?"

"You heard of a creep called Tewis?"

The name has no effect on the kid and he ain't no actor.

"Who is he?" he asks. "One of your marks?"

A quick shake of my head. "A client of mine. An ex-client as it happens. Soon to be ex of this life if I can find him. I just wanted to judge your reaction. He might've gotten to you first and I need to be careful but I think you're clean."

"He sounds dangerous."

"He is… I want you to do a job for me."

"Sure. Anything. *For a price.*"

I smile. "There's a file wedged in my wafer. Stuck fast. Encrypted. I need it out of my head, asap."

Dynamo's blue eyes search my face, as if trying to peer inside my skull. "I can give it a go. But I'd need to see it for myself, to get the measure of what we're dealing with. Tewis is after this file?"

I nod. "Seems like he'll move heaven and earth to destroy it. The only problem—I'm in his way."

"We'll need to return to my lab."

"No way."

"But all my equipment is there."

"No."

"You gotta understand. I want to help you but without my tek, I'm useless."

I take a sip of tea. "I've my own place nearby," I say "a hideout. You can bring what you need there."

A quick shake of his head. "It isn't that easy. I can't… even if I…There's just no way to do that."

I've trapped Dynamo and he's afraid. But he hasn't the guile to try and trick me. And he's genuinely afraid of getting on my bad side, so I make the decision. "Okay. We'll do it your way. Return home now and I'll follow you."

"Will I be in any danger?"

I lean forward and fix him with my meanest stare. "You try and pull any nonsense, and I'll burn your face off. Understand?"

He swallows. "Sure."

"Good. Now get your shit outta here."

4

NO RED dots while I follow Dynamo home.

It's possible Tewis knows about my associates, that he's having them watched. He could even be waiting back at Dynamo's den, hoping the tek-boy would bring me back to an ambush. It's unlikely, granted, yet he somehow knew about Angie.

Damn! I'd been sloppy with her… but a chick like Angie can do that to a gal.

I'm reminded of the goon at her apartment and his half-assed attempt to off me. From what I've seen of Tewis's methods, he ain't subtle. If he'd had Dynamo followed, his attack would've come in the bar—he wouldn't miss a chance like that and I don't think he's the type to play the long game, which gives me the advantage.

Dynamo enters the crumbling tenement he calls home and I hang around outside in the shadows for the required amount of time. Satisfied all is okay, I call the single elevator and ascend the thirty or so floors up to his room. The only way in and out… unless you possess an augmented exo that is.

I crouch, sliding the door open, laser on standby. Dynamo's den is empty, apart from a nervous looking Dynamo and his extensive tek stacks.

"You're sure putting the sweats on me, you know that?" he says.

His den is an open-plan apartment. The only other room is a small bathroom, the door open—empty. I stand up and holster the laser. "A gal can never be too careful."

Dynamo relaxes. "I have my own security system should anyone try to creep up on me." He nods his head to a screen from which a camera angle shows the building's foyer, the fire escape, elevator, the alleyway below, roof, and various other shots. He sits on a battered office chair and powers up his screens. "I take it you want this to be quick?"

"As quick as it can be. Encryption ain't one of my skills."

"That's why tek-boys like me exist."

He gestures to a couch and I dutifully lie down. He places a monitor on my forehead and goes back to his screens.

I've been here before and had a similar procedure. From my position, I've a great view. Dynamo is suddenly all action. Gone is the nervous twenty-something, in his place is an artist totally in control. His hands wave through the air as if conducting a vast and complicated orchestra, his fingers occasionally typing on an archaic keypad.

My wafer appears on the main screen and below it a list of folders. I don't even have to tell him which is the offender, nor remind him all the other folders are private. I'm the top of the tree in my profession and Dynamo is no different in his. There are few boundaries on this world but people like me and Dynamo recognise and respect them.

"What the hell is that?" he says, eyeing the offending file with an excited raise of his eyebrows.

"That's what I want you to find out."

A few more hand gestures, and the interloper glows red. "Was this flash-dumped?" he asks, not taking his eyes off the screens.

"Yeah."

"You were lucky it didn't fry your brain."

"I don't believe in luck."

"You're right. This wafer is top-of-the-range. The best ripped tek money can buy. You know some of these components come from the Key Systems huh? All held in perfect balance by a SLASH-STAK bio-controller, and a host of other bits and bobs. I installed and designed this baby myself and when it comes to wafers, I know my job."

I laugh inside at Dynamo's unconscious arrogance. "You think the flash-dump was an attempt to kill me?"

"Could be. But why encrypt the file? No. Whoever sent this wanted you alive."

"You can open it? Get inside?"

"There ain't no file Dynamo can't get into… Shit!"

"What is it?"

Dynamo leans into his screens, squinting. "The wafer has fused with the bone-tissue of your skull. It's the heatsink I designed."

"What about it?"

"It's supposed to 'float' on top of your frontal lobe. This has become a part of your brain and skull."

"Bad?"

"Brain damage is minimal, so no. But you won't be able to remove it. Not without some serious surgery from someone who knows their shit inside and out. And guess what? There ain't no one like that on this backwater planet."

I shrug. "That's not important now. I just need to know what's in the folder. How long will this take?"

"Shh!"

Being shushed by a kid like Dynamo irks me but I forgive him. He's in the zone. Doing his thing. I sit back, close my eyes, and let him get on with it…

"Jane!"

My eyelids part to reveal Dynamo's face next to mine. "Did I nod off?"

"Yeah, it was kinda cute actually."

"Back off, Bud!" I push him aside. Behind him all the screens are flashing red. "What the fuck?"

"I managed to open the folder," Dynamo replied. "And whatever was inside took over my system… or tried to," he added, sounding more impressed than upset. "My tek stacks are protected. Walls within walls and then some. Whatever was inside the folder was trying to get out."

"It didn't make it?"

He shook his head. "I'd stake my rep on my security cols but I think it's still a good idea we get out of here."

"Tell me what you found," I say, stumbling to my feet.

"An invasive program of some kind," Dynamo replies, flinging a section of wafers and other tek into a satchel. "I'm guessing military or something else. Programmed to attack."

"Did you get it out of me? Or make a copy?"

A shake of his head. "The contents are hard-wired into your wafer, happened in the flash-dump. And like I said, you can't get rid of it without serious medical intervention." Dynamo runs over to the window and pushes it open. "Come on. Down the fire escape."

I rip off the monitor and follow him out. The kid clatters down the stairway. But other than his urgent, metallic footsteps, the area is quiet. No approaching vehicles, and a quick glance at my phone tracker shows no guns in the vicinity.

A thought crosses my mind. Is Dynamo double-crossing me? Did he put me to sleep and arrange this little scenario? It's possible but the way Dynamo is rattling down the steps tells me otherwise. He's genuinely freaked.

Instead of dropping down, I use the exo to jump across the street, landing on a rooftop of a smaller block below.

Dynamo is still a good ten floors above me.

I check my wafer. The folder still won't open.

Damn!

Things are going from confusing to downright infuriating. I wanna run, to get away from here. But I've put Dynamo in danger, he at least needs my protection and could still be useful. I'm about to jump up to him when the world explodes in a ball of blinding white.

5

I WAKE up coughing, covered in dust and rubble. A quick onceover tells me I'm not injured.

I stand, brushing more dust from my coat and stare in disbelief at the scene in front of me. Dynamo's tenement has gone. Disintegrated. Cut cables spark and water gushes from many broken and exposed pipes. There's no explanation other than the building was hit from orbit.

What the hell is in my head?

In the distance, I hear the approach of emergency vehicles.

But they can do nuthin. Dynamo, the block and all its inhabitants have gone. Broken apart at the molecular level is my guess.

I can't hang about. Whoever blasted the building from orbit may have the capability to see me standing here. And I'm the target. Or whatever's in my head.

Plan two didn't work out for me.

Only one option is left—*go find Tewis.*

Ten minutes later, I'm a long way from the destroyed building. I access the news channel via my wafer but the streams are quiet. It means only one thing.

Whatever is going on here—is government sanctioned.

I enter the second of my hideouts—a cellar under a row of shops and slip inside the fusty smelling room.

After what happened to Dynamo and his building, I can't stay in any one place too long. My visit is a quick one. I grab a stash of illegal bucks, recharge packs for my laser and exo, a range of grenades, flash-bombs and gas pellets, and a few extra guns with ammunition. What I can't wear, I place in a holdall.

As for my appearance, I decide to stay as a man—swapping my dust-covered clothing for something less conspicuous. I even change my hat. Then I'm back out on the streets again.

The back alleys somehow feel more dangerous. Instead, I head towards the centre of town, down one of the many high streets. They aren't exactly crowded but there's safety in numbers.

A chirrup from my phone. A quick glance tells me it's Tewis. I answer the call.

"Hi there," I say with forced calm. "You getting all sweaty that I'm still alive? Cos I hope so." The guy has been able to call in some pretty big guns. He's connected and, despite my plans for revenge, getting to Tewis ain't going to be as easy as I'd hoped but he doesn't have to know that. "And guess what? I'm coming for you, understand?"

"I'm afraid Mister Tewis won't be making any more phone calls," replies an officious sounding woman. "In fact, Mister Tewis won't be doing much of anything anymore."

"I can't say that news makes me sad," I reply, my mind racing.

Of course! Tewis was too small to be behind all this. Especially after the strike from orbit. Bigger players are involved, that much is for sure. "Who the hell are you? And what's all this about?"

"I can tell you in five simple words. Alpha. Renegade. Purple. Angst. Drumroll."

"Huh? What the hell is that?"

"Just a little something for you to ponder on. I take it you're the girl causing everyone so much trouble?"

"Trouble is my middle name, as is 'get to the bloody point.'"

"Quite. You've heard of the Galactic Secret Service?"

The question takes me aback. The Galactic Secret Service is a ghost organisation. A name bandied around the backrooms of gangster hangouts, seedy barrooms, millionaire clubs and political headquarters as the main reason behind any number of imagined gripes. These gripes ranged from shipment seizures and disappearances to assassinations and regime changes.

"Yes, we do exist," the woman continues. "And we are here on this shit-end planet of yours, which must highlight the seriousness of your situation. Now, before we talk further, I've got a little question for you… You've been on this line for over thirty seconds. How come we can't track you? That's impressive."

I decide to bluff this out. "I'm an impressive sort of a gal. Now what's the damn lowdown?"

"Before we move onto that, I've another question for you. Do you want to live?"

"You're threatening me?"

"No. Not a threat. More of a choice. You've done a good job of surviving so far. You've shown yourself to be resilient, resourceful and your augmented tek is borderline genius but believe me, without the protection of the Service, you won't survive the evening."

"I can do without your protection," I say, wondering why I don't hang up but I'm intrigued. "I saw what you did to that building."

"You think that was us? The service isn't beyond blowing up civilians when deemed necessary but it's those who want to destroy the information inside your head that are responsible."

"So you're not the bad guys, huh?"

"Let's just say some other bad guys are out to kill you. Today, it's us bad guys from the Service wanting to keep you alive."

"For the wafer inside my head?"

"For what's on the wafer, yes."

"This is all fine and dandy but I'm running low on trust tonight. So forgive me when I tell you to *go to hell!*"

"I thought you might be like this, so here's a little bit of encouragement."

A sudden, high-pitched whine from the earpiece makes me wince and the phone becomes hot in my hand, sparking like a firework, and dying.

I throw it into the gutter and stalk quickly away. I have no idea where I'm going but standing still seems like inviting trouble.

The bloody Galactic Secret bloody Service! They actually exist?

Going to any one of my hideouts is now a mistake. Staying in one place also seems like a dumb idea. Sooner or later they will catch up with me. And besides, I have everything I need on me.

There's nuthin for it, I'm gonna have to improvise. I pull up my own schematic of the sewer system, what I've christened the Rat-Run, and superimpose it over the street. Most of the shops are closed for the evening. I duck down a side alley and find my way to a set of tradesman's entrances.

There's no lock in this city that I can't tek-crack. Within moments, I've let myself into the back of a shop.

I find the alarm system and disable it before it can trigger. I take out my laser and punch a hole through the floor, quickly dropping into the sewers.

I don't want to admit it but I sometimes feel more at home here in these pipes than I do elsewhere. They should call me The Sewer Rat not Quick-Kill Jane. But I digress, all my considerable brainpower is telling me one thing, and one thing only…

I'm done for.

The Service or the friends of Tewis will find me. It's just a matter of time.

The only thing I've got to bargain with is fused into my head. And to try and bargain would literally be serving my head up to them on a plate.

Maybe this is how the marks feel after I've caught them? The terrible sense of no way out. And worst of all. I'm missing Angie and her wonderful pies.

I take a left, a right and, pushing full power to my exo, run as fast and as far as I can, heading for the city outskirts in as roundabout a manner as possible.

You may try and corner Quick-Kill Jane but she ain't too proud to run away. As to where I'm heading, I'll work that out when I get there. But I'll find something. Come up with a plan. I've never yet failed to come out on top.

I access my wafer and play the last conversation over again. I'm sure I missed something in the heat of the moment.

What did the woman say?

Alpha. Renegade. Purple. Angst. Drumroll…

What the hell does that mean—! But it's too late. Before I can curse my own stupidity, the folder locked inside my head unzips and all hell and damnation breaks loose.

6

THE OVERPOWERING smell of ammonia under my nose and I'm jolted back into consciousness.

I'm tied to a chair in a white room with soft edges and even softer lighting. A deep hum from behind the walls irritates my hearing.

A quick glance down shows I've been stripped and placed in a black skinsuit of some kind.

Without my exo and nanomesh armour, I might as well be naked.

Twin wires are attached to my temples, connected to a large tek stack.

I remember the folder opening in my head and the wave

of horror emanating from it. I unconsciously access my wafer again. The folder hasn't been removed. For now, it's inert but threatening.

What the hell was inside there, and how the hell did I get here? Wherever here is.

A tired woman in her forties, wearing a similar black skinsuit revealing a honed physique, stares at me intently while leaning against a white table seemingly extruded from the floor. She possesses beady eyes sitting under a wrinkled brow, above which perches long black hair twisted into a rough bun. A sense of controlled power emanates from her and, although she's no looker, there is something about her.

"Hello," she says.

I know that voice. The woman from the phone call… I'm in the clutches of the goddam Galactic Secret Service!

I wriggle, trying to get a sense of my bonds, aware that the gravity has increased. I'm either on a different planet or this room has artificial grav.

"They call me 'Mother'," the woman continues.

The woman ain't the type to be changing diapers. "I never had a mother," I say. "I never needed one. I grew up on the streets and found my own way in the world without a damn family. But it's no sob story—all the hard knocks were dished out to any and everybody who got in my way."

Mother ain't listening. Her eyes narrow. "You sure are one difficult girl to catch," she says. "But credit where credit is due. You led us on a merry chase alright. Luckily, we were mostly one step ahead. Mostly. We thought we'd lost you when that cityblok was fragged from space. But no, you turned up again."

"And here I am, wherever here is," I reply, searching the room for anything that might aid my escape. The place is more of an office than a holding cell. But I'm relieved to find my equipment laid out on a shelf to my left.

Nanomesh, exo and the rest.

I just need to get untied and dressed, and I'll be back to being a one-girl army. "And if you think I'm gonna let this pass, you've another think coming, you get me?"

Mother shrugs. "You might want to stop the threats and start giving out some thanks for saving your stubborn ass. You were in a hell of a mess down on that planet of yours."

I snort but the information jolts me—I'm on a spaceship. I've finally got away from Plenty. Just not the way I envisioned it would happen. From a practical perspective, I'm trapped—even if I do manage to get free of these bonds and out of this room. "So where are we, still in orbit?"

Mother sits back on the desk and hits me with a quizzical look. "I'm asking the questions. And you have me flummoxed. Just who are you? I'm pretty sure you weren't christened with that ridiculous name you go by… *Quick-Kill Jane?* How very quaint."

She picks up a sheaf of plastic sheets. "You've no DNA profile. Well, nothing that can be left behind or traced, which is quite some trick, don't you think?"

"I have no idea what you're talking about," I snarl at her. "The cops have never scanned my DNA cos I ain't never been stupid enough to get caught. Even so, I ain't the type to leave such obvious evidence lying around. And if there's a prize for the most ridiculous name, you'd win that hands down."

Mother's quizzical look remains stuck to her face, as if my words have no impact on her. "I might expect to see something like this in the Key Systems," she continues, planting a hand on the curve of her thigh while her eyebrows furrow. "Or on the mediscan of some antigov rich-kid from one of the Gaiaspheres but not from some cheap assassin in the back end of nowhere. How'd you afford it? The procedure costs more than the GDP of your whole goddam trashcan of a planet."

I've always prided myself on my ability to read people face-to-face. Mother doesn't appear to be lying. If anything, she's surprised by what's she's found. I'm also shocked by the information—mainly because it ain't true. "There ain't anything augmented about Quick-Kill Jane," I announce. "I'm perfect and untouched. Just as nature intended.

"You're telling me you don't remember the procedure?"

"What possible reason would I have to lie?"

She takes in my words with a rise of her eyebrows. "If that's the case, there is only one conclusion—shortly after you were born, someone hid your identity. As to who or why, I have no idea but they sure went to a lot of trouble over you."

"What do I care?" I reply. "You think I'm like every other orphan who dreams they're some lost princess? Give me a damn break. And besides, why should the Galactic Secret Service care one jot about—how did you put it?—*some cheap assassin in the back end of nowhere?*"

"How old do you think I am, Jane? Forty? Fifty maybe?" she asks. "Well think again. The Service doesn't pay well but they have a great medi-plan. I'm over a hundred years old and seventy of those years have been with the Service. I've survived all this time because of my gut. My instinct. Some might call it clairvoyance or telepathic insight. And all my insight is telling me there's more to you than…" she stares intently into my face. "…than meets the eye."

"I know who I am and that's enough for me," I reply. If I only had my laser, I'd burn that quizzical look off her face. First I need to get untied and to get out of this place. "Now, tell me… what the hell am I doing here? After what happened when I activated that damn file, I pretty much thought I'd wake up dead."

Mother puts down the sheaf and grimaces "You nearly did. But you are the resilient type. What we in the Service call a 'survivor'. You also show a disdain for authority and an almost paranoid lack of trust—which I personally find admirable. But trust is what I need from you."

"You ain't getting anything from me."

"Sure, trusting the Service is not always the best option. But in this instance, you need us—or, more importantly, you need me. I'm in your corner, although you don't realise that yet. There are some quite nasty people desperate to retrieve what you've got stuck in that stubborn head of yours. So let me be honest, the Service doesn't care one single jot about you. To them, you are just a container, and very much expendable. My orders were to retrieve the missing data and get it out of the system and back to headquarters. And believe me, it would be a lot simpler to cut your head open to do that. But after such a long time in the Service, I get a certain amount of leeway. I'm putting myself in the firing line by keeping you alive. So cut me some slack."

Mother is telling me pretty much what Dynamo said earlier. There's no way to access the file without removing the wafer from my head. I don't trust Mother, her intentions are all too foggy but I must admit that what she says is plausible—and most of all, I don't wanna die. "Okay," I say. "I get it. You're keeping me alive. So why keep me tied up?"

"Once we intercepted Tewis, we found out everything we could about you. And you know what we came up with?"

I shrug. "Not very much."

"Exactly. That's impressive right there. After we brought you aboard, I had time to check out your tek. You designed all that by yourself?"

"Sure. There ain't no walk-in armoury on Plenty. I had to improvise with what I could find. And I like to tinker."

"You sure do. Which means you're dangerous. You will be kept in restraints until we can get to headquarters. We're en route via voidwarp and I've scheduled surgery to get your wafer removed. If you survive the operation, we'll talk again. I think we may be of use to one another." She pushes herself up to her full height, looking to leave.

"You ain't gonna tell me what's stuck in my head? Even if I say 'pretty please'?"

"That's better. You will learn that if you ask nicely, I will try my best to answer."

"So what's in the damn folder?"

"Quite simply… we went fishing."

7

A LOUD reverberating bang rocks the ship. The room jolts sideways and Mother is thrown to the floor.

My chair is bolted down, my restraints preventing me joining her. The white light of the room suddenly flashes red and sirens blare.

"Status update!" Mother bellows.

A voice over booming speakers: *"Three cruisers, a fourth closing in. Took us by surprise."*

Mother straps herself to her desk chair. "How'd they find us so quickly, Captain?"

"The Cabal must've tracked the shuttle bringing the package from the surface, and followed our wake into voidwarp. Inertial dampeners are offline and we—BRACE FOR EMERGENCY MANOEUVRES!"

The Cabal? The name rings a series of bells inside my head. They are as mythical as the damn Galactic Secret Service. A sort of super-mafia.

Another jolt, and the background hum increases in volume. I'm slammed into my chair, my spine crushed by a sudden upsurge in gee, knocking the breath out of my lungs. More gee, flinging my head in every direction. Like some kind of rag doll.

"Two more cruisers ahead. We're not going to be able to hold them off, Mother," the Captain blurts over the com.

Mother is all controlled calm. "How long do we have?" she asks, her hands sweeping over what I guess is a desk readout.

"Two minutes, maybe three…"

"I'm afraid you're going to have to keep those ships occupied for as long as you can, Captain. You know the contingency."

"…Yes, Mother," the Captain replies after a short pause. *"Inertial dampeners are now back online."*

Mother unstraps herself and comes over to me. Without any preamble, she cuts me free. For a second, I consider kicking her aside—an automatic reaction—but I sense she has a plan to get us out of this. I damn hope so.

"Follow me!"

I don't need telling twice.

Mother opens the door and we race down a corridor, rocking side to side from multiple impacts, red lights flashing.

We arrive in a hub-room hung with similar skinsuits to the one I'm wearing.

Mother punches at a control panel. A door opens. We dive inside an escape vessel of sorts. Long, thin, and barely large enough for the two of us. The door slams shut and the dash flashes into life.

"Strap yourself in." Mother punches at more buttons and the craft begins to hum. "We're ready, Captain," she says into the com.

A sudden jolt of gee and we're ejected out of the ship, followed by a booming explosion seconds later.

"This is gonna be rough," Mother barks. "Brace!"

Everything goes black. My mind is wrenched from my skull to be scattered across the cosmos like so many broken shards. I want to scream but I remain trapped, inert, until… *I'm back.* "What the—!"

"Quiet!" Mother orders, wrestling with the controls. The ship bucks but comes under control.

I peer over her shoulder. Star maps and navi-readouts. "Where are the other ships? What the hell happened?"

"A contingency measure," Mother answers. "In case of emergencies. We took an escape raft and were jettisoned just before the captain blew the ship. A loss of many brave men and women. But they knew their duty. Hopefully we weren't tracked. We dropped out of voidwarp at the same time as the explosion… I did say it was gonna be rough." She punches at the navicom with quick fingers. "This ship is one big voidwarp engine with room for one or two passengers. But we aren't clear of danger quite yet—we need to evade those pursuing Cabal ships. It's only a matter of minutes before they work out what happened."

"Then let's get outta here," I reply, trying to control my voice but I admit it, recent events have jolted me somewhat.

The Cabal—a loose collection of illegal gangs, mafia families and violent, secretive underhand groups of organisations of all types—want me dead. It's one thing to piss off a few hoods and local kingpins but the mythical Cabal? That's a lot to take in.

Mother saved my life—I know that she's protecting what's stuck inside my head but I can't ignore the fact she kept me alive against her orders. I'm not sure if I would've done the same if I was in her shoes.

Do I trust her?

No. Not for one moment.

Right now, she's calling the shots and seems to be actively trying to keep me alive. And Quick-Kill Jane ain't too stupid to realise sometimes she's gotta go with the flow.

"We don't possess the power for an immediate jump," Mother replies calmly. "We have to wait for the engines to recharge. A few minutes but if we can get out of here before those cruisers arrive, there'll be no way to track us."

"A waiting game?"

Mother nods. Outwardly, she is cool personified but I can plainly see beads of sweat on her brow.

"Headquarters is out of the question," she says. "I've plotted a course for the Outland Systems. Sometimes the best place to hide is amongst the unwashed… but we have to get there first."

I drum my fingers against my thigh, missing the sure presence of my laser, yet I'm still capable of putting a tight arm around Mother's throat, forcing her to tell me what all this is about. Even so, my sixth sense is telling me that would be a bad move. I get the feeling she may be as dangerous as I am. I try a different tack… "Are you gonna explain to me what the hell is going on? And what exactly did you mean by *fishing?*"

A small laugh escapes Mother's tight lips. "We put our line in the water, dangled our bait and waited to see what sharks would bite. That file you have stuck in your head… was the bait. Although it's less of a file and more a piece of highly volatile but effective code. A half-aware information gatherer. Or to put it another way—an intelligent spy working on behalf of the Service."

"Intelligent?"

Mother nods, her eyes still fixed firmly on the voidwarp readout. "You've heard of Encephalic tek?"

"Sure," I reply. I might not have had an education back on Plenty but everyone knew about that. "Artificial intelligence was banned hundreds of years ago. They're supposed to be illegal."

"Remarkably illegal but we in the Service have a certain leeway with what's lawful and what's not. The code welded into your wafer isn't a full Encephalic intelligence—not even close—although it has objectives and self-preservation skills." Mother shrugged. "We call it a *Ceph*. And for a Ceph to function properly, it needs a certain amount of suitable hardware… A few years ago, we created our own little illegitimate operation. Designing, manufacturing and supplying illegal tek to anyone and everyone willing to buy it. We flooded the illegal market with high-quality wafer components of our own particular design, making it easier for this operation to work."

A name flits into my mind, complete with a rotating logo. "You mean the Secret Service is behind SLASH-STAK? The part of my wafer Dynamo was bragging about? I have damn secret service tek welded into my head?"

Mother nodded. "Yep. One and the same. The problem… SLASH-STAK was far too successful. And, as supplying top-class tek to a growing bunch of dangerous illegals was starting to raise a few eyebrows, we were forced into entering the second part of the operation without being fully prepared. Under the guise of SLASH-STAK, we arranged a robbery. An 'audacious strike against the Secret Service', or so the Cabal was led to believe—the theft of a supposed list of our operatives and operations. The file was indeed 'stolen'. Or what they thought was a file. It was our burrowing worm. Our information gatherer. The Ceph. Like I said… we went fishing."

I digest her words. "Okay, the Ceph is part of your operation, of your plan. I can see that. It makes sense. Sure it does. But what was the Ceph doing on Plenty, a planet in the ass-end of nowhere? Inside some low-life scum?"

Mother turns away from the readouts, contemplates me for a few seconds and shrugs. "As your friend Dynamo discovered, the Ceph can't be copied or cracked. It was passed around from one underground organisation to another, exactly as we anticipated, while collecting as much intel as it could. But as I said, SLASH-STAK was an unprecedented success—too damn successful. Soon after the Ceph was 'stolen', our plan was leaked. All hellfire was let loose as those compromised organisations used their considerable resources to find and destroy it. The Ceph has a certain amount of guile. It tried to hide. Flitting from one illegal wafer to another. Seeking an opportunity to call for help. Until it became wedged inside you."

"Okay," I say, taking in the information. "But that doesn't answer why I was contracted to kill Rollo Barla. Why employ me when they had all that firepower circling in orbit?"

"Like I said, the Ceph has a certain amount of guile. We'd lost it for a few weeks. It did what it was programmed to do—the Ceph went underground. That's why it ended up in the backend of nowhere. But the bad guys weren't idle. The Cabal panicked and began eliminating anyone and everyone who may be the carrying the Ceph in their augmented SLASH-STAK wafers. There's been a plague of assassinations, hundreds over the last two weeks. That's how you became involved. Tewis wasn't sure what he was looking for, but he was ordered to eliminate anyone with an illegal wafer and to data-beam anything unusual to his superiors."

Mother pulls her lips into a tight smile. "Six cruisers—a mishmash of mafia families, clanships and illegals—voidwarped to your planet in the last hour. We followed them, arriving shortly after, masking ourselves as a family merchant vessel. But we were just as blind as the bad guys who were looking for you—until the Ceph sent us a message, that is. Courtesy of your friend Dynamo. But in contacting us, the Ceph revealed its position to the Cabal ships and they destroyed the building you were in. Then it was just a matter of who could get to you first. We had one advantage though, the Ceph broadcast an encrypted message, allowing us to get to Tewis first. You were tough to catch, granted… but here you are."

A beep from the com. Mother's head darts back to the readouts. "Multiple incursions! The Cabal will be here in moments but that's all the time we need." The navicom flashes green and Mother punches the voidwarp activation code.

This time the lurch into voidwarp is not as jolting. All my sensations slip backwards and forwards and loop around themselves then return to relative normal. Sure, the experience isn't particularly nice but neither is it so injurious.

The stars of voidspace stream past us on the screens. I've seen them many times before, on the streams but not for real. They are nuthin like what you see on a cold, clear night from Plenty. The spectrum of human eyes is too narrow. But in voidspace, the stars are revealed as vast, luminescent, jellyfish-like structures, floating past us as if we're underwater, not in a wormhole. "It's beautiful," I hear myself saying.

"It's your first time in the void," Mother says. "Everyone reacts the same."

I never thought I'd miss Plenty but now, in this moment, all this is a little overwhelming. I shake my head, deciding that to survive, I'm gonna to need to adapt. Having nostalgic thoughts about a place I spent a lifetime trying to escape from doesn't sound like Quick-Kill Jane. "Tell me, where are we heading?"

"I mentioned the Cabal… we're now entering their heartlands. I've set a course for the Barrens."

Clever. *Always do what the enemy doesn't expect.*

Back when my escape plan had been simple, the Barrens was going to be my first destination once I left Plenty. A place to meet the right people and to enhance my skills and my fortune. And Mother is taking me right there. If it wasn't for this damn Ceph stuck in my head, I'd be elated. For now, I'll need to hold off until Mother can sort out my wafer. Having to rely on somebody irks me but, unfortunately, Mother holds all the cards. "You got friends there, huh?" I ask.

"The Barrens is a hive, full of paranoid off-gridders, pirates and clans. You should fit right in. But I also know my way around. It's where I grew up."

"You came from there?" My voice sounds more incredulous than I intended.

Mother laughs. "Where do you think service operatives are made? At some elite training compound where only the best of the very best end up?"

"I suppose so, yeah."

"Well think again. My childhood was… problematic. But I'm like you, a survivor. I was a master-thief and an assassin. Until the Service caught up with me."

"Well more fool you."

"Fool?" Mother says, turning to face me. "It's not me getting shot." She pulls out a blaster and fires point-blank into my chest.

8

I AWAKE, groggy and uncomfortable. I'm lying down—or at least I think I am—my body feels heavy and I'm unable to move even fingers or toes. I must be somewhere in high-gee or held by some powerful restraint field.

And then my memories come flooding back in the bright flash of a blaster discharge. I was shot!

"How is the patient?"

I recognise the voice immediately. It's Mother. I try to curl my fists but, again, I'm powerless.

"Under stasis," replies another voice, male and ancient-sounding—nothing more than a reedy whine. "But all readouts are well within acceptable parameters. The procedure was a resounding success."

"Thanks Abe, I knew we could rely on you," Mother says. "Time to revive the patient."

"He's already listening to us," the man replied.

I'm confused. I thought they were talking about me. Who is this 'he'? Some other sap? Sudden panic floods my mind. Am I dead? A disembodied consciousness trapped in some mad scientist's lair? Mother shot me at point-blank range with a blaster. Even my nanomesh wouldn't have protected me from such a gun.

She killed me… *Didn't she?*

"Release him, let's see how good you did." Mother again, a pleased tone to her normally efficient words.

A weight is lifted from my body and I gasp for air, my chest heaving. I try to lift an arm but it's too heavy. I'm also aware of my heartbeat—a loud, slow thud, reverberating from inside my chest. I try to speak but my mouth is dry. I cough—the sound is different—it's not my cough. What the hell is happening to me?

I struggle to part my eyelids and they finally peel apart. Harsh, bright light slams into my brain.

I try to speak again but the only sounds I make are low and guttural—like some brain-damaged ape.

Slowly, my eyes adjust. I become aware of an aged man staring at me. His face a mess of vertical wrinkles cutting deep into his skin. His eyes, watery and surrounded by thin red veins.

Again, I try to lift my arms—I want to strangle him and then Mother but the effort is just too much.

"It will take you some days to regain any semblance of strength," he says. "But you are breathing on your own and your bodily functions are very much in the green. In the meantime, you need to rest and re-orientate."

I feel pressure against my neck and I slip into unconsciousness.

The next few days are spent flitting in and out of drug-induced sleep. My waking periods are characterised by what feels like physio, my limbs massaged by some machine whilst electrical impulses make me jerk and twitch.

After I don't know how many more days, I wake again. It takes me long minutes to make sense of where I am—the drugs slowly being leached from my system, I guess. But finally, the blurs resolve themselves and I find myself in a small room, sitting up in bed. Mother and Abe are here, both looking at me.

"Welcome back to the land of the living," Mother says.

"You shot me!" I blurt, but something is wrong. My words are not my own. They sound harsh and loud. I raise my hand and baulk at what I see. It's not my hand. It's too large, the fingers fat like sausages.

"What the hell have you done to me?" I growl.

"Saved your life," Mother replies. "With the help of our chief *meat technician,* Abe, here. But you don't have to thank us just yet."

"It will take you a short while to adjust to your new body," Abe says, "but in a week or two, you will be up and about and able to leave us."

I stare down at the bed. A hideous ape is lurking under the bedsheets.

"I know it's an imposition," Mother says matter-of-factly, "but with the Cabal looking for you, there was no way I could enter the Barrens with you in tow. I'm afraid I had to dump what remained of your body in voidspace. But I kept your head and… *here we are.* As for the gender reassignment, that's standard procedure for a new agent."

"You've turned me into a goddam man!" I croak, finding this difficult to process.

"Can it!" Mother replies harshly. "You're not on that backwater planet no more. Your issues with gender are old-fashioned and out-moded. But don't worry, your proclivities remain unchanged. You will still have the same sexual urges but they are now confined within a male container."

"You bastards," I spit, staring down at my spatula-sized hands. I curl them into twin fists.

"That may be," says Mother, coming closer—close enough for me to put my hands around her throat and squeeze the life out of her. I want to but, more than anything, I want to hear what she's got to say.

"I know how much we become attached to our physical selves," Mother continues. "You are still intrinsically you but this…" she puts one thin hand onto my arm—it looks tiny in comparison to my vast biceps. "…is the male version of Quick-Kill Jane. If you're going to work for the Galactic Secret Service, you need a completely new identity."

"You really think I'm gonna work for you after this?"

"I'm sure of it. First off, we recovered the wafer from your head and replaced it with something far superior. Secondly, we reassigned your gender ID. A complicated procedure for those not diagnosed with gender dysfunction before puberty—but as you might have seen in the streams, it's also become a fashionable procedure that the rich and sexually promiscuous are happy to endure for the thrill of the different. Here in the Service, it performs another function. All new agents are gender-reassigned and their DNA homogenised. They become entirely original individuals, retaining everything other than the body they had before."

"But I didn't ask to become an agent," I snarl back at her, aware of an edge of animal violence I've not felt before—those active male genes, I guess. But I'm sure the old me would still want to rip Mother's head off, even if I needed my exo to do it.

"No one is asked," Mother continues. "We are all *recruited.* And before you start flexing all that new muscle, you'd better realise that if not for the Service, you'd be dead. I saved you and gave you a chance at a brand-new life. And I must admit, the male version of yourself is impressive. I told Abe to give you a body to match that iron-will of yours and he's certainly come up trumps."

I'm flooded with an intoxicating mixture of emotion. Betrayal, loss and—most of all—*anger*. But at heart I'm a logical pragmatist. The only way I survived on Plenty was to roll with the knocks and not let anything or anyone defeat me. To turn every setback in to an advantage and to take every chance at revenge without looking back. Above all, Quick-Kill Jane is a survivor.

"There's one more thing," Mother says. "Abe managed to find a strand of your original DNA in that brain of yours. When we get the time, we'll chuck it through our tek stacks. You never know, you might be a princess after all."

"Don't bother," I reply. "I know who I am. I don't need no goddamn backstory."

Mother shrugs. "As you wish but we'll keep it on file for you."

I review the facts and can't ignore them. Without the intervention of Mother, I'd be dead meat. I'm still alive—not in the way I wanted to be—but I can play the waiting game, even if it's a different heart beating in my chest. And the less I know about what they've put between my legs the better.

"Can I ever get Jane back?" I ask, guessing Mother's answer.

"The old you?" She shakes her head. "I incinerated the body and dumped it into voidspace. "But if you live to retirement, the Service has a great medi-plan, or didn't I mention that? When you retire, you can start again, live any life as you wish, as anybody you want to be—within reason—with a few mega-bucks in the bank courtesy of the Galactic Secret Service. And with that DNA we found, we can even grow your old body back... if you still want it."

I take in the information with a nod of my head. A body is just a body to Mother and Abe. I get that. But I've been violated and I ain't never gonna let that wash. I have to admit it, they've got me but Quick-Kill Jane ain't nothing if she's not resourceful. I'll find my way through all this and come back for revenge. First, I must play their dumb game with a goddam smile on my face. "You're holding me as a hostage while I go and do your dirty work for you, is that it?"

Mother nods. "That's exactly it. Although for someone with your talents, it won't exactly be work. More like a helluva lot of fun. You'll need some training—how to use that new body of yours for starters—but once you're done with that, you'll pretty much work on your own. You'll become an independent special agent operative. And, let me tell you, you're quite the looker, despite the dumb expression plastered all over your face. We'll send jobs and missions your way and, if you do well, I may even let you take me on a date." She laughs.

I try to pull a smile on what I guess is my new face but my lips feel as clumsy and oversized as the rest of me.

"The name 'Quick-Kill Jane' might've suited you on that dead-end planet we rescued you from but it won't do for the Service. We will need a codename."

I shake my head as vigorously as I can manage. "You've taken everything else from me but you ain't taking my name!" I blurt. "I'm Quick-Kill, that's all I've ever had that's been mine and mine alone."

Mother contemplates my words for a moment and shrugs. "Okay, your codename from now on is *Quick-Kill*. Keep it secret. It's for Secret Service use only. A way for you and other operatives to identify one another. The Service will issue you with any number of false IDs but your codename will always remain the same. You understand?"

I lean back and laugh loudly. I'm still angry, and this body is going to take time getting used to but another emotion has joined all the others vying for my attention—*elation.*

I didn't expect that. But I know why… I finally did it. I got my ass off Plenty, got myself a new life and… got myself a new body. It's not how I envisaged escaping, and living life as a man is gonna take some getting used to, but I'm up for it. Although, there's no way Quick-Kill is gonna bend the knee for the Galactic Secret Service for long. "Okay," I say. "I'll do it. How long before I can get my old look back?"

Mother shrugs. "Seventy or so years, give or take a decade."

"Then I'd better get started."

"I knew you'd adapt quickly to the situation. You are a survivor after all—a one-in-a-million that the Service is always looking for."

I openly scoff.

"Maybe the odds are not that high but we service men, women and all shades in between, come from the same stock. So believe me when I tell you that all your thoughts of payback, punishment and whatever else you are feverishly planning in terms of revenge, are a waste of time. Every agent has lain in a bed similar to your own and, in coming to terms with what's been done to them, has planned what you're planning. I won't tell you to forget that, it's who you are. It's why you've been recruited. But you will find the Secret Service hard to shake off. You've spent most of your life working on your own selfish goals. Today that has changed—you now work for the greater good. You've been recruited."

"What next?" I ask, my new voice a guttural growl.

"First off, I suggest a shave."

I rub a hand across my face. My chin feels enormous, jutting out of my face like a slab of granite, bristles rasping against my skin. "This is gonna take a lot of getting used to."

"After that," Mother continues, "we have a little job for you. Nothing too strenuous but you will need to be at the peak of your strength. You'll have four weeks to learn how to talk and walk—without falling over that brand new dick of yours." She salutes. "Welcome to the Galactic Secret Service, mister."

I sit back and groan. Seventy years before I can get my old body back? No way in hell! Mother has underestimated me. I ain't like her or any of the other saps the Service has 'recruited'. I'm not one-in-a-million, I'm one of a kind…

I'm Quick-Kill!

THREE:

THE PETROL REDHEAD

THE POWER of life and death lives in my right hand. The mastery over another's fate is the ultimate supremacy. The freshly struck match. The yellow, burning flame.

Pure unadulterated power.

Fascinated—we both watch with mesmerised eyes.

Trussed up in his hole, my prisoner who is soon to be no more, cannot remove his stare from the spluttering flame. I am his judge and jury—and now I am to be his executioner.

I have chosen a stunning location for his demise. Some people say Wales is a bleak place. Far from it. It is one of the most beautiful places in the British Isles. And one of the most uninhabited, which suits my purpose perfectly.

As to the manner of his end?

I have chosen petrol.

You think that I'm maybe unhinged and barbaric? That's for you to judge. But I, more than most, understand what petrol is capable of doing… *of hiding*. And as you will soon find, *petrol is my signature*.

Now don't get me wrong, I'm not some messed up, bitter and twisted woman.

Far from it.

I just believe that sometimes there's a price to pay, that's all.

You may think that I've gone a little too far, that my kind of retribution is harsh and unforgiving—if that's the case, we aren't going to get along at all. And so be it. But hear me out before you make your decision.

It started two years ago. Everything seemed so simple in that faraway time. As a successful TV personality, I'd come a long way from the motor-racing circuit where I'd wasted so many years.

Don't be surprised—racing has been in my blood from the start. I easily thrashed my older, more competitive brothers in our early karting days. It was the beginning of my success and where I earned the nickname that has followed me to this very day… *The Petrol Redhead*.

I fucking love that name.

To be the first British woman to win a permanent seat in

Formula One was an achievement.

Sure it was.

But my gender had nothing to do with being a racer. No. I was in it for me. For simple respect. For the speed. For the winning.

I've never traded or relied on being a woman. If anything, being regarded as a redheaded beauty was more of a hindrance to my career.

Yeah, I'm hot. Damn hot.

Even now, in my forties, I turn men's heads. And yet, I avoided the glamour rags like the plague—not that the popular press didn't publish pictures. You know what I mean?

At first… flattering—me on the beach, me out in a party dress, me showing accidental nipple. And when I wouldn't play ball with them… me looking fat, me with cellulite, me acting like a bitch.

I ignored it all with aplomb.

As I always said: *The only difference between me and the other drivers is my twat and my tits.* I'd tell that to any sexist journo who'd ask.

That quote became famous, even if they had to use asterisks. But what's between my legs makes no difference when I arrive at Turn One at one-hundred and fifty miles an hour with twenty-one other cars all vying for position.

In those early days, only two things mattered to me: *Winning* and *respect.* And nothing's changed in the intervening years, except that my list has a new addition: *family.* Mess with my family and I'll mess with you. Understand?

And sure, I was a talented driver… but not talented enough. Don't get me wrong, I was damn fast, worked hard and had a single-minded focus on winning and nothing else, but I came to the slow realisation that no matter how hard I toiled, I was never going to be a champion. I was faster than half the field, but just not fast enough to get the attention of the teams that mattered. The teams at the front of the grid.

And believe me, it hurt.

To lack that little extra, known throughout the world as 'the-bit-that-counts,' was difficult to come to terms with. But I still believed.

And then came my season from hell. Collisions, retirements, mechanical breakdowns and a slew of penalty points. You name it. It all happened to me.

The press had a field day at my lack of form, blaming it on my 'attitude'. On my sex. On imagined affairs and… well you get the picture. My sponsor pulled out and I was left on the scrapheap. Replaced by a *younger more exciting driving talent*—or so the press put it.

An everyday story in my sport.

Only other failed racers will understand how I felt. Having done everything. Having made all those sacrifices, having invested in all that self-belief…

Call it ego, call it bullheadedness, call it being a fucking prick. But it took time to accept that my racing career was over.

In need of something to fill the gap until the 'next drive', I landed myself a temporary TV job reporting and interviewing for one of the main sports' networks.

A racer on the ground who knew what-was-what and who took no shit.

Behind the microphone, I suddenly came alive. I asked the questions that the viewers wanted to hear and, astoundingly, got all the answers.

Soon my talent got me into sports presenting and finally hosting a late-night hard-hitting TV chat show.

To find that one thing you are good at, to become what you have always wanted after trying for a lifetime to be something else—*how can I possibly explain the relief?*

I was thirty-six when I finally, in my own eyes, became who I wanted to be.

You must understand that success has been central to me. *Always.*

I remember meeting my husband. He was so unlike all the other men. Not ambitious, not using me as some kind of trophy, and not wanting anything from me other than myself. A kind, generous, sexy man who was perfect for me in every way.

He didn't care about my success, my two-million Twitter followers, or the press who always hounded me. He liked *me.*

The real me.

Knew me inside out from our first meeting. Not that other face I was forced to wear in public.

I had seven happy years with him and produced two, fine-boned, intelligent children. Children I never wanted until I met him.

I look down at the match. Half burnt, my story half told.

Yes, my life was perfect.

I can hear you laughing. That statement always precedes a fall from grace… and what a fall it was. How did it happen?

Didn't you read the papers? *You know what I did…*

My network sent me to Birmingham to cover some sports awards thing. A weekend job and a nice little earner.

It should've been a bit of fun. But it was ruined by one of those young and dynamic, twenty-something presenters. For 'dynamic' read 'irritating, arrogant, sexist prick'. You know the type. 'All mouth and no trousers' is the saying.

But I'm no bitch—far from it. I offered my advice and help in a professional way, like I would to anyone else. His reaction… "Thanks… but I don't need no help from an old girl like yourself. Things have moved on since your day. Comprendi?" …said to my face.

To my face.

He might as well have kicked me in the tits.

You know what I did?

On the outside, I was all professionalism. Yet I undermined that nasty little prick at every opportunity. Nothing noticeable, but enough to show him up. The night was long, and I did what I had to do. When we were finished, myself, the producer and a few other staff ended up at the hotel bar. The prick was chauffeured back to London.

More fool him.

Always chat to the backroom boys, is what I say. I learnt that back in F1. Keep the mechanics happy. Press the palm. Smile at their shit jokes… do everything to keep them on side.

Money in the bank.

If you've not worked in telly before, you won't know how everyone likes a drink. We sat in the bar until the early hours. Chatting, drinking, chatting some more. And all the time, there *he* was.

Have you guessed who he might be yet?

Here's a clue. He must have been twenty-five, twenty-six. Tanned, gorgeous, with broad shoulders struggling to break free from an open-necked shirt.

My-oh-my, how he smouldered.

He sat at the bar on his own, until, thankfully, the producer asked him to join us. After some subtle prompting that is. He ordered a whisky on the rocks and knocked it back like in the movies.

Fatal.

I'm no prude. I've had my share of fun and games over the years. And why not?

A girl has to eat.

But since my marriage, there has been only my husband who I love dearly. I'd looked, like we all look, but this guy...?

It's hard to describe the kind of beauty in a man that makes you stop open-mouthed and stare. That makes men gape too—a mixture of jealousy and unrestrained admiration flushing their annoyed features.

This guy did it for me, heart-thumpingly so.

He turned to me with that now famous smile, running his tongue over moist lips. You know what I imagined him doing…

We got talking. He seemed genuinely surprised when I told him I worked in television. I was impressed—he liked *me,* not the fact I was a TV personality. I couldn't believe my luck. It was one of those rare opportunities that come once in a lifetime, that sure bet with the most beautiful guy you have ever seen—or so you say afterwards—*but he was beautiful.*

I'm not vain, but time was catching me up. Soon, a boy like him would not see me at all, and that thought grated, regardless of all my considerable common sense.

But it was more than that—and don't pretend that you don't know what I mean as we've all been there, yeah?

After years of faithful marriage, with life happy but a little boring, it's impossible not to crave a little excitement, isn't it? And then, out of the blue, you meet someone new and that aching bud of anticipation returns, burning deep within, thrilling along nerves, shuddering up and down with a hot fire desperate to be quenched.

God, how I wanted him. And, of course, who would ever know?

Don't laugh!

I know some of you are judging me. That I brought what happened on to myself. But don't fool yourself that in my situation you would have gone back to your room, horny and alone.

No fucking way.

I took my fill like any normal woman and was grateful, and you would have done the same.

When he went, it must have been about five in the morning. I wasn't sorry to see him go, nor was I guilty. I'd done nothing wrong. Sexual betrayal is nothing compared to the betrayal of love.

I went home to my husband with renewed vigour for our relationship. I was on top of the world. This night of passion had done something special and I was grateful.

Two weeks later, late on Friday night after my weekly chat-show, a journalist friend of mine phoned and told me everything.

I went to the toilet and sat down. I was shaking. I couldn't believe what had happened.

The Sunday paper said it all:

MY SORDID NIGHT OF SEX WITH
LOVE-CHEAT PETROL REDHEAD

Ex-Page-Seven-Hunk tells of drugs & bondage session...

I forced myself to read the story. You may or may not be the same as me—I have a healthy attitude towards sex and life—but to have all those intimate details drooled over by friends, colleagues, and strangers, and to feel the stare of their lecherous eyes?

The squalid horror of those words still burn me now.

As to what happened next? You know the pathetic drill for losers caught out in this way… although I was more pathetic than most. I lost my job and most of my fortune in an ill-judged libel case and stupidly fell into drinking.

Finally, my husband left, taking the kids. It was the lowest of the low.

And there *he* was, on all the chat shows, furthering himself, furthering his career.

Only one word was on my lips: *Revenge.*

Two years, I said to myself then. Two years is not too long to wait.

I pulled myself together and wangled a job on Northern-Ireland radio—no need for passports you see. Forward thinking, I call it. And although the pay was not as good as I was used to, it was more than enough for my plans.

Two years.

And as that deadline approached, my head began to race with *The Plan.*

I'm not a violent person by nature, nor cruel. I just believe in retribution, in people who've done wrong having to pay.

You understand?

I stare at the slowly dying flame. It too, is part of my retribution. I look into the hole and smile my most winning smile.

I have practised this face many times while imagining his terrified, pleading, beautiful features.

Bliss.

Often on the TV, you hear the phrase 'shallow-grave'. Not this. I dug it personally with clothes and tools bought in a small town two-hundred miles away about a year and a half ago. The petrol at about the same time.

It was not hard to lure him. He was as ever self-centred—making love to his own ego, unworried when that tramp actress he was screwing was not waiting for him at his out-of-town den.

I heard him arrive, singing his latest pop song to himself—woefully out of tune. Waiting upstairs, I chuckled to myself.

It sounds simple, but chloroform is what I used. I stole it for just the same purpose two years ago from my make-up department. I remember looking at that bottle and smiling, sometimes on a daily basis.

I rented a little isolated lodge in Wales by phone. Money sent through a bogus account I'd set up for myself years ago when such things were easier, and I'd had a mind for the secretive and underhand. Not that I was either—I just loved the thought. I was pleased to find that my alter-ego at the bank still existed. After the money was paid, I closed it.

Easy.

Crime thrillers are my pastime you see.

The lodge is mine on a two-year lease and I never visited until I had reason to. An easy trip from Liverpool in the small estate car I bought privately.

It's amazing how people don't recognise me in the wig and the fat-suit that went missing from Props. And with a pair of sunglasses and make-up, I'm a totally different woman.

Wales is a beautiful… but many don't know that even in this day and age, it's also a wilderness. I spent many weekends finding the perfect spot.

Did I tell you about my love of technology? I chose a suitable site and set up a few hidden time-lapse cameras. In the previous eight months not one soul had passed.

Not one.

A sudden breeze in which the flame flickers. It does not falter but grows. I have decided to wait until it burns my fingers. I have told him this, recited in detail what I am going to do on a regular basis since his abduction.

He is naked in the hole, trussed up, hands behind his back. I left him there for the night, letting him get to grips with what I was going to do. He had to be naked, just for the humiliation. By far the best bit was removing the gag and allowing him to plead with me. I videoed it before leaving. A pure indulgence I know, but so enjoyable on the way back to my secluded cottage.

I think he guessed I was for real when I dropped the memory card in with him, and poured the petrol, slick and greasy, over his naked, trembling body.

Striking the match—oh, how he tensed—so beautiful he was!

"So charred you will be!" I whispered, stifling a laugh.

He was almost hysterical in the hole… in the pit… *in his grave.*

The flame flickers against my fingers.

"Ow!" I say, just for effect.

It doesn't burn me. No. I am wearing my old fire-resistant racing coveralls. I know all about petrol, about burning and fumes and, well, I just have to watch.

I drop the match into the hole, igniting the petrol before it touches him.

Pleasure is a strange thing.

I can't explain the considerable delight as he burns—screaming through the gag. All too soon, he stops moving, his face tightening and his once-magnificent jaw snapping.

The police never found him, and I wasn't interviewed. I've even got my career back—not as successful as before, but making a good living all the same. My husband talks to me ever more increasingly, and with rehab behind me, I get see the kids regularly.

Life is good again, but know this…

Never, ever cross the Petrol Redhead.

FOUR:

HOW TO MAKE IT UP TO JULIA

IT WAS difficult. I didn't know what I had done to upset her in the first place. We were always so very much in love. Sure, we'd had our arguments like most couples, but there was never any hint of a problem, not until three months ago.

I'd come home after work and everyone was waiting for me. The kids hugged me like I'd been away for a month, not the eight hours since breakfast. Julia was cold and distant in a way I'd never seen before.

We haven't made love since then. She insists I sleep in the spare room.

Why?

Of course, I've slept there before on the odd night, but if we had our disagreements, we'd learnt to solve them before bedtime. The spare room was a rare event for me as we both hated being apart.

Just a normal couple… or so I thought.

This was more than that not sleeping together. She could not bear to let me touch her.

I'm not the nervous type, nor the kind of man to balk at confrontation or to sit back while events pass me by. I've always been driven and successful because of it. And yet, there was a fear inside of me so large, so terrifying, that I was unable to act.

In my heart of hearts, I knew Julia didn't love me anymore, and to confront her directly would allow this terrible truth to escape into the world. So instead, I bought her presents, made sure I was doing my bit around the house, left the damn toilet seat down, helped with the washing up and watched my drinking. All to no avail.

It was as if she despised everything about me.

Occasionally, I'd catch her looking at our photographs and crying—and unable to face the truth, I would slink away unheard.

And it was not just Julia. We'd always had a great social life and a wonderful group of friends. Now, we never saw them. No phone calls, nothing. And I soon learned not to contact them myself—as soon as they saw my face on the vid, they'd freeze and make lame excuses. It was obvious that they all knew we were having problems—or God forbid—they guessed Julia was having an affair. That possibility had been growing in my mind for some time.

It couldn't be true.

Not Julia. We loved each other for Christ's sake!

But that niggling doubt grew inside of me like an ulcerous tumour leaking bile into my mind with every disgusted look, every secret tear.

Work was a totally different matter. I always had problems with management. My style was, shall we say, 'abrasive'. Not my intention, you understand, but with busy deadlines and work arriving in flurries, I'd get the job done regardless of who I trod on.

I was aware of this trait, and seemed to be unable to change my behaviour. As a result, I was not a popular boss or colleague—the effective Rottweiler who did a great job keeping everyone in line.

Nowadays, things had changed. My staff were more relaxed around me. We joked and laughed at the cooler, and others in the department, who I'd barely talked to, sought out my friendship. Many clients, who had previously only been just business acquaintances, now actively invited me out on social occasions.

Work was going well.

It was just my home-life that was all shot-to-pieces—and I didn't know why—or at least, I didn't want to know why.

Only the kids gave me any joy. Aged four and five, they delighted in me as always, although Julia never liked to leave me alone with them.

Did she despise me? Was that it? Was I keeping her away from some secret lover? From some other life? Did she hate me for being such a faithful, loving husband?

My anger was hard to control, but I managed it. I had to. I'd rather have Julia in my life hating me, than no Julia at all—there then might be a chance she would come back to me.

And so that was my life. Coming home day after day to a cold, lifeless house where the only love I felt came from my kids, and the only friendship came from colleagues at work.

I couldn't go on like this. Who could? There was only one thing for it—a holiday to sort everything out. I'd book us away for a few days and try to get things back to normal.

Maybe away from the kids and our suburban existence, Julia would realise what she was putting in jeopardy.

I'd had a few credit card problems recently. They all had to be changed due to some annoying identity hack—you know the sort of thing. But nothing could have prepared me for what happened when I tried to book a romantic Dubai holiday.

Sitting in my office, I went through the normal on-line channels only to fail on the last step. Guessing it was this problem with the cards, I phoned the agent. We went through details—times, hotels, and when I came to pay? …A long pause.

"Is it the damn card?" I blurted, trying to control my anger. "I'm afraid this has been happening off and on now for months."

"No, no. It's not your credit—I'll put you through to our manager…"

"Hold on, I—"

A few clicks and whirrs.

"Ah hello, Mr Hackett, how can we help you today?"

"I thought I was booking a short trip to Dubai. But I can assure you… I have no credit problems. Quite the opposite, if I'm honest."

"No, no Mr Hackett, your credit's fine. It's your passport."

"What's my passport got to do with you? You're a travel agency, not the damn Home Office."

"That's right, but I think you might need to check it."

"Huh?"

"All I'm saying, Mr Hackett, is that we can't possibly book you a holiday abroad. We have many romantic locations within the British Isles if you would like to reconsider?"

"Don't be ridiculous, I just want to go to Dubai. End of story."

"As I said, I'm afraid we're not authorised to do that. Goodbye."

He put the phone down!

It was the same at other travel agencies. As soon as I entered my details, the process either stopped, or I was informed that the destination was no longer available, or that my credit had been rejected.

Rejected!

The day had gone slowly after that. I quelled my natural desire to phone home to ask Julia to check my passport. I was sure I had at least another four or five years left on it. It was only Dubai, not bloody Cuba!

The morning dragged. I had a few meetings—datavised mainly from Tokyo—and the project I was supervising in Java. Come to think of it, I'd normally visit these locations at least once every six weeks. I'd not visited in months.

That was odd in itself.

It was okay to be a project manager via the virtual meeting place, but I always liked to be there in person to put a bit of stick about. And now that I remembered, I had mentioned a work trip a few times and been knocked back.

Things are just too busy James, we can't afford to lose you to Japan again, Bex, my boss, had told me after my last request.

Funny how I'd forgotten about that. Bex was very similar to me, brash, abrupt, and always got the job done.

I walked into my secretary's office. "Schedule me on a quick in-and-out visit to the Tokyo project will you Sue."

Sue looked up from her desk. "Are you absolutely sure, Mr Hackett? You do have a lot of work coming up."

I stood there amazed. Sue never answered back—it wasn't in her job description. As to my schedule, I knew it inside-out. Visits like this were factored into the job.

"I beg your pardon," I answered, rounding on her. "Just book it, Susan. You can do it now while I'm here."

I don't want to sound like the office bully, but work is a black-and-white thing for me. Of course, I lean to the left politically, I always have. I believe in equality, fairness, respect. But I also believe that if you're paid to do a job, you do what you're told, if not, you're fired.

Black-and-white.

But Sue, who had always been in awe of me, didn't react. She picked up the phone. "I'll call Bex."

I trembled with rage. "Don't you dare!"

Sue ignored me. I went back to my office and sat down, fuming. *What the hell was going on?* Sue had never acted like that before. Sure, she'd been more relaxed recently. If I was honest, she'd been like a timid mouse for so long that the change had been a relief. But this was out-and-out insubordination.

My phone buzzed. Bex's face on the vid-screen. But just a still—she'd turned off the live-feed. In terms of office etiquette, this did not bode well.

"James, I hear you're trying to leave us again?" she said in her rich Jamaican tones. "That just won't do."

"And why ever not? It's never been a problem before."

"We need you here," said Bex, her voice peculiarly slow and adamant. "You are the heart and soul of the business. Remember?"

Maybe she was right. Did I really need to go? Maybe I did have too much on?

"Sue says you're also very busy at the mom—"

"I want Sue out of my office. I don't care what you do with her, but she has to go!"

"Why is that, Jim?" The tone was quizzical.

"It's her attitude these days, she's just… I dunno. There's just a lack of respect. If I ask her to do something, I don't want a damn debate, I want it done. You of all people understand that, surely?"

There was a pause. "She's a great asset, James. That description doesn't sound like Sue at all."

"Don't you get it? Her attitude's all wrong!"

"James… Jim, look, you've been under a lot of stress. Don't blame Sue for keeping an eye on you. It was at my request."

"Stress? Are you mad? I've never suffered from stress in my life. Not till now when I find everyone is ganging up on me to stop me doing my job properly. And how dare you go behind my back like that." I shook my head, clearing my mind of an inexplicable fog. "I'm going to Tokyo, and that's final. I need to see things first-hand. That's my style Bex, we both know that. So put me on a plane today, I can be back tomorrow evening."

"I'm afraid that's not possible, Jim. Please don't make me pull rank on you. I really need you here. Why not take the afternoon off, calm down a little and come in fresh tomorrow?"

"If you can spare me for the afternoon, you can definitely spare me away for a few hours in Tokyo."

"Jim, go home. I'll phone Julia."

"What has Julia got to do with anything?" It was a fair question. Julia had her own career. She never wanted to play the doting wife. Our working lives were separate and that was the way we liked it… *wasn't it?* It surprised me that Bex even knew her name, never mind had her phone number to hand.

Bex sighed. "Jim, you were a good man, you really were."

"Were? You're surely not sacking me, are you?" I said jokingly, although inside I was genuinely worried.

"Don't be silly Jim. Just a slip of the tongue. I'm very busy, so this is not advice but a direction from your boss. Go home." She put the phone down.

"Shit."

Sue came in and stood by the door a few minutes later. "Your wife rang, she's expecting you back at the house."

I didn't say anything. Julia should've been at work. If she was waiting at home, something serious was going on.

I left the office and spent a long time sitting in my car, thinking, replaying what had gone on. It made no sense, none of it. Finally, I drove away. It was only when the battery light on the runabout began to flash that I grudgingly headed back home.

Julia was waiting for me. The kids, who should have been back from school, were nowhere to be seen.

"Jim, we need to talk."

Ignoring her, I ran upstairs. I was hot all over, nervous in that sweaty way I normally get before flying. I went into our wardrobe, took down the box where we kept all our personal documents and routed through it. My passport wasn't there.

"You won't find it, Jim."

"Why not?" I asked, my heart thumping in my chest, wondering how Julia knew what I was looking for.

"I'm so sorry Jim," she said, beginning to cry.

"About what?"

"About the holiday you planned, about…" she looked around the bedroom, shaking her head forlornly, and visibly crumbled, "…about all this."

"How can you know about the holiday? I went over to her and, as usual, she flinched from my touch. "What the hell is going on?"

"I didn't know it was going to be like this. I was thinking of the children… you see that don't you? I was messed up. Christ! This is all messed up. You have got to realise that I'm sorry for what I've done, very sorry. Okay?"

A knock at the door downstairs.

"That's for you." And from nowhere, she started sobbing. I'd never seen her so distraught.

"I'm not going anywhere until you tell me what this is about."

"Just answer the damn door!"

Something snapped inside of me. I'd been a fool for so long—hiding my head in the sand instead of facing the problem full on. "Okay," I said, "but when I come back, I want us to sort all of this out, okay?

"Goodbye Jim," she said.

Trembling, I went down and opened the door.

A fat man in a white boiler suit and clipboard. "Mr Hackett?" he asked, smiling.

"Yes," I answered, ready to slam the door in his face and go back upstairs. This was no time for a sales pitch.

"About your missing passport…"

"Huh?" What did this man have to do with any of that?

"Yeah, there's been a bit of a mix-up, if you could come to the van with me, there are a few papers to sign and everything will be okay.

I looked behind him. Parked on the roadside was a white Ford. Across the road, my neighbours were looking out through their windows, some standing on their neatly trimmed lawns.

"It will only take a moment."

I stared into his eyes, giving him my full attention. What I saw confirmed my suspicions. He was lying. "Okay, but make it quick," I replied.

"This way," he said, the smile returning to his face.

The man turned, and in that moment, I pushed into him, knocking him over. I tried to run, my heart readying for escape.

The man was quicker than I thought. He wrapped his hands around my ankle. I fell over, kicking at him. Out of the corner of my eye, two men carrying long sticks jumped out of the van and rushed towards me. I scrambled to my feet. One of the men touched his stick to my back. I felt a sudden jolt in my kidneys and fell like a sack of potatoes.

"Sorry about that, Mr Hackett," the fat man said, getting to his feet to supervise the two others, his breath rasping with the effort. "We've all got our jobs to do."

"Julia!" I shouted weakly. There was no answer from the house. "Help!" Even my neighbours didn't come to my aid.

The men strapped my feet and my hands to a stretcher before loading me into the van. The fat man got in with me and closed the doors. He bashed a hand on the inside of the cab, and it pulled away.

"Now that wasn't too bad, was it?" he said taking out a sandwich box and a flask. "I thought you'd put up more of struggle though, a big chap like yourself."

"What the hell is going on?"

"You've been returned, Mr Hackett—happens more often than the company likes to admit. But since the dollar investment is low and the insurance returns so high… well, why not."

"Is this a kidnap?"

Laughing, the man put down his flask and picked up his clipboard. "James Hackett. Return Order. Signed and stamped today by a Mrs Julia Hackett. I was there when she came in. Tasty. You're a lucky fella."

"Julia did this?"

"Well yes, she is the executer of your estate, well, the deceased James Hackett's estate that is. I'm afraid you're not who you think you are."

"Deceased? I'm not fucking dead!"

"I'm afraid the paperwork says you are." He smiled inanely. "Sorry, my little joke. You died months ago—the real Mr James Hackett that is. I think it was a plane crash or something. Very nasty by all accounts. It looks like you had your insurance up to date otherwise you wouldn't be here."

"You mean…?"

"Yep, you're a Replacement. Memories stored during your last medical were close enough for the cloning procedure to be carried out without any major interruption to your life. That's a top med-package your company gives you."

I didn't believe it. This couldn't be true, it just couldn't. "You're lying," I whimpered.

"Of course they didn't tell you, it's the shock or something—total mental breakdown. That's academic now of course."

"But I love her."

"You were probably getting quite a few problems with credit cards and officialdom in general yeah? It's because you're legally dead. All that passport nonsense was due to the fact that Deadies—you in this case—are not recognized as full humans in other countries, not yet anyway. Religious intolerance I call it. Deep hypnosis therapy should have put you off travel for life, but you are intelligent and driven. It never works out too well for people of your type. It's the one time that being thick really pays off. So don't be hard on your wife, it's difficult to live with a walking corpse."

"No…"

"That's the way it goes sometimes," the man continued obliviously. "I believe she really, really loved him though, that much was apparent."

"She loves me, I'm him."

"*Was him,*" the man said, opening his sandwich box and smiling. "I'm afraid the real you died. I'm sorry it's the not the news you wanted to hear, but with what's happening next, well, they think its best you know."

I cried then. I sobbed for Julia, for my kids and, most of all, I cried for myself. "What's going to happen?" I asked after the fit had passed, not wanting to hear the answer.

"You're to be decommissioned."

"Oh Christ!"

"Yeah, I know, not a nice way of putting it. At least it will be over quick." He unwrapped a syringe pre-pack and jabbed it into my shoulder. "This will help. Relaxant."

"Something has gone wrong somewhere, you've got to listen. I'm definitely me."

"'Fraid not, and, I guess you secretly know it."

I said nothing. It all made dreadful, awful sense.

"Listen, Bud—you were lucky right? You got what most of us don't get, yeah? A chance to say goodbye."

"But I didn't say goodbye, I didn't know—no-one told me," I wailed.

"You got kids?"

I nodded.

"Then you got to see them again. I'd say that for a dead man, that's not a bad achievement."

"I'm not dead!"

"That's one interpretation. The law says otherwise."

I tried to struggle against the bonds, but the straps were immovable. "I won't—I won't let it happen…"

"I'm afraid it already has. Sorry."

"What?"

The man nodded his head towards my shoulder. "That wasn't a relaxant, but I think you've guessed that, a clever man like yourself… We're off to the crematorium." He took a bite of his sandwich, smiled sadly and patted me affectionately on the side of the head. "You're nearly there…"

His smiling, half-sad face began to fade, and in its place came a slow, all-encompassing blackness.

"I love you Julia," I whispered.

FIVE:

BALANCING THE BOOKS

"**I'M NOT** the type to gossip," said Deirdre over the pristine, white tablecloth of the exclusive restaurant.

"That's the kind of sentence usually followed by a b—" Dan began.

"But Jane's a real bitch."

Jane. Four letters. The tenth, first, fourteenth and fifth numbers of the alphabet. Adding up to the number thirty. Or one-hundred and one thousand, one-hundred and forty-five if written in sequence. Or an even seven-hundred if multiplied. Dan's brain did the mathematics effortlessly, unconsciously finding sequences and patterns.

Deirdre took a large gulp of the vintage red wine Dan had chosen especially for this meal. He'd brought it and its sister bottle to the restaurant earlier in the day. The Maître d' was more than happy to serve such a distinguished wine for a small 'corkage fee' and was even happier when Dan rounded up the figure to something far more pleasing to his numerical way of thinking. Some numbers were not intrinsically lucky, but they had other properties that Dan admired. And why shouldn't the man benefit from his getting the numbers in the correct order?

"You don't know her, but you know the type. All gob and no knickers. I don't mind people, I'm as open-minded as the next woman, b—"

"But..." said Dan with a cheeky smile.

Deirdre ignored him. "...But I have to sit opposite her at work. And controlling? You don't know the half of it."

"What is it you do again?"

"It was all in the email. Didn't you read the email?"

Dan smiled, "Yes, of course." *Three paragraphs. Twenty-four words, thirty-seven words and one-hundred and eighteen words. All adding up to one-seven-nine. A prime number.* "I just wanted to hear it from your lips. We are actually here after all. In the real world."

Deirdre took another gulp of her wine and rudely gestured to the wine waiter for a refill. "It's boring. A boring job at a boring company. I turn up, do as little as possible, and go home."

"And I suppose that Jane is always trying to get you to do things, huh?"

"So you *do* know the type? Nasty, skinny, uptight cow. And you should see the way she dresses. The girl's a slut. Plain and simple."

The wine waiter, a small man, brown-skinned with a warm face showing a mix of Indian and Chinese—on his nametag: 'Peter'—appeared and poured a splash of wine into Deidre's glass costing, by Dan's estimation, two hundred and thirty-seven pounds and eighty-two pence.

"Call that a refill?" Deidre sneered. "To the rim, I'm gonna need it."

Three-hundred and thirteen pounds, forty-seven pence, Dan revised.

She pulled a mock grimace in Dan's direction, her large purple earrings swinging to-and-fro from under the weird umbrella of her over-dyed, plum-tinted hair. Deidre appeared to love the colour violet. Her lipstick and shoes were also this hue, as was her voluminous dress with its rather lurid pattern of enormous flowery blooms.

A spiral pattern of eleven flowers (a Fibonacci prime) increasing in size—a perfect representation of the Fibonacci sequence. The Golden Ratio.

Dan had been on many first dates. Tonight was his one-hundredth and twenty-second. They seemed to bring out the worst in people. But that was what he looked for. It was his game. His secret pleasure. And Deidre had all the hallmarks of being an A1, tip-top candidate for his purpose. Single, no kids, or so she said. But kids were important. A showstopper—*mostly*.

He chose her carefully, scrolling through the dating sites for just the right flavour. Deidre's profile was almost classic. A brief introduction followed by lists of what she didn't like including all the normal things: *selfish bastards, jerks, farting, football, dogs, cats, smoking, beards and not treating me as a lady* and a few more off-the-wall pet-hates such as *talking when I'm shopping, phoning me during my soaps, not keeping your car clean* and, bizarrely, *antique fairs and clock-collecting.* All within *two-hundred and six words*—the smallest number to contain all five vowels once.

The clock-collecting made Dan laugh. A clock had led him directly to his present vocation as a serial dater and to this date. Not that he told her that of course.

He smiled. Hers was a long list of hates, leaving no room for anything she liked, which Dan guessed, was pretty much nothing and no-one. The astounding thing? This wasn't her first date. Other men—very possibly sad, desperate, and lonely men—must have hoped there was something lurking under such a defensive profile. Dan surmised they were as disappointed as he was elated. In her defence, the title of her little online missive was more positive: *Forty-something and looking for fun*. Although he imagined 'fun' in Deidre's world consisted mainly of getting sloshed and bad-mouthing everything and everybody, before passing out on the sofa in front of one of her many soaps.

Yes. She was perfect.

Most of Dan's existence upon planet Earth had been spent as a low-level accountant commuting daily to the City of London. But he didn't mind. Dan was obsessed with numbers, their relationships, and their power. Numbers were everything to him and he counted *everything*. If he needed to find out how many bottles of his favourite Domain Grand Cru he'd drunk in the last ten years, he'd open up his master spreadsheet and there would be the answer. If he wanted to know the exact number of years, months, weeks, days and minutes he'd spent at work, it was all there—even the cumulative time he'd spent on toilet breaks or talking to that lovely temp, Angie, who he had totally failed to get off with.

Counting made sense of everything to Dan. Filling in all those empty electronic cells gave him real purpose. On finishing work, he looked forward to his commute, to taking out his Notebook and updating his many sheets. Bliss.

His was a simple, happy, relaxed and *numbers fulfilled* life. And it would have been perfect if not for one, constant, irksome problem…

Other people.

He didn't despise people *per se.* He wasn't anti-social, or indeed bad company when forced to talk to them. If anything, his social skills were significantly more adept than anyone else he encountered, but he simply had no interest in them. They were a distraction from his numbers. And any distraction from what he saw as his primary purpose ruffled him. For the most part, he coped well, but there was one type of person he couldn't get along with at all. They were what he liked to call the *Misfits.* They were the awkward numbers. Numbers that had no symmetry or elan. His life was infested with them. Rudely intruding into his world and making a mess of his tidy, blessed spreadsheets.

It seemed incredible to him that people could go through their lives so belligerently, without a care or concern for how their anti-social, selfish behaviour affected others. Every time he was abused, bumped into, or shouted at, something hardened inside him. He never said anything, never complained. That couldn't happen. He was English and terribly middle-class. But inside he seethed, planning elaborate revenges on all those dreadful people who had made his life a living hell…

And so Dan did the only thing he could do. *He counted.*

He counted the number of times people had sat next to him on the train, shouting the petty dramas of their egotistical little lives down their phones blissfully unaware of others around them. He took note when people walked into him, expecting him to get out of their way, telling him he was a 'fucktard', 'a stupid fucking idiot' or a complex mixture of other insults and expletives. Just for being quiet, polite, or trying to be helpful. He counted their words, the number of times the same letters appeared, the pauses and the *fucks.* He recorded everything, entering the details meticulously into his master spreadsheet. He'd work for weeks on end, until the numbers added up, until he could find their number and put a line under it. Only then, could he move them to the 'deleted column' and relax.

Dan was nothing if not meticulous. An essential quality in an accountant and the reason he was kept down. That and his middleclass English reserve that never complained when louder, less qualified colleagues were promoted above him. He was too valuable to be wasted in management, where, as Dan saw it, the main skillset was the ability to attend pointless meetings, take Fridays off, and talk in loud, purposeful, and incomprehensive corporate patois.

But work was behind him now. He'd retired at the exact age of fifty-three and two months—*a rather neat hendecagonal pyramidal number*—with a tidy pension, substantial savings and a polite *thank you* to everyone he'd worked with over the years. Dan hadn't expected anything other than a slow, boozy decline into travel, fine dining, and old age. But on the occasion of his retirement, his raft of guilty managers, finally realising his worth, perhaps, bought him an antique, miniature carriage clock. A beautiful, worn, peculiar thing. And Dan's life took a new and unexpected direction.

"…puffing herself up for that Mr Edwards, who she is all over like a sticky rash. You listening to me?"

Dan came back to himself and smiled. "Of course, Deidre. You're still chatting about Jane. That… um *cow*, you work with."

"I thought you were drifting away. Men do that, you know? Stop listening when a lady is talking. I'm not the type to let them get away with it."

"I can see that. But be assured—I find you stimulating company."

"Aw, you say the nicest things, Daniel."

"I prefer to be called Dan, if you don't mind. Three letters instead of six. Odd components not even. Three is a more powerful number."

Deidre shrugged "Well, I prefer Daniel."

"Of course you do."

"You'll get used to it. I had a boyfriend called Dan. I didn't like him. You don't want to remind me of him, do you?"

"I suppose not."

"You're very easy to talk to, but you know that, don't you?"

"I've always had the knack for conversation. *Agreeable*, people say."

"I do like people who always agree with me!" She laughed as if making a great joke. "The other Dan never did. He had a right gob on him."

The first course arrived. Salmon Carpaccio. Dan beamed. A flawless circle of delicious *Salmo salar. Radius one point two seven three two three nine five four four seven inches. Circumference? A perfect eight inches.*

Deidre stabbed at the raw salmon with a fork, as if harpooning minnows in a barrel, and stared curiously. "They're serving raw stuff here? What is this place?"

"Try a mouthful."

She gingerly put the morsel in her mouth, pulling a face like a bulldog chewing a wasp. "That's just weird," she said, her large, make-up caked jowls quivering as she spat the offending morsel back out onto her plate. "Yuck."

"I know the chef," said Dan. "He'll be terribly upset." He placed a tasty sliver of salmon upon his tongue and savoured the delicate flavours. *Six mouthfuls, six chews each and six swallows. Six-six-six.* He chuckled.

"Why didn't you tell me what I was ordering? You're supposed to look after a lady."

"There's a few more courses to come. I'm sure you'll find something you like."

"Not too many, I hope, I'm watching my weight. Although, if they're all like this rubbish, I'll soon be skin and bone."

Dan hadn't mentioned Deirdre's weight. She'd put down 'average' for body-type on her dating profile. And Dan agreed—she was averagely overweight. But physical shape meant nothing. It was not what he was after, nor why he was here.

Deidre's hands made a fist beneath her chin and she stared. "You're not very much like your profile picture. I know everyone tells a few white lies, but, to be honest, you're a lot older than I was expecting… and wider."

Dan was eating and too polite to speak with his mouth full.

"And your hair... you're grey."

Dan swallowed the sixth mouthful of salmon. "Silver, I like to think. But yes, my profile picture is from about ten years ago."

"Hmm. You fellas will try any trick to get a leg-over." She giggled loudly, so that others in the effete, quiet restaurant looked over at their table. "But I'm gonna have to tell you now, you're not my type okay? Way too old and past it. What were you thinking? That I wouldn't notice?"

Dan's kind, blue eyes stared into hers, holding her attention for the first time that night. "But it's about what's inside, don't you think? That's what I've found is the most important. How all the parts of ourselves add up, multiply and divide to create a whole. And may I say that you're my type. Very much so, Deidre. That must count for something."

"Ain't you the smooth talker. But I'm honest, I pride myself on it. I'm always honest to everyone about everything. So you won't mind me saying that grey hair reminds me of my granddad and that ain't attractive. Like I said, you're way too old and fat for me to be interested."

"I've always liked honest people, Deidre. Some people say it's not honesty, but rudeness. That their opinion is more important than other people's feelings. That they don't care who they hurt. But it's what I appreciate the most in people."

"You do?"

"It's an admirable trait. I'm sure others love you for it."

"…They do, yes. It's a sign of quality in a person. I'm always telling people that."

"I'm sure you are."

Deidre stared at him quizzically. "You're certainly a funny one, Daniel."

Dan took a delicious twenty-eight pounds and fifty-six pence sip of his wine, savouring both the flavour and the price. "I should hope so."

"You remind me of someone, you know that?"

"I do? That does sound very promising. But I can assure you, tonight is the very first time I've laid these eyes on your face."

The next course arrived. Pan-fried sea bass fillet on a bed of celeriac mash.

Deidre looked at the fish with mistrust. “I’ve never been a fan of foreign muck,” she said, “I prefer a curry or a pizza. Can’t go wrong with that.” She sniffed loudly at the fish, taking an experimental mouthful and, liking what she tasted, shovelled the whole plate down in a few mouthfuls.

“I enjoy meeting new and interesting people. Don’t you?” asked Dan, watching the food swim around in her mouth as she chewed.

Deidre shrugged and took another loud slurp of her wine. “Depends on who they are and how much dosh they’ve got!” She laughed hysterically. “You can certainly treat me again anytime you fancy. But not this awful place. And that doesn’t mean you can have your way with me. You won’t change my mind about that, not once it’s set.”

Peter cleared away the dishes. “I hope our entrée selection was to sir and madam’s satisfaction?”

“It was wonderful,” said Dan.

“You could be a bit faster with the wine,” said Deirdre.

“Of course, madam. I shall make sure your glass is always full.”

Peter left with their dishes. “What a toadying creep.”

“You think so? I find Peter to be very polite.”

“It’s his type. That’s the problem.”

“And just what is his type?” said Dan, controlling the sudden edge in his voice.

“Not his colour, I’m not racist. But he’s an immigrant. They all are these days. I bet he’s an illegal. They probably pay him with food scraps and a bed in the basement.”

“Peter picks up our used plates and doubles up as our waiter, but he is a trained Sommelier. He’s probably forgotten more about wine than I’ve ever known. We are in *Felipe’s*, one of the best restaurants in London. I eat here often, and I know Felipe personally. He, too, is a numbers man. He takes the greatest care in selecting his staff. Restaurant professionals come from far and wide to work for him.”

"Well you can tell Felipe from me, his restaurant sucks. And you won't get into my knickers by dropping names. I'm too classy for any of that."

"You've made that perfectly clear, Deidre. Repeatedly. Let me thank you again for your constant honesty. And now that we've solved that little issue, why not tell me a little bit more about yourself."

"I'm sorry Daniel, but one of my rules is to never give too much away on a first date. I prefer to be enigmatic."

"Yes, you've certainly been… um… *enigmatic* so far. Very much so… although you were very forthright about Jane, your unfriendly work colleague."

"That's because she's a sly one, always finding work for me to do. She even tried to get me to stay late. Can you believe that? Just because I didn't arrive on time. I told her. *I've got an important date at some posh place and I'm not gonna miss a free feed.* You should have seen her face. What a picture."

"Again, I'm overawed by your forthright nature."

"It is free though, yeah? You are paying?"

"Of course. I'm old-fashioned in that respect."

"Good. Cos there's no way I'd fork out my hard-earned cash for this posh rubbish. You decided to bring me here, Daniel, so you can pay. It's only fair."

"Yes, as I've already stated, I'm more than happy, as you might say, 'to fork out my cashola'."

"I only brought enough money for a taxi. I said all this in my email under 'Date rules'."

All the numbers relating to Deidre's four emails flew through Dan's head in a most agreeable way. "Yes, your emails were fascinating reads."

"We could've gone for a pizza. I know a nice place. Cheap. Better and more filling than these over-priced titbits."

"It's a shame you don't like the restaurant. It's my favourite place to eat in town."

"You bring all your dates here then huh?"

Dan shrugged. "Yes and no."

"What does that mean?"

"The question raises a paradox."

"A para—*what?*"

Dan raised his hand and the waiter came over. "Peter—"

"That's not his name. He won't give his real name," interrupted Deidre.

Dan ignored her. "—Peter, how long have you worked here?"

"Ten months, sir."

"Have you seen me before?"

"Yes, sir. Many times."

"And how many times have I brought a companion?"

"Sir always dines alone."

Dan indicated for Peter to leave. "You see? I only eat alone and yet here you are. A paradox."

"I'm not sure what you're getting at."

Dan sat back while Deidre fidgeted. A long pause. "Tell me something about you, from your past. You don't have to be enigmatic with me. It can be anything. The further back the better."

The change of tack seemed to unsettle her. "Huh?"

"Think back along the span of your life to a memorable event and tell me about it."

Deidre reached a fleshy hand around her wine glass. "Something funny?"

"Something that happened at a New Year's Party or a birthday."

"You mean when I've been drinking?"

"Possibly, I'm just interested in an actual date. Numerals are my thing, you see. It's all about the numbers."

"You trying to work out if I'm lying about my age, you sneaky bugger? Well a lady never tells."

"But Deidre, you're forty-four."

"How do you know that?"

"The Internet."

If Deidre was taken aback, it didn't show. "Do you research everyone you date?"

"Oh yes, yes I do. I always like to check the integers. And the

Internet is so useful don't you think?"

"With that hair, they ought to call you the 'Silver Surfer'! But you're starting to sound a little creepy. I don't have to stay you know. I have my rules, Daniel. If I feel uncomfortable, I'm outta here. It's a taxi straight home."

"I hope you will stay, Deidre. I love learning about new people. About what makes them… *them.* Call it a quirk of mine, but I enjoy hearing people's stories."

"I don't like talking about my past. It's gone. Dead and buried."

"Then what have you got to lose? What's in the past is safe isn't it? It can't hurt you. As you said, it's gone. Finished."

"I dunno. There's something you're not telling me."

Dan took a thoughtful sip of wine and placed the glass precisely back on the indent it had made on the tablecloth. "I can't put anything past you, can I Deirdre? You're a canny one that's for sure. So let me come clean. You found me out... I'm a sort of freelance journalist, although that sounds a little grand. My hobby is writing blogs, articles and features… and meeting people."

"A journo?"

Dan gave a half nod. "I'm interested in the stories of people I meet on dating websites, on first dates. I take them out, feed them, water them, and get them to tell me an interesting story from their past. The stories will be anonymous, but I like to know a little bit about my subjects, hence the Internet research."

Deirdre appeared more intrigued than angry. "You're gonna tell everyone my intimate secrets?"

Dan gave a firm shake of his head. "No, it doesn't work like that. I only use gender, age and a date—and I tell the story anonymously. The stories are linked by the numbers in the tales themselves. I can make numbers add up and have significance. My particular expertise and a great little angle."

"So you… you date fellas as well?"

Dan wasn't expecting the question. "Why, yes. Although I don't actually *date* anyone. I'm here for their stories, that's all.

Plain and simple."

Deidre's face dropped. "So you didn't fancy me from my profile?"

"Of course! One of the perks of writing this piece is meeting exciting and interesting women."

Deidre didn't seem convinced. "So you want a story from me and it'll be published?"

Dan nodded. "In one of the women's magazines. I don't know which one yet, but I can email you the details."

"My mates will get to see it?" she asked eagerly.

"Oh yes… So you'll do it?"

"You are paying, aren't you? I suppose I could break my rule and let you get your way." She shrieked in amusement at her own joke.

The main arrived shortly after. Roast quail and seasonal vegetables.

"Where'd you get the chicken from?" Deidre nudged Peter with a sharp elbow. "Looks like it's shrunk in the wash!"

Peter carried on professionally, despite a grimace of pain.

Dan laughed politely.

After the food that, despite protestations, she savoured to the last sucked bone, Deidre agreed to tell him the story of what she called her 'eighteenth birthday bash'.

"You're right. I am forty-four. I was eighteen on the twentieth of February—you can work out the year for yourself—and to celebrate, me and the girls went for a weekend in Brighton. It was gonna be a wild-time, but something ruined it, good and proper." Deirdre took another swig of wine. Dan indicated for Peter to decant the second bottle.

"You stayed in a hotel?" Dan removed a little black book from his jacket pocket, unscrewed the top of an expensive fountain pen, and began to inscribe a long list of numbers.

"Yeah, I'll never forget it—The Viceroy Lodging House—they sent me a nasty letter about damage or something. It sounded posh, but it was a shithole, nothing like it said in the brochure. So we treated it like a shithole, plain and simple. I remember telling that smarmy girl on reception that the bogs didn't flush properly. Not that they did anything about it. It was run by some jumped up family. The girl was up the duff. Probably some stag got her that way. The place was full of fellas. Not that we minded!" She laughed louder than before. Some of the other diners were getting annoyed.

Dan sat back, enjoying the spectacle. "Go on," he said, basking in the magnificence of her ego.

"Well, we arrived on the Friday night, the nineteenth. Got off the train and went straight to the hotel. Found out we'd been ripped off, but we thought, fuck it. Let's go out and get pissed. And that's what we did. I was a teenager after all… and almost legal."

"As interesting as it sounds, your story doesn't quite have what I'm looking for. Young ladies out on the um… piste, shall we say, is a rather common experience."

"But something weird happened that weekend. Something I haven't thought about for years. I'm not sure what made me forget it."

"That's how the memory works," said Dan leaning forward. "But a little jog here and there and snap! It all comes flooding back."

"I picked up some fella in one of those beachfront nightclubs, left the girls, and went back to his place. I was sick all over his bed. But we still did it. He was fit as well. Nothing like what I have to put up with these days." She flicked disappointed eyes in Dan's direction. "Anyway, I woke early. He was snoring like a trooper, so I left him to it and made my way back to the hotel. It was a quiet morning... so I decided to walk along the beach. It was cold, but not like you'd notice. Serene. A gentle mist coming off the sea. No other people about. The sun was rising. And then I met this strange fella."

"Another party-goer?"

"No, he was old. White hair, overweight."

"Oh yes?"

"He sort of just appeared out of nowhere. Gave me a bit of

a shock to be honest. I wasn't worried. But you know what was weird? He knew my name. Called it out. I didn't know him from Adam. I asked him his name and—" Deidre's mouth hung open, her jaw slack.

"What is it?"

She shook her head in confusion. "He said to call him… *the Silver Surfer.*"

Dan donned his best surprised look. "That's quite a coincidence, Deidre. How peculiar. But do go on."

She said nothing, going pale.

"Deidre?"

"It can't be," she said.

Dan called Peter over. "A glass of water, please… quick. What is it, Deirdre?"

"I knew I recognised those eyes. It was you, all that time ago on Brighton beach."

Dan sat forward, his face a perfect mask of confusion. "Listen to what you're saying, Deidre. That's impossible. If I was there, I'd have been in my twenties. Not an old man. It can't have been me. It's just a coincidence. These things happen all the time. I may include it in my story, if you like?"

Peter arrived with the water and Deidre downed it in one. "I'm sorry," she said finally. "Of course, it's a fluke. It has to be. I don't know what I was thinking."

"I'm so sorry to have upset you. Are you okay? I can get you that taxi if you want?"

"No, I'll be okay. Maybe a… *brandy coffee?*"

Peter took the order and hurried away.

"You've got me worried, Deidre," said Dan. "Just what did this man do to you—my doppelganger?"

She frowned. "Well, nothing," she said after a long pause, coming back to herself. "It's what he said."

Dan scribbled furiously, filling the notebook page in his fast, precise hand. "Go on."

"He told me it was his job to rid the world of those people who… *whose numbers were not worth adding up.*"

"How odd."

"I laughed, told him he was drunk. But I knew that wasn't the case. He was so calm. That's what I remember, *that's what frightened me.* He told me it was the day of my eighteenth birthday. That it wasn't too late to change my life. I thought it was some prank set up by the girls, how else could he know all that stuff about me? But no. He was too serious. That's when…"

Peter arrived with the brandy coffee.

She took a sip, thick cream covering her top lip, wiped away with the back of her hand. "…when he threatened me."

"No!"

"He said if I didn't change, if I was still found wanting, he'd come back and… *balance the books.*"

"If you may pardon me, that's hardly a threat."

"But he did this…" Deidre drew an imaginary knife across her throat.

"Oh dear. That does seem a little melodramatic. But I can see you believed him."

"I did. It was the way he said it. I was hung over and half-asleep. He put the willies up me good and proper. He told me, as a start, to go and apologise to the pregnant girl at the hotel otherwise… *he'd be back.* And then, he was gone, like he wasn't there at all."

"And did you apologise? To the girl?"

"She was on reception when I returned and could see I was shocked. Made me a cup of coffee and sat me down. I found out her husband had been killed recently. That she had no money and was forced to work there. I gave her all the cash I'd saved for the weekend."

"And you felt better?"

"At first, yeah. But after I went back home, the more I thought about it, the more angry I became."

"Angry?"

"Well, it's obvious isn't it? They were in it together. How else could that old bloke know my name? He was her father or even her boyfriend. It was a scam and I fell for it. I phoned the hotel up and told them that little tart had defrauded me. Demanded that she was sacked."

"And did they… sack her?"

Deidre shook her head. "I don't know, I hope so."

"They sound like quite a pair, conniving together like that."

"Is that a good enough story for you?"

"Actually, it's perfect." Dan took out his miniature carriage clock. Small enough to fit easily into his pocket. It was an intricate device. Not only did it possess a clock face, but a series of many rotating numbers like a combination padlock, expertly worked in gold and silver. The numbers had fascinated Dan. It had taken him two years to work out what they were for and that the clock was not what it seemed. It was no antique, that much was for sure. Where it came from, Dan could only speculate. He was sure that it had reached his hands by chance alone. A retirement present bought by a junior no doubt. Luck had brought it to him, and his lifelong love of numbers had done the rest.

Some may have seen the odd timepiece as a power to right wrongs and do good in the world. Others certainly would have seen it as a route to personal glory and supremacy. But not Dan. No. He preferred simple asset management. Putting the numbers straight. Others might call it an eye-for-an-eye, but Dan was not so prosaic, he just wanted everything to add up.

"What's that?" asked Deidre.

"A gift," he replied. "From work."

"It's a bit tatty," said Deirdre, coming back to herself. "I hope you complained."

He raised the clock and held it before her. "You see these numbers? …*They're yours.*"

"Mine?"

"Oh yes. They are quite clear. Numbers never lie. Numbers never shout at you, or bump into you on the street. And I can always make them add up. You know, I've had many, many people sit opposite me on this table."

"But you said—"

Dan raised a finger. "The rich, the poor. Snobs and oiks—the whole gamut. All I had to do was find their numbers and move them to the deleted column." He spun the tiny clock in the palm of his hand. A flicker of lights, and Dan slumped back in his chair, nearly falling to the floor, his chest heaving.

Peter hurried over to the table. "Is everything alright, sir?" he asked.

Dan nodded. "Ignore me. Just another one of my turns, you've seen them before."

Peter nodded. "Yes, sir."

"I really ought not to dine alone," he added.

"No, sir," said Peter, standing by the empty chair opposite Dan. "I'm sure there are many ladies… or, if I may be so bold, gentlemen, who would be more than happy to dine with you."

"That is very kind of you, Peter."

"Is sir ready for the dessert?"

"No Peter, I'm quite sated. Be a good chap and get me the bill. Add the usual tip for yourself. And Peter…"

"Yes, sir."

"May I book a table for the same time next week?"

"For how many people?"

"Two. It's not my favourite number, but I'm feeling lucky…"

SIX

RACE TO THE RUN-TO

THE GLEAMING hellijet flew over the oasis. A fertile circle of land containing a small natural lake surrounded by huge dunes. Vegetation thrived for hundreds of metres, iridescent trees, hardy shrubs and grass-like meadows. It stood in the sand of the Amazon Desert like a large emerald eye with a pupil of pure blue. An explosion of jungle green amongst the featureless, coffee-coloured landscape.

Morgana cheered. "Well done, Cadet Hermans," she said, her sandy-coloured bob bouncing in time to her eager, precise words. "For a cadet to discover an oasis. Wow, I'm jealous." She saluted.

Blue, named after his intense and peculiarly large blue eyes, shrugged. He couldn't care less about the oasis. Sure, he'd been disappointed and a little upset that the humans in his time had pretty much cut down the world's most important rainforest, but that wasn't his fault. Just because he'd time-travelled, against his will to the twenty-fifth century didn't make him the Amazon's destroyer. More importantly, it should've been his turn to fly, but the sticklike Ganymedian, Hermans, had to show off with is 20/20 plus vision. Corvus, who sat next to him, said nothing.

"Well done indeed," intoned Captain Sekhmet, a wide smile plastered over her wide, serene face. "This will make a fine addition to your record."

Hermans brought the hellijet to a controlled landing on one of the sparse grassy meadows below a large dune and they disembarked.

"Cadet Hermans with me. Cadets Blue, Corvus and Morgana stay here with the Helli'," Sekhmet ordered, much to Blue's disappointment. The Ganymedian smiled in apology before stalking off into the trees and disappearing.

"Where did all this come from anyway? I thought this was supposed to be a desert?" said Blue kicking at the sand.

"An interesting question," replied Morgana with gusto.

Blue groaned inside. Morgana loved any opportunity to flap her lips.

"The Amazon is a dust bowl," she began, "but water from underground springs supplied from permeable aquifers sometimes reaches the surface. No one knows how or why. The sand is full of old seeds and insect pods left over from the mother of all rainforests. As soon as moisture arrives, life explodes out. Sounds simple, but the process is vastly more complicated. The eggheads are stumped. This is why Hermans' discovery is so brilliant. They can learn loads from this place. Some think it might be possible to rebirth the jungle."

Blue had forgotten Morgana's voice. She pitched it even higher in the open desert. An irritatingly noisome blurt of over-emphasised vowels and sharp consonants. She carried on for a while but Blue's disinterest, meant she soon lapsed into an uncomfortable silence. Corvus stood a few feet away, his arms crossed. Making it very clear he wanted nothing to do with either of them. Blue guessed the arrogant black-haired boy was still peeved at him. Blue had nearly killed Corvus, Hermans and himself, in a hellijet accident during flying practice the day before and Corvus hadn't talked to him since.

A long time passed. Far too long. "Where the hell are they?" Blue asked finally.

Corvus opened his mouth to speak but changed his mind.

"I'm going to investigate," announced Blue, walking off.

"We can't," said Morgana. "We were ordered to stay here."

"He's right," agreed Corvus begrudgingly.

"You think so?"

Corvus grabbed Morgana and dragged her along. "Let's go."

They ascended a grassy dune, disturbing a multitude of fat beetles that lurched clumsily into the air, crashing into their legs, trying to escape. Smaller flies, a cloud of black dots, flew into their eyes and mouths. Bugs crawled and scuttled everywhere.

"Well this is just, great," Blue whispered, swatting at the air.

Herman's elongated sandy footsteps led down the other side to a line of thin trees growing in number and size surrounded by a sea of shrubs and vines. Muffled shouts and yells came from further ahead, hidden by tightly packed vegetation.

Hermans and Sekhmet!

They ran towards the voices, trampling plants underfoot,

pushing through exotic greenery, disturbing even more and larger chattering insects before entering a tree-shadowed glade that surrounded a deep pool of bluest azure. The sounds of shouting became louder, until, in the distance on a small shore, they spotted Hermans and Captain Sekhmet fighting with what appeared to be an invisible enemy. Blue was a good fifty feet away, yet the fear on Hermans' face, as he swung a heavy branch around him, was obvious.

"Stay back, Morgana!" shouted Captain Sekhmet. "Stay back all of you. That's an ord-" Sekhmet lost her footing and fell to the ground. A wave of sand-coloured writhing shapes engulfed her.

"Crawlers!" Morgana shrieked, running forward under a wide arch of vine-entangled trees.

"Cadet Morgana, no!" shouted Hermans. He tried to fend off even more of the voracious insects. A crawler, a giant millipede the size of an outstretched arm, landed on his shoulder, sinking chitinous fangs into his lengthy neck. Hermans wrenched the insect away and, kicking the crawlers aside, bent over Sekhmet, pulling the bugs off her, stamping on them with stilt-like legs.

A crawler reared at Morgana's feet. She kicked it viciously in the head. She ran to the aid of Captain Sekhmet and Hermans.

"Be careful, Morgana," warned Corvus, "they're everywhere."

Blue stared at Corvus and nodded. They followed her, the heavy sound of falling crawlers thudding around them. They joined Morgana who had reached Hermans' side and dispatched as many of the creatures as possible.

"This One tried to stop them. Unfortunately, he was somewhat outnumbered by the voracious and rather irritated insects," Hermans rasped in his curiously formal, sing-song voice, clutching at his wounded neck. "This One should have protected his captain."

Morgana sank to her knees to examine Sekhmet. "That's not important now, Hermans."

Corvus kicked a still twitching crawler. "How bad is the captain, Morg'?"

"She unconscious. Covered in bites. We have to get her back

to the Run-To. Otherwise…"

Blue had no memory of how they managed to haul Captain Sekhmet past the crawlers to the hellijet. It was a blur of shouting, dragging, smashing, swatting and fear. By the time they arrived at the ship, her golden skin was ashen, her breath short and rasping. Hermans collapsed into a fever soon after and drifted into unconsciousness. Blue jumped into the pilot's seat and cycled the prop.

"No way!" shouted Corvus.

"Huh?"

"Maybe you missed it, Buddy-boy, but I have my wings. There's no way you're gonna fly me again, not after what you did."

"I-"

"No time for argument," said Morgana. "Corvus, get on the radio and tell the Run-To we have an emergency. We'll need serum ready. Blue, come back here and give me a hand."

Corvus pushed Blue aside and took over the control column. "Hab Control, Hab Control," he said, bringing the hellijet to life. "This is an emergency, over."

Static.

Corvus cycled the frequencies. Still no signal. "The damn radio's down."

"Try again in the air," ordered Morgana.

"No probs," replied Corvus.

The hellijet lifted off. Blue clambered into the back to join Morgana. Captain Sekhmet was deathly, whilst the fang marks on Hermans' neck had turned black. Blue shuddered.

"Hab Control, Hab? You dig me?" Corvus continued on the radio. More static. "We have an emergency. Two with crawler bites. We will be at the Run-To in…approx. eighteen minutes. Hab Control, do you read me?" Corvus repeated his message over and over. No reply.

"Anything we can do?" Blue asked Morgana.

"They need serum quick, or we'll lose them both," she replied with tears in her eyes.

Long minutes passed until, with a whine, the hellijet lurched violently sideways.

"What was that?" Morgana shrieked.

"I don't believe it," whispered Corvus. "I don't jazzing believe it."

The hellijet rocked. Corvus, struggling with the controls, bounced on his chair like a rag doll. A high-pitched squeal behind the sound of the engines. Sand whipped against the cockpit window.

Blue climbed over the seats and sat next to Corvus. A sludge-storm swirled above the desert. A living thing of whirling sand and ice—peculiar to the future and this now decimated region. They were about five minutes from the landing field, the shrouded shape of the Mound faint in the distance. Wind snarled at the hellijet.

"We'll have to turn back," barked Corvus.

"Nowhere close enough," said Morgana. "If we don't land in the next few minutes, Hermans and Captain Sekhmet won't make it."

The rapidly growing storm transfixed Blue. "I can fly this."

"Don't be stupid. You'll kill us all," sneered Corvus.

Blue pulled his attention away from the squall and looked straight at the raven-haired boy. "We can't let Sekhmet and Hermans die… We can't."

"But to fly into a sludge-storm is suicide."

"No. I can see inside it," said Blue. The calm certainty of his words surprised him. "I can see wind patterns, pressure lines and speed vectors. I can fly within them."

Corvus was adamant. "We'll all die."

"If you were injured instead of Hermans," implored Morgana, "wouldn't you want Blue to try? Captain Sekhmet said Blue is the best pilot she's ever seen. And I dunno, I trust him, okay? We knew when we signed up there would be danger. If we are going to die, let's at least go out with honour… trying to save lives."

"We're not going to die," insisted Blue. "I can get us there. I'm not making the same mistake twice."

"This is not about skill," said an unconvinced Corvus. "Nothing can fly in a sludge storm." As if to prove his point, a violent updraft slammed into the hellijet knocking him sideways. Blue grabbed the control column and slid into the pilot's seat.

The hellijet immediately stopped bucking.

Corvus stared at Blue as if for the first time. "Hey! How you doing that?"

"Like I said, I can take us home." The golden craft twisted in the volatile winds, yet Blue, somehow kept control. "What do you say? You gonna let me try?"

Corvus leant back in the seat. His hands shook, his normally confident eyes full of anxiety. A quick flick of his head and sudden determination replaced his fear. He set his jaw and smiled. "Why not. Let's give it go at least. But if you can't handle the stick, we turn back. Agreed?"

"Agreed."

"Strap in the passengers," Blue ordered, his mind becoming absorbed with contours and vector lines, eddies and pressure changes.

They spiralled closer to the landing field.

"I think we're gonna make it," said Corvus.

As if in response to Corvus' words, a strong gust upturned the hellijet.

"Hold on," yelled Blue who, rather than wrestling the controls, let the flying machine be carried this way and that. Seconds later, the straining craft righted itself and Blue was again in control.

Wet sand began to block the windows. With a grinding rasp, the prop stopped spinning and the jets spluttered.

"I knew it," growled Corvus. "I damn well knew this was a stupid idea."

"Don't listen to him Blue," said Morgana. The fuse jets screamed in protest. "You can do it."

The sand build-up was disastrous, clogging the hellijet's essential systems, sticking to the outer hull, making the ship heavy and impossible to manoeuvre. With a deep breath, Blue turned off the fuse engines and the hellijet dropped from the sky like a stone.

"What are you doing?" howled Corvus in alarm.

Blue had not been idle since yesterday's near disaster. "I vowed to never make the same mistake again. I've learnt my lesson. This time I know the schematics backwards… and then some." Blue pulled the Fuel Dump lever.

"No," protested Corvus. "We'll never restart the prop."

Ignoring him, Blue cycled the fuse engines and the fuel ignited. A massive explosion erupted below the hellijet, bright orange flames searing the cockpit windows, burning away the sand and bathing Blue in arcane red and golden light. In the reflection from the cockpit window, he looked as if he was made of fire rather than flesh, blood and bone.

The flames did not engulf the craft. Instead, the flying machine rode on the back of the fuel burn like a cushion. They descended, landing with a controlled thud. The blaze died, replaced by the cruel whip of sand and sludge.

"We're here," whispered Blue as if from a dream.

Corvus sat open-mouthed, too amazed to speak. "How?" he managed.

"Break out the tarps," ordered Morgana. "We must get the casualties to the Run-To now."

"How are they doing?" Blue asked, coming back to himself.

Morgana shook her head. "Not good."

They busied themselves with the tarps: thick plastic-like blankets used as shields against the grating sand. Blue put Captain Sekhmet on his back, whilst Corvus and Morgana carried Hermans between them. They left the hellijet and, with Blue leading, they struggled blindly through the devastating storm, the grit whipping at their exposed feet. They found one of the many Run-To doors and pounded for all they were worth.

A shocked ground crew let them in. "Where in space did you come from?"

"No time," replied Blue. "These two need serum now. Crawler bites."

A group of medics took Hermans and Captain Sekhmet away,

Morgana going with them.

Blue brushed sand from his face and rubbed at his sandblasted feet. As his eyesight recovered from the sludge-storm, he became aware of Saturn Squad and the ground crew staring at him with a mixture of confusion and amazement.

"Blue flew us in," explained Corvus with a dry croak. "He saved Captain Sekhmet and Hermans." He faced Blue and offered him his hand.

Blue took it and they shook. Around them, Saturn Squad and the ground crews erupted into spontaneous applause.

Blue ignored them.

Morgana had returned, her face a mask of grief.

"Did they make it?" Blue asked, but he already knew the answer.

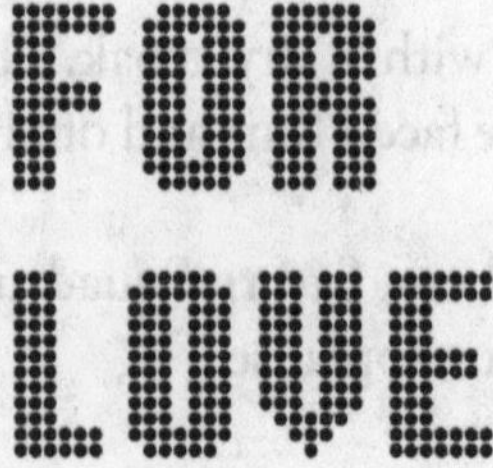
SEVEN:
FOR
LOVE

THE BLOATED pod-like body inflated, turning, as she watched, from shiny green to purple, before exploding into a mist of tiny, fly-like buzzing creatures that hurriedly mated and died. And where they fell, more green pods began to grow and expand, ripening under the bloated, red sun. It was a desperate, repeating display copied by nearly all the life-forms on this doomed planet.

All too late, thought Mylin, who found only sadness in this frenzied show. Her sorrow was a constant companion now, something she had learned to live with after the crash. She no longer averted her eyes from the crumpled gossamer sails of the ruined lightship whose flesh-clean bones jutted through the now thick, choking vegetation. Instead, Mylin took solace in the knowledge that she would soon die here, joining the dead ship on this ancient world that was also soon-to-die.

The planet had stopped spinning many millennia ago—Mylin lived in a never-ending day of purple skies punctuated by long streams of cruel orange-red sunlight and brilliant stars, of beautiful undulating horizon-wide auroras and the flash and crack of tailed lightning, of scorching rain and weird hails. She could do little except watch this awe-inspiring display.

The hot earth, a tangle of crawling vegetation, suddenly brought forth squat mushroom-like buds appearing from under the choking green like the heads of so many bald men. They burst with startled gasps and alien shrieks. A revel of noise, of rattles and clicks that played helter-skelter with her hearing. It seemed that in its death-throes, this fertile world was making a last attempt at life, pouring its remaining resources into a series of overwhelmingly exotic displays.

Had this place always been so alive, so vivid? Thought Mylin, aware of Raymon nibbling at her exposed toes. Smiling, she bent down and picked him up.

The ground rocked under her feet, the earthquakes were coming faster now. Shaking, rattling and groaning, and Mylin was reminded of the death throes of her kin who all died on this planet. Friends, family and lovers consumed and lost. Every one of them dead and gone forever.

Raymon squeaked, trying to burrow into her hand, his humanlike, fur-covered face full of fear.

"I'm here my love," she soothed. "I'll never let you go."

Raymon was a nervous creature whose bizarre evolution had produced weakness and predation in equal measure. He fitted comfortably in the upturned palm of her hand. Mylin stroked him gently, thrilling at the feel of his thick, luxuriant fur, murmuring and whispering comfort and reassurance in the heavy air.

Raymon was all she had left now.

The light-ship had come down heavily, splashing itself against this crippled world. Mylin was one of the lucky few to escape with their lives, but she had still grieved painfully at its passing. Even now, she could hear the echo of the ship's terrible screams reverberating in her mind.

The survivors, dishevelled, crumpled and dumbfounded, somehow struggled on—the same stubborn human instinct that had taken humankind away from its humble beginnings to populate the cosmos—striving, fighting for life against the odds to put their indelible mark upon the universe.

They returned to the ship, salvaged, built, and made love and life upon a condemned planet they had come halfway across the galaxy to find.

Raymon snuggled against Mylin's palm. His adorable whiskers tickled and thrilled, his fear now gone, his eyes half-closed in rapture at her touch.

How long does this planet have left? It must be getting close to its end now.

Time had never been on their side. The old sun was unstable, growing ever large, and this world would soon be consumed. And that's how it should've been. The survivors also consumed in this cosmic apocalypse.

But there had been a more immediate threat. A deadly force had devoured them one by one. Something unexpected and seemingly benign had brought death into their little huddle of shacks.

Raymon chirruped hungrily. She fed the creature, taking motherly pride in his greedy sucking movements, in his fat, healthy body now pressed against her naked breasts.

Devotion was a strange, wonderful and powerful emotion evolving eons ago solely for the nurture of weak, yet demanding offspring. It not only imprisoned parents but also joined them together—a time-served survival mechanism remaining intact throughout the ages.

This same force joined humans together in friendship and shared purpose. It had pushed humans far past their humble beginnings on Earth and out to new worlds and experiences. Mylin smiled. It was ironic that this single powerful human virtue was responsible for the downfall of the survivors.

Momentarily contented, Raymon snuggled up to her, his rich fur tickling against the welts of her thickly ridged maltreated flesh, the skin glistening with leaking wounds—as if her body was weeping tears for what it once had been, for she was still young and had possessed a fine-limbed beauty.

The children were snared first, falling prey to the emotio-telepathic need that made it impossible to deny their greedy furred friends, allowing them to drink painlessly from outstretched fingers.

It seemed natural for the settlers to take the Raymons in, to feed and nurture them with their own precious blood. For they too were flesh and bone—the only mammalian survivor on a world turned awry.

Even when the children began to look malnourished and pale, even when they began to die, it became impossible to resist the wonderful, needy Raymon. None could forsake these gentle companions who had come to mean more to them than life itself. And, one-by-one, they had all perished.

A wave of affection for this world, for Raymon and for their dead ship that had nourished them on their long journey, washed over Mylin. It wasn't the end they had come here for, but they had travelled to Mother-Earth for one thing, and at the finish it mattered only that humanity should make peace with itself, with its past, with everything and to die for the one over-riding emotion that defined them as a species.

"For love..." Mylin whispered as Raymon purred hungrily at her dry breasts.

EIGHT

And they were taken to the Isle of Asbit, to his dark red, twisted tower whereupon evil was put unto them.

They grew in size and mind, came to know what they were, and to feel unimaginable pain and suffering.

But they escaped, thrived through terrible adversity, and the Margolyn became their home…

And it was in this forest where they met the harna…

The Yarn of Gard, Cairn.

i. Kretch

"NOW YOU are what I call a nice bit o' weavery!"

Vareena pushed back her long lank, blonde hair and eyed the obnoxious drunk with defiance. He had been causing trouble since she and her hooded companion had entered this shantytown tavern. It was a rough place, but Scowl's cold iron—a metal that put dread into all—and his ever-present hood, meant such squalid accommodation was the norm. They had not yet seen the room. It promised to be as dingy and unkempt as this over-filled bar.

"A toast! A toast to—?" The drunk stared at Vareena expectantly.

She turned away from the greasy-blonde ruffian whose face was red and stained, his fighting weave muddied. One hand rested on his thigh, the other proffered a dripping mug.

"A toast to the loveliest bit o' skin that has graced this bar in a long time." He drank from a wooden tankard before lurching towards them and sitting down. His breath stank of stale ale.

Vareena scowled, her lip curling in revulsion. Her features spoke of refinement and nobility, a natural beauty whose gruff-looking fighting-weaves gave an almost boyish allure. Many other eyes had caressed her lithe figure, but only Raza was fool enough to ignore her worrisome companion.

"Now darlin', give Raza a chance!" He laughed, a lecherous grin twisting his features. His attention turned to Scowl and the blank, iron-blue eyes staring through two ragged slits in his hood. "What 'ave we here?" he asked, sitting back. "Hey lads, I think this one's shy."

There were few laughs as most found the shrouded figure worrisome.

Raza turned his attention back to Vareena. "So, what's your story? Let me guess—a rich man's piece down on her luck, or some courtesan looking for some rough?"

Vareena sat back and smiled. Scowl had seen the expression before. He shook his head in warning.

"Cos if it's a bit of rough you're after, I'm your man." Raza licked at a well-worn hole in his top lip, his tongue missing whatever jewellery usually decorated the space.

"Go and find some urine-smelling pigsty to rot in, you drunken idiot, or you'll feel the flat of my blade."

"What?"

The slap came without warning and resounded loudly. "I said, get lost."

The dark tavern exploded in laughter.

Raza appeared nonplussed; the slap only seemed to encourage him. His eyes narrowed. "Thinks you are better than us, do you? Well maybe you are, and maybe you're not. But maybe this will make you think otherwise." He produced a small lump of yellow metal from his stained weavery. It caught the dim cresset-light, gilding his features in amber.

Gold.

She was intrigued, suspicious. Gold was a forbidden substance; and these were miners.

"Not so haughty now, are you?"

Vareena shook her head, trying to rid herself of a sudden dizziness.

"Put that away, Raza," grumbled the Innkeeper, an overweight, baby-faced man whose bald pate shone with a thin pall of sweat. He wore a stained apron and little else. "You know what Jessop will do to you if he finds out."

Raza continued, undaunted. "I eat girls like her for breakfast, know what I mean?" He made an obscene gesture with his tongue.

Vareena grabbed the fleshy protuberance with swift fingers, twisting viciously. The drunk's eyes popped, but he still smiled. "You'll learn some manners when talking to your betters," she said in clear, noble tones. She pushed him backwards. He fell with a clatter, breaking the wooden chair.

Scowl closed his eyes and groaned.

Raza rubbed his tongue with relish. "I like a lass who puts up a fight." In one quick movement, he was back upon shaky feet, an inelegant but well-kept stone sword held threateningly in his outstretched hand. "You'll pay for that, my young lady—with a kiss!"

"Raza! For the sake of the Gyre, let the girl be!" shouted the Innkeeper.

"I can look after myself." Vareena pushed their table over and sprang into a fighter's crouch. Beer and their uneaten meal crashed onto the floor.

Scowl cursed under his breath, covering his long curved blade of iron with his cape.

Vareena brandished Scowlsbane, her well-carved and balanced sword of magnificent white. Such unblemished stone was rare indeed and worth a king's ransom, but the value was not just aesthetic. Crystal purity gave strength to the blade, preventing it from shattering during battle. Black-fenneral was its master, but the best sword was only equal to the flesh wielding it. Vareena was a trained fighter.

Bowing to the encircled crowd, Raza made a flourish with his arm. Vareena's booted foot sent him flying. He hit the floor hard and lay there for a few moments. When he got up, all trace of humour had gone. Someone put a friendly hand on his shoulder. "Leave it man, come 'ere and share a drink." He shrugged it off, eyes ablaze with anger. Blood leaked from a cut lip.

"Raza!" warned the Innkeeper.

Vareena measured her opponent. *Drunk yes, but lithe with a balanced physique. His sword is well oiled. As is he. I'll have some fun teaching him manners.*

The drunk crashed in upon Vareena, not expecting the sudden shift of weight that took her beyond his thrust and gave room and time for her to slap him across his backside with the flat of her blade.

Unable to resist this second opportunity, she kicked him to the floor again. He jumped up with a spring, flying at her. Vareena dodged, tripping over the upturned table. She regained her balance just in time to parry a vicious slice to her throat.

Raza battered murderously upon her sword. Hot sparks from both blades bathed the drunk's enraged features in a dancing array of flashing shards. They revealed something evil in the man, some debased thing inhabiting his leering, creased face.

Vareena crumpled under this fenneral hammering, parrying with defensive grace. Raza sweated heavily, his breath laboured. The barrage faltered, Vareena slipped under his blade and punched him in the face with her hilted fist. He went down, yelping like a dog, his sweaty hands clutching at a broken nose. His sword fell with a clatter.

"That'll teach you to watch your words in future, if nothing else. Now get out." She kicked his blade to the door, and returned to the table.

A few moments later, the ruffian was thrown into the street. Raza lingered outside for a while, moaning and shouting with equal vehemence, before disappearing into the late night of cold winds smattered with snow.

Vareena righted their table and sat down with her sable-weaved companion. She patted her sword, staring at him with pride and expectancy. As usual, his features were hidden—she could not fathom his thoughts.

"Next time flirt, and save yourself the trouble." His voice was cold and emotionless.

"Flirt with every smelly drunk just so you can eat in peace? I'd rather die."

"If you go on in your present manner, you probably will. I was nearly forced to intervene; and iron is the nemesis of delving, not drunks. I had wanted to talk to the man. There was something about him."

"It's not my fault we've to stay in this dive. I've enough wealth to afford better lodgings. It's you they don't like."

A few men looked up.

"Keep your highborn voice down. Soon, we will be in Palim. You can then find more luxurious rooms."

Vareena dreaded reaching Palimara's capital. They were to part there, or so he had said many weeks ago, before their long passing of *The Grikes*—a vast, broken land of exposed, cracked rock. "I'm sorry." Her hand reached out to his masked face but, as ever, he pulled away. She stared at their spilled food. "Oh."

"Yes, I'm afraid our dinner is on the floor. Perhaps your great wealth can pay for a replacement, Mistress Vareena of Keep Krall."

She was about to tell him otherwise, when a shiver shot down her spine.

Scowl's head twitched towards the wooden entranceway, his keen but misshapen nose sniffing the air.

A gust of wind, and the door opened to a hairy monstrosity. An animal was framed there, a deformed creature whose large eyes took in the tavern scene with one great sweep of its bull-head.

"Kretch!" Vareena gasped, her hand again moving to the sure white fenneral at her side.

Ill-wrought ears pricked and pointed in her direction, while eyes, fringed by abundant fur sought her out.

A demon straight from childhood fairy tales, a bugbear akin to the bogeyman that haunted deep night, darkly lit rooms and forbidden holes, stared right at her. The Kretch were monsters from myth, used to frighten children into obedience. But here was the monster made real. She drew breath to shout, but Scowl covered her mouth with his gloved half-hand and shook his head.

Vareena was terrified, but the men in the tavern showed only resentment. *They are used to this creature's presence.* She guessed they would not tolerate it for long.

The Innkeeper remained unmoved, his expression grim.

The thing lurched forward, uneven legs twisting in unnatural but well-practised rhythm. Muscles bulged and knotted awkwardly. One leg had too many joints. The other was thicker, nothing more than fur-wrapped bone covered in a dense network of arteries and tangled lines of rope-like sinew. It shuddered and shook as it lumbered closer. The movement sickened Vareena. It was impossible to make sense of the dark-grey, furry limbs.

The tavern became hushed as the creature approached the bar. Long muscled arms brushed against chairs and tables. It wore a weave of some kind, beaded with red, azure, orange and grey. Vareena gasped, for at its side hung an enormous wedge of roughly-hewn fenneral. She possessed a passion for weaponry of all kinds and this was a magnificent specimen. A mixture of pure white and black banded stone. The true beauty had not been realised by the carver and, intentional or not, its roughness served as a sharp reminder of its function.

"What on Arn is it?" Vareena whispered through Scowl's stunted fingers.

"He is a kerrish."

The name meant nothing to her.

The creature spoke, its voice low and un-Arnish in cadence, reverberating from within its enormous barrel-like chest like a growl. "Innkeeper, Ya'ousa search for one called Raza. To him, Ya'ousa must speak. You seen Raza?"

"I've told you, we don't want your sort in here. Get out before I kick you out myself!"

"Ya'ousa must find Raza." The kerrish glanced around at all the upturned faces. "He miner. Ya'ousa just want speak." A short, stubby snout opened to reveal a set of white, canine teeth and blackened gums.

Vareena shuddered.

The Innkeeper's eyes flicked at Vareena and Scowl with silent warning. "I have never seen nor heard of this Raza."

"You speak untruth." The animal sniffed, his black nose crinkling. "Ya'ousa smell lies in your breath and sweat. Tell Ya'ousa where Raza is, and Ya'ousa will not return."

The bulging head brushed the ceiling with fur. A powerful creature, yet Vareena sensed vulnerability. As if the stares of so many hate-filled eyes somehow weakened it.

The fat-bellied innkeeper shook his head. He reached down under the bar and produced an evil-looking wooden club. A rustle behind the kerrish, and the other men readied their weapons.

A change came over the creature then, a calmness. Scowl cursed before getting up and pulling Vareena behind him.

"Ya'ousa thirsty. Long way back to his camp. You give Ya'ousa water."

The innkeeper patted the club into the palm of his hand. "We don't serve the likes of you in here. Now go while you still have the legs to carry you."

"A drink of water and Ya'ousa will leave in peace, yes?"

The Innkeeper's expression turned to one of grim violence, but before he could act, a nasal voice spoke from the shadows. "A mug of water for my friend." Scowl moved out of the smoke-filled murk and stood next to the peculiar creature.

Animalistic eyes searched the hooded features with a mixture of unease and wonder.

"Are you deaf? A mug of water," Scowl repeated.

"I don't serve his kind. He ain't natural. You'd best to keep out of this if you know what's good for you."

"And what is good for me?"

The Innkeeper swung his club, but Scowl caught the wood in his perverse-looking half-hand and wrenched it from the astonished fat man's fingers. He nodded to the kerrish and, grabbing Vareena, they made a rush for the door. A few men tried to stop them. The lump-like paws of Ya'ousa knocked them aside as if they were children. Scowl whirled the wooden club around him like a living thing.

They burst into the street with an angry mob in pursuit. "What are you doing?" shrieked Vareena. "Why are you helping this creature?"

Scowl ignored her.

Raza appeared, his face full of anger, a group of ten men standing at his back.

"So, you're in cahoots with this inquisitive Kretch? I should've guessed. Come on lads, let's finish this here!"

Something in his manner angered Vareena. Before, Raza had been a loud and harmless drunk, now, with others to support him, an evil streak showed itself. Vareena took a deep breath and threw herself straight at him, slashing and hacking at his blade. He stumbled backwards in shock, parrying. A whirl of flashing blades in which Raza was but a minor player. A shiny object dropped from his hand, distracting him. Vareena plunged her sword deep into his rib cage, crunching bones and twisting viciously. Blood spurted, bathing her in crimson. Raza gurgled for a moment, and crumpled to the ground. Reaching down, she grabbed at the object that had been the cause of his downfall and hid it in her weaves. She pulled the fenneral free and stared into Raza's lifeless face. The horror of what she had done hit like a thrown rock upon the back of her head.

The mob howled in derision at the sight of the dead miner and charged towards them.

"You little fool!" Scowl shouted, snatching her sword from her limp fingers and throwing the club away. "We might have been able to disappear into the night, but now these men will want revenge."

Ya'ousa unleashed his bludgeon of fenneral. "Follow!" he barked with command. The kerrish broke through the massed men, and rushed down an enclosed alley. Scowl doubted this strategy but had no time to consider its merit. They reached the back wall of a squat, wooden building. Ya'ousa flung himself onto the roof.

His legs are not as weak as they seem, thought Vareena.

Ya'ousa lowered a muscled arm and scooped her up before she had time to protest. Blackbeak needed no such assistance and ascended to the roof with ease.

They ran across the rooftops, disturbing more inhabitants below. The mob grew in size and volume, filling the narrow streets with howls and shouting. Ya'ousa remained unperturbed. In one deft movement, he bounded down into a bramble thicket and revealed a hollow, a hiding place.

The horde rushed past.

A few minutes later they were on their way again. This time the kerrish lead them upwards, away from the shantytown of Fisk and its angry inhabitants.

ii. Fire

"YOU EAT." The kerrish thrust a rough wooden bowl at Vareena.

She examined the contents with worry.

"It good."

The creature had strung only a few words together since their escape, but they had willingly followed him to his camp hidden in a small glade on the hillside. It looked down on the red-orange fires and thick smokes of the small shantytown they had so recently departed, a long brown stain upon the thin covering of snow. Fisk sat to the north-west of Palim.

Ya'ousa's tent, constructed from skins and tanned pelts held together by a tight latticework of thongs, was foreign to Vareena. Roughly painted marks adorned its surface, enormous paw prints of blue, red, orange and yellow on the white, black and tan of the furs. A haven of warmth. She allowed herself to relax.

Ya'ousa came back with another bowl, and stared at the cross-legged hooded man whose sable weavery somehow fitted these outlandish surroundings. "Ya'ousa not mention before but why your face covered?"

"He prefers it that way," said Vareena.

The kerrish ignored her. "Is insult to Ya'ousa, insult to his tent, to his food."

"Forgive me, Ya'ousa. I wear my hood against the hatred of other men."

"Hatred? Yes, Ya'ousa know of what you speak. He sees it across the lands of man. Aversion, loathing—all these things. Yet kerrish too are not free of this evil. Ya'ousa say, remove hood. Let him see who you are, let him judge."

Scowl placed his hand on the hilt of IronScythe, and caressed the delving metal.

Vareena sensed the meaning: only iron had ever been his friend. She was young, an annoying hindrance to him, but she understood his pain.

Blackbeak nodded and in one deft movement, the hood was gone.

A single stranding burned in the hide-encased darkness, flickering in gentle homage to the wind gusting outside. Warm orange light bathed Scowl's naked face in velvety hues and delicate shadow. Even this lambent glow could not diminish the abomination revealed lurking there.

Ya'ousa studied the smashed, misshapen features—the blackened beak-nose, the crooked eyes and leering mouth—with curiosity.

Vareena, intimate with Scowl's looks, still shuddered involuntarily. Such heinous, viscerally repellent features would always shock. *But I have grown to care for them.*

"Yes, Ya'ousa thinks he understands. Men do not like difference. They want everything to be same. Is why they do not take to kerrish. Too much deformity in us bred from our beginnings many, many passes ago. But from adversity comes humility. From hardship, comes strength and resolve. Yes?"

Scowl cast a wry eye in the direction of the furred face. Ya'ousa's long, white whiskers twitched proudly against black and grey striped fur. He nodded.

With her perfect limbs and fine features, Vareena felt guilty listening to these words. She had tried to understand Scowl, to understand what effect appearing as an atrocity to other men and women might have upon her own sensibilities. But it was impossible. She was his antithesis, his opposite, and that was as close as she could ever get.

"I am different," Blackbeak croaked, his face blushing in uneven red over the thick welts of his scarred flesh. Under his cowl, he was confident, powerful. Exposed like this, his embarrassment made Vareena's heart melt.

Taking the stranding in reverent paws, the kerrish lit a small bowl of incense. "We eat now." The collection of dried leaves, seeds and berries fizzed and spluttered, filling the air with vapours not conducive to eating.

Vareena coughed and her eyes watered.

Ya'ousa paid her no concern. He joined them, bending his legs awkwardly.

She studied her food again. She dipped in a wooden spoon and took a wary sniff of the contents.

Scowl caught her expression. "My companion's trust is not so easily given. She is a curious sort, and eager to find out who you are, my friend."

"I didn't say that," Vareena protested, forcing a spoonful into her mouth.

"But question is on your mind, yes?"

Vareena nodded, not bothering to hide a grimace at the taste of the grim broth.

"Where Ya'ousa comes from, fighting together proves friendship. After battle, we share food as sign of trust. Only then are formal introductions made. But Ya'ousa bow to man's way." He put his bowl down and placed enormous paws on his chest. "This is Jantiff Ya'ousa of Totu Cland. Powerful Cland. Ya'ousa is kerrish from Northern land of Skourass, wherein sits beautiful forest of Margolyn." He spread his arms around him in a magnificent arc. "Big forest. Mother to all Ya'ousa's race. Home. But you, man-girl, you called Ya'ousa by other name."

"Kretch?"

Scowl glared at Vareena. “Forgive her, Ya’ousa, she does not know what that word means.”

“Yes I do,” she answered, spitting out bits of food. “The Kretch are animals who come from holes of delving. As a child, Melaina, my nanny, told me they came at night to eat naughty children.”

“Ya’ousa is no Kretch! Has never been. They were an evil from long time ago. No more Kretch, they gone. You understand?” Ya’ousa’s breath rasped in the smoky gloom. “Yes?”

“You give Ya’ousa the worst insult, Vareena,” said Scowl.

Vareena sat back, a worried expression on her face. “I’m sorry, but how was I supposed to know? I’m not like you, Scowl, who has knowledge of everything, every place and everyone. You are no older than me. When did you find the time to become so informed?”

Blackbeak shrugged. “All I know I learnt upon the Bacchust Isle.”

The kerrish made a gruff sound in his throat. “Ya’ousa never heard of such place.”

“It’s a myth, a fancy of old befuddled sailors,” interjected Vareena. “The island doesn’t exist.”

“I awoke there.” Scowl stared up into the shadowy recesses of the tent. “Although my memories are sparse.”

“Then you, too, must have been befuddled,” Vareena mocked. “‘The beautiful but lost Bacchust Isle’ is a familiar theme of those who make a feeble living begging down by the docks in Fangarra. A fable from the dreams of the deranged.”

Blackbeak dismissed her comments with a shake of his head. “You wanted an introduction, Ya’ousa. Then let me give it. I have many names, but most know me as Scowl.”

Ya’ousa bowed. “And what of the man-girl?” he asked, impatient with the exchange. “Who you?”

“I am Mistress Vareena Krall of Oldiva,” she replied in her finest noble tones.

“Good,” the kerrish boomed. “We share food and introductions. We now friends.”

Silence descended while they ate. In the quiet of the meal, the dying face of Raza came repeatedly to Vareena's mind. An odious part of her psyche had revelled in the death. Blood still stained her weaves. Its salty smell pulsed within her nostrils, even under the burning incense. *I killed before, when escaping Keep Krall. A necessity, but I wanted to kill Raza.* A thrill shuddered through her, akin to those first few nights with Steward Allon, her only lover. But this was lust of a different kind. She had not been herself since entering the seedy tavern. She was tense, fevered and her heart thudded over-loud in her chest.

After they had finished, Ya'ousa took their bowls and scrubbed at them in some dark corner. He returned and crouched upon a cured hide. Vareena tried to read his features, but could glean nothing from his animalistic expression.

"Tell me Ya'ousa," said Scowl. "What was your interest in this man, Raza?"

The kerrish cocked his head to one side as if debating the merits of this question. "Ya'ousa must find him. Is all."

"I killed him," said Vareena, ashamed by the hint of pride coating her words. "The man was a letch and a fool."

"Raza was the dead man?" Ya'ousa shook his bullhead and the light left his eyes. "Then all Ya'ousa has done now turned to dust." His claws pulled into two, enormous fists and Vareena feared he would hit out at her.

"Why were you searching for him?" asked Scowl. "And in such a dangerous tavern?"

"Enough. Before Ya'ousa answer, he too has question: Why you help Ya'ousa, why you put yourself in danger for kerrish, eh?"

"The answer is a single word—*gold*."

Ya'ousa scowled, his paw reaching for the smooth haft of his fenneral club. "Then you are like him, like all men. Ya'ousa tried to ignore what is against your thigh. Delving metals are not hidden easily. Leave now. Go, or Raza shall not be only casualty this night!" He bounded up, his club swinging in one commanding claw.

Scowl did not react.

Why is he not afraid of this monster? thought Vareena, grasping her blade.

"Sit down, Ya'ousa," Blackbeak commanded. The club hung only a sword width from his ruined nose. "Yes, I am interested in gold, but my interest is in returning it back to the earth, where such evil belongs."

"Why should Ya'ousa believe? You like other men hungry for delving metals."

"Raza was a troublemaker and a drunk. Yet before Vareena sent him on his way, he showed her a lump of the forbidden metal. The miners tried to hush him up, and I have a nose for such things."

Vareena fingered her weaves guiltily. The gold weighed in her pocket. Knowing it was there thrilled her.

"Another name was mentioned: *Jessop*."

"Jessop! Yes, Ya'ousa has heard speak of this man."

Scowl motioned for Ya'ousa to sit. "We fought together, shared food and honour. Our trust is proved. Your own laws bind you as I am bound to my bane of iron. Put your club away, Ya'ousa my friend, and tell me your story. I may find a way to help."

The mound of foreboding muscle and fur, pondered these words. "Trust is never easy for kerrish, despite pretty speak. But Ya'ousa put away his fenneral."

"You will trust me. I swear upon my iron that my words are true."

"What is the worth of trust when all hope is gone?"

Vareena couldn't control her curiosity any longer. "Why were you looking for Raza? The man was an idiot, a drunken fool."

The kerrish turned sorrowful eyes towards her. "Ya'ousa search for his Clandsriders, his brethren. They are slaves in some mine of fenneral near here, in broken region known as *The Grikes*. Evil men make them work in deep dark holes. Many mines in this land. Ya'ousa not know where to look. And no one will help a Kretch." He paused, his face showing pain even underneath its thick covering of grey fur.

"Continue," whispered Scowl. "We are your friends."

"Ya'ousa employ thief who visited town where mining men

go. Fisk. He found nothing until he met Raza, bragging how he tortures kerrish. The thief befriended him, but learnt little more. They returned to his lodging, and when Raza fall under spell of man-beer, Ya'ousa's thief search his room. All he found was map. He bring map to Ya'ousa, but it useless. Mine is marked but no scale, no orientation." He unrolled a ragged, brown parchment scrawled in black indistinguishable scribing. "With Raza dead, Ya'ousa now give up hope. He must return to home, to Margolyn."

Vareena pushed the enormous paw aside, surprised at the softness of the fur and squinted at the map.

Ya'ousa's bony snout jerked turned towards the tent's opening. He sniffed the air. "Many men come."

A twig snapped in the distance, voices murmured. A shout, and the tramp of many feet filled the hillside.

"Seems men will not leave Ya'ousa alone. Seems Scowl has another chance to prove friendship and trust."

Vareena's eyes widened in sudden discovery, her finger resting at a strange mark upon the map. "Scowl, I—"

A flaming brand exploded in the tent's entrance.

iii. Death in the night

YA'OUSA JUMPED backwards, eyes bulging. A torch landed on the roof of the tent, another burned at a wall.

Vareena rushed to stamp out the growing blaze. A large brand hit her a glancing blow and rebounded into a pile of weaves. Ya'ousa's furry paw dragged her away from the flames.

"Come out, Kretch!" an angry voice screamed, while others jeered. "You're going to pay for what you did to Raza!"

Within the passing of those words, the fire found hold, burning quickly at the cured hides. Flames erupted on either side of Scowl, forcing him away from his companions and escape. Red embers fell around him, framing him in yellow and flickering orange.

Vareena feared he was trapped, but something flashed at his side.

IronScythe.

Did she glow? It was hard to tell amongst the growing conflagration.

Ya'ousa dragged Vareena into the cold night amidst angry shouts of the men and women who had come together for this burning. The mob boiled with hatred at their appearance. Their detestation echoing in hissing, barking tones.

Trapped inside the scorching leathers, Scowl stood motionless. Somewhere in his lost past those same voices of hate had united in aversion against him. He had nothing but a half-formed memory from childhood, but it was strong enough to fill him with rage.

Raising the She-blade, he stared in confusion at the glowing metal. *The IronLight again? Why?* He slashed through the smoldering leather of the tent wall. A man waited for him, his mouth a leering rictus of hate that turned to horror as his eyes caught Scowl's exposed features. A stifled scream and IronScythe found her mark, planting herself in his throat. Blackbeak twisted her, driving the gurgling, dying man down on his back, grating her against the bones of his neck; letting her relish the death.

Many torches glowed. A huge crowd had come for a kerrish burning. Yet IronScythe had her own particular fire.

A deafening, animalistic roar and, to the left of him, Ya'ousa and Vareena were revealed as figures as if in a dream. The girl struck out with her blade, catching an unwary attacker in the face. He fell forward. She elbowed him in the guts, hacking at his head. He crumpled, blood splashing.

Ya'ousa jumped aloft, spinning high in the air, striking out with his wedge-like lump of fenneral. Smashing arms and legs, crushing shoulders and thighs. And when the men grouped against him, those legs bent again to take him far away from their angry blades.

Scowl had no time for contemplation. Men drew in on him from all sides. IronScythe flashed and stabbed like lightning from a black whirling cloud. Heads and limbs fell thudding onto the hillside. None could escape the intent of the eldritch blade and its shining, devastating light. Blackbeak stole life from the fallen with murderous grace. A man with a smashed leg put up a defensive arm. IronScythe removed the limb before pinning him to the ground in a quick thrust, silencing his pleading voice forever. A moan to his left, and again the She-scythe struck—vicious and brutal maybe, but superb, wondrous and deadly.

A group of seasoned warriors with tanned skin and swords glistening with cleaning oils, made a stand against him. Even their coordinated efforts could not resist the berserker in their midst. Scowl shrieked and charged. The men stumbled and fell, and he was soon to find his mark.

With their fighters slain, and the bright blade twitching for their doom, the mob panicked and ran. IronScythe was not sated; she craved more blood. She sliced at thighs and necks, ripping through the air to cleave nerve and sinew, muscle and bone. When the hillside was empty, she returned for the wounded. The pleading men's cries only fuelled her efforts, and they too fell into ruin.

Ya'ousa appeared at Blackbeak's shoulder. IronScythe swung at him. The enormous kerrish parried with his club of fenneral. At the touch of the curious white and black stone, the IronLight vanished and Scowl collapsed to his knees exhausted.

For a moment the man-animal stood with his weapon raised in anger, but as his eyes opened to the destruction around him, the rough bludgeon fell to his side.

The tent was nothing more than a few smoldering rags. Ya'ousa kicked around in the ashes, stooping to pick up a burnt corner of the map, his big mop head falling to his chest. "Gone," he said, letting the singed bit of parchment fall to the ground.

A noble voice rang out behind him. "No Ya'ousa, I can find your mine, I know I can."

"But how, Man-girl?"

Vareena felt sick, was as appalled at her own ability to kill and maim, as she was awe-stricken by the carnage staining the hillside. But that unmistakable feeling of power had engulfed her again, and she was powerless to resist. *Is it something to do with the peculiar light surrounding Scowl's blade or that lump of gold in my pocket?* Dead faces accused her with blankly staring eyes. In a convulsive movement, she grabbed the kerrish and held him tightly. “Let’s leave here.”

Enormous arms enfolded Vareena.

“Darkness would have been done tonight,” Blackbeak said. “But iron is the reward for all those foolish enough to let hatred dominate their lives.”

Vareena laughed, high and nervy, mixed in with sobs and hysterical sounds. She never understood his simple justifications. “What was that light surrounding your blade? I have seen you fight before, but you were turned a mad-man.”

“The Ironlight,” Scowl rasped. “A rare thing, usually. Yet twice, recently, I have suffered its uncommon glow.” The close-set uneven eyes stared into Vareena.

“It is not my doing,” she said, fingering the lump of gold within her weaves. “Is it?”

“I cannot ignore Fulminara’s prediction, nor your destiny.”

“What is the IronLight?”

Blackbeak considered her question for a moment, cleaning IronScythe by stabbing the blood-drenched blade into a snowdrift. “Something invested in iron. I do not know more.”

The kerrish bowed. If the exchange had intrigued him, he did not show it. “Again Ya’ousa is in your debt, Scowl. Your trust is more than proved.”

“Please, for the sake of the Gyre, let’s go,” said Vareena with impatience.

Blackbeak studied the smoldering remains of the tent. His hood was gone, burned with everything else.

“Man-girl, you say you can find mine?” growled Ya’ousa, as they hurried into the night.

Vareena was still shaky. “Something hidden in the fold of the map. I glimpsed a drawing.”

“Tell Ya’ousa.”

“A lith-stone.”

“What?”

Scowl pointed his ugly features towards the kerrish and

nodded. "The lith-stones belonged to an ancient past before delving, to the Golden Age. Some call them 'Travellers Stones'. Columns of rock, now mostly fallen and left in ruin—their secret is lost upon the cold winds of time, Vareena."

Her head shook with irritation. "For once, you are wrong my friend. If we can find one of these liths, I'm sure I can find the stone marked on the map."

Blackbeak's head twitched, shrugging. "The secret has been lost, it—"

"No Scowl, listen. Below each pinnacle is a squat building—a bolt-hole. A place to hold up against the night and the worst of the weather. Carved on each building is a mark. A symbol that tells you where you are. This sign points to others, and the direction you must take. We need to find one of these liths as a point of reference."

Ya'ousa stopped, one great paw covering his mouth, his gruff voice shaking. "Ya'ousa saw such a stone two days past. Old it was, broken. He seen many on his travels. Tell Ya'ousa secret, he needs to know."

"It's not that easy to explain, nor to understand."

"If at all," interjected Scowl.

"Kerrish try!"

"I once knew the cypher, but it was a long time ago, an idle fancy when I was a child. I'm sure I can work it out if you take me to this lith-stone. What do you say, Scowl?"

Blackbeak snorted, his head shaking in resignation. "Where there is gold, there is always delving. Besides, word of this night will surely pass to other towns, to Palim. And I am—unmistakable. The roads will be watched. We can only expect trouble if we continue. We travel with Ya'ousa."

"Good. We go tomorrow. Under light of sun. Ya'ousa tired. He sleep now." He found a sheltered hollow and fell immediately into slumber.

Vareena and Scowl spent a cold night huddled under gnarled, leafless bushes that provided scant protection from the freezing wind. Tomorrow and the rising Sun was all that mattered.

iv. Harna

"HARNA LIKE sky and trees above, they do not care much for stone," boomed Ya'ousa with pride. They entered a rocky crevice forming a natural hollow in the hillside, magnifying the many grunts and murmurs, the chewing and grinding of flat teeth.

Before them were four creatures of such preposterous design that Vareena's mind could not at first fully comprehend them.

"The kerrish riding beast," said Scowl in explanation. "Harna. I have heard of them, but never seen one with my own eyes."

The animals came alive with hollow hoots and croons. Wide nostrils flared at the end of stunted snouts, long tongues lolled out of peculiar mouths. The largest of the bunch—enormous and bulky, with massive flattened paws covered in dense hair of white and tan set against the black flesh of its muzzle—lurched towards them on strong but cumbersome legs. A low stubby head shook with unrestrained joy. The creature's movement was a mess of unbalance and wasted energy.

This is a riding beast? thought Vareena. *The back legs are too small and squat, compared with the powerful forelimbs twice the length.*

The creature charged and Vareena yelled in alarm. Scowl stumbled backwards, his hand coming to rest upon IronScythe.

"Do not worry," shouted Ya'ousa, a laugh contained somewhere inside his barrel voice. "These beasts not cause hurt. No. This is Taatchi, of the Forest." The beast slid to a sudden stop, splattering the kerrish with mud and grass. Ya'ousa slapped the creature's forehead that sloped backwards to a ridge of pointed bone and guffawed. Taatchi tried to bite him with snapping teeth. *"Ygirrit tu ankum, ya ellasteer bak!"* chided Ya'ousa in his native tongue, giving Taatchi a wry glance.

The harna murmured in response, lifting his head to examine Ya'ousa's companions.

Vareena glanced at the face and let out a yelp. Taatchi jumped back, nudging closer to his master.

"What is it, Man-girl?"

"The eyes—" She was lost for words. They were large, set far back into the enormous head, protected by many eyelids and flaps. A grey iris surrounded by white. Like—*human eyes.*

"Ah yes. They stare. They study. They have eyes of men! See, are not Ya'ousa's the same?"

Vareena pushed back her lank hair, and studied the kerrish's face. Outlandish. An enormous man-animal, deformed in limb and movement. Fur-covered, wet-nosed and snouted—long, yellow teeth poked from his maw in an attempt at a smile. A horror by any other definition. Yet something special dwelled in his brash expression and intense brown eyes. *But they are the eyes of an animal. Nothing like what I just glimpsed.* She nodded politely.

"We kerrish do not share same origin as harna. No. They much older than us. Wiser. Yet we are like kin."

Taachi spat, and then seemingly chuckled. Ya'ousa laughed also. "Now we choose your rides." The kerrish had changed. His grim personality softening in the presence of these animals.

Vareena's eyebrows leapt upwards. "Rides!" she cried, staring after his enormous back.

Ya'ousa returned with a young sturdy beast three heads taller than Vareena, but younger and smaller than Taatchi who stood with comical authority.

"This is Purl, which means *murmur of hidden forest stream.* He now yours, Man-girl."

"Mine?"

"Gift of harna is sacred thing. He is unridden. Purl yours for life. *Tella fuh bontek, ah foh rewk unt pffe sah!"*

Vareena stared on dumbfounded. "—What?"

"Ya'ousa says *ride long and ride free!* Is always spoken at the *Giving."*

"How can I thank you?"

"No. Do not thank Ya'ousa, thank Purl. Ya'ousa will now go and choose a mount for your friend. You need be alone for a while. Come Scowl."

They left.

Purl turned away, pretending indifference. His hair, shorter than Taachi's, was silken and striped in bands of dark grey, crested with a black, pleated mane.

Beautiful.

The creature spat. A well-chewed bolus whizzed past her ear. Vareena didn't allow herself to be intimidated. She slapped his flanks as Ya'ousa had done. The harna carried on chewing. She rested her left hand upon his front knee where fur did not grow, unconsciously stroking. Purl hummed, nuzzling. She pinched the loose skin. "You like that, Lad?"

Purl turned to examine her. His eyes were a deep blue, irises surrounded by white. Human eyes trapped within animalistic flesh. They stared into her, measuring, yet Vareena had no desire to turn away. A sound akin to a chuckle reverberated in Purl's mammoth chest. *Is he laughing at me?* His wet nose pushed at her weaves, sniffing—stopping at her gird-belt where the single lump of gold lay hidden. He shook his head, blowing out air with a disapproving hoot, before comically nudging her off-balance. She fell on her backside with a shriek.

Ya'ousa and Scowl returned with another harna. Older than Purl, but not much larger. The harna's short sleek black hair caught the early sun revealing a tight well-honed musculature. A breeze played with its brilliant snow-white mane blowing it across an expansive flank.

"Burrstone!" announced the kerrish with pride.

Scowl stood at Burrstone's side, his warped features inscrutable. *Is Blackbeak incapable of any emotion? Is he not similarly amazed by this kerrish gift?*

Vareena found her feet, brushing ice from her weaves. Something about Scowl's harna spoke *female.* She perceived no sexual difference between such beasts; the dissimilarity radiated from within. "A black beast for the Blackbeak. Nice."

Ya'ousa nodded. "Yes. Good fit." The kerrish put his paws on his hips and stood rock still, only his enormous head moved, sweeping from Vareena to Blackbeak, and back again. "You understand this no simple gift? In return for harna, Ya'ousa demand your help rescue his comrades. Yes?"

The barest of nods from Scowl.

"You put a lot of trust in me," replied Vareena. "What if I can't read the lith-stones? What if—"

Ya'ousa raised a dismissive paw. "You help Ya'ousa or not?"

"I will do my best."

"Good. Now we start. There no trick to riding. Is easy. One lesson is all. Harna enjoy carrying you, they love burden. Kerrish not ride otherwise. It help, however, to be confident. To think what you do at all times," he said, pointing at his head, a stubby claw showing them the importance of the information his words could not properly convey.

They nodded.

"You only need learn not to fall off."

"Fall off?"

"This first lesson, Man-girl. Listen. One day you fall. Like season of the Gyre, it will come! If you ready, you not much hurt, yes? But riding easy part. True nature of riding is *look-after* of animal. Harna need care, attention." His bullhead jerked towards four sturdy saddles protected from the weather by a rocky overhang. The largest was more ornate, the wood stained black and decorated with intricate beadings matching the beads upon Ya'ousa's weavery. The seats held many pockets and bags from which brushes and combs protruded.

Ya'ousa then spoke about feed, exercise, tack upkeep and clothing. They listened, repeating his words while fixing ropes, reins and saddles. He checked their harna, adjusted straps and ties, and led them away.

Although nervous about the lesson, Vareena was full of pride as they left the rocky hollow, pleased at the new way Ya'ousa treated her. *To think only yesterday, the kerrish race was unknown to me. Creatures of a childish nightmare. Ya'ousa is nothing like the Kretch I know so well.*

An enormous paw reached down to her leggings and tugged. "Too tight. Leg weaves must be loose. Is same for you Scowl-man.

Material gathers at knee and rub. No good. Change soon, yes?"

They walked for an hour westward, skirting the broken land of *The Grikes*, and came upon a small twisted forest bordering a low plain. Most trees had lost their covering of green, although isolated saplings, hungry for the sun's rays, still kept their yellowing leaves.

Vareena was keen to get in the saddle, though nervy. Scowl remained distant, unmoved.

"We learn to ride now." Ya'ousa led their mounts around in a tight circle while they studied the harna's untidy bounce and outlandish movement. "Only in speed do they become Margolyn's greatest gift," he said, as much to the vast vault of the sky as to the two novices.

The harna behaved in an almost sarcastic, superior, way—as if they were in touch with a greater world of which Vareena knew nothing. It made her want to ride even more, to prove she could master them. *And yet, for all their muscle and bone, for all their constrained power, they are clumsy creatures.* Awkwardness dominated their form. They struggled against their own muscles and weight like the cumbersome strongmen of her dead uncle's court. The stubby back legs lurched and staggered, occasionally tripping and snagging each other. *How can any rider stay aloft on such a beast?*

Then came the time to mount. Scowl jumped up in a single bound. Confident and relaxed, a smirk crossing his ruined features.

Vareena placed her foot in the extra leathern stirrup used for mounting. The mountain of flesh rose impossibly high above her. "I can't," she blurted.

"You mount," said Ya'ousa. "He ready."

"I'm not sure I—"

"You mount. Purl yours now. Remember, he sturdy, but is uncomfortable for him if you not mount with care. Watch. Grab mounting pommel here, take weight on right arm, see? Try to avoid your weight dragging saddle towards you. If you mount bad, harna expel air and is chance saddle will slip. Look out for this."

"I don't think I can reach."

"He not bend for you. If cannot climb up like Ya'ousa show you, then get helper. Always mount easy. But Man-girl not need helper, Vareena big enough without."

Scowl turned away, his smirk turning into a smile.

He's loving this. But, if he can do it, so can I. And following Ya'ousa's simple reassuring directions, she pulled herself clumsily into the saddle—and nearly slid off the other side.

Ya'ousa adjusted the stirrups for her leg length, and against her earlier assumption, the saddle felt secure.

The kerrish was last to mount, his steed grunting with sudden effort. Up to now, the harna hadn't moved. When Ya'ousa gave the command to trot, the world jolted and jumped like the shaking lands common to the season of Blaze. Vareena forgot all his instruction. She pulled on the reins in panic. Purl's nose lifted and he came to a halt.

Ya'ousa chuckled. "Riding is always shock, but true grace comes from speed. We go faster soon. First, we try again."

Vareena clicked her tongue.

Purl, pricking his flat, comical ears, lunged forward.

The peculiar gait of the harna thrust her backwards, then forwards and, as if this was not enough, flung her up and down. Vareena clung on for dear life. *No one can ride like this. It is too uncomfortable, I'll throw up my breakfast if we don't stop soon.*

Ya'ousa motioned to go faster.

Vareena wasn't sure she could take much more, but at the barest flick on the reins, Purl doubled his speed, and with speed came a new fluidity. Vareena was no longer thrown this way and that.

"How is it?" shouted Ya'ousa.

"Good," answered Scowl.

"Faster?"

"Yes, let's go!" Vareena whipped the reins and Purl hooted in response. She darted past Blackbeak in a rush of pounding paws and flying snow. She glanced backwards. Burrstone was matching Purl paw for paw. Gone was clumsiness. In its place: a lithe, effortless bounce. *Purl is holding back, he is capable of much, much more.*

Burrstone trumpeted with pleasure.

Vareena's thighs began to ache. She clung on too tightly. "I'm sorry, Boy," she said, relaxing. Purl responded and, for the barest of moments, she received the strangest sensation—a four-footed impression of security, as if she understood what it was like to be Purl, to be harna. He monitored each little jolt of speed, silently asking Vareena if he was going too fast or too hard for her. How he communicated such thoughts, she could not fathom, but Vareena felt protected, perched as she was, upon the massive, racing animal.

Scowl, riding astride Burrstone, thumped past, his beast's paws showering her in snow and ice. A silent urging from Purl and—the race was on.

"Faster!" she squealed, releasing all control to her animal.

They charged across the powdery snow, the acceleration flinging Vareena back against the raised saddle. They raced neck and neck, until, with a subtle understanding, the pace dropped and they came to a shuddering, jolting stop.

Ya'ousa rode up to them. "Always," he said, with a rough approximation of a smile, "they take to it as if they were born for it! But remember, is not rider who important but harna under you. Without him, you could not ride like wind. You both need practise. Never should harna adjust to you, but you to him. They struggled with you. Always *listen*. Harna speak to you in thought and feeling, a feeling you can trust forever."

"Thank you, Jantiff Ya'ousa," said Vareena, tears in her eyes.

"Hah! The greatest of gifts, perhaps, bar one, and only *Thank you?* Yet Ya'ousa understand. It feels right. It feels good. We not go too fast now. Harna prefer speed—they like the wind in their hair and can travel vast distances in great hurry—but must start slow always. Find rhythm, then comes speed. And Arn is a smaller place."

He spoke again. They listened to his words, corrected their posture, concentrated and thought; and rode again.

There was no need for reins this time as both harna responded to their silent urging in an exultant burst of speed that took them past Ya'ousa and his harsh laughter, and hurtled them towards their goal.

v. Liths

THE FIRST sight of the lith-stone lying in ruin around this little hillock, thrilled Vareena. A growing excitement gave her a sensation of invulnerability. She leapt off Purl and ran towards the lichen-stained boulders of deep black, veined with a pale limning of blue. Beauty still lived within this tumble of fractured, jutting stones and low stumps. The once-majestic pinnacle had fallen long ago. Only its cracked, flattened bottom was visible from beneath mud and vegetation—like a giant's foot had toppled the column and smashed it into the ground.

The base building, nothing more than three immense blocks topped by a flat slab roof, stood awry, as if the same giant had attempted to push it over. The structure was broken, riven by the intense seasons of the Gyre and split by its own weight. One wall lurched free of the others, lying at an angle and although covered in mud, moss and yellowy lichen, Vareena spied an array of eroded glyphs and symbols. *Yes,* she thought. The vague outlines made sense to her mind. *I can use this as a sentinel. A starting point.*

"Be careful, Man-girl!"

Vareena ignored the kerrish. *All I need is a dagger or poniard, a wet rag and—*

A huge hill-boar charged from its lair close to the fallen column. Vareena tried to dodge and took a glancing blow, falling onto her back. The black-haired, squat razorback squealed in anger. Twin tusks jutted from the feral-pig's lower-jaw like two scythes; it twisted, preparing to charge again.

Scowl raised his poniard of iron in his half-hand and readied to throw. A furry paw knocked the wicked dagger from his grasp.

Blackbeak glared at the kerrish with confusion, his other hand finding IronScythe. "What are you doing?"

Ya'ousa's answer was to toss back his grey-furred head. A bizarre sound, like a soothing roar, escaped from his throat; a weird, animalistic cant. Behind him, Burrstone, Purl, Taatchi and the other harna added to this threnody. Each produced a peculiar un-Arnish lament. A harmony not of two notes, or three or even four, but many.

The hog slid to a stop, black ears twitching. Its dreadful tusks were only inches away from the bemused face of Vareena.

A discordant tune reminiscent of old forests and silent, imposing trees filled the air. The harna sang what sounded like an ancient lament—*a warning*. The pig snorted, beady eyes turned towards the riding beasts in confusion. Hot breath escaped from a flat snout in twin fogs of frosty air. The song changed, became gentler. The boar's breathing slowed and, with a defiant snuffle, the creature retreated backwards to its hole.

A bark from Ya'ousa, and the refrain ended. Vareena reeled, grasping for a balance she already had.

"Ya'ousa is sorry, Scowl." Intent brown eyes fixed upon the poniard lying on the ground. "Is not kerrish way to kill, unless unavoidable."

"Never touch my iron again!" Blackbeak rasped, dismounting and landing in a crouch. He grabbed at the dagger, holding the grey blade close to his chest, his gloved half-hand curling protectively around the curved hilt. Burrstone was agitated, as if she shared his anger. At the touch of his iron, his mood softened. He stood up. "But it is not my wish to kill when unnecessary."

"Ya'ousa react without thought, is Jantiff, is high in Cland. Is difficult for him to change ways of lifetime."

"The matter is at rest."

Ya'ousa nodded respectfully, flinging himself off his harna and approaching Vareena. "Is safe now. Silly razorback will stay in hole. Will not come out." He lifted Vareena up with a strong arm.

"What was that song?" she asked, staring in awe at the harna. They seemed pleased with themselves, chomping on bits of exposed green with loud, snapping teeth.

The kerrish shrugged, enormous shoulders rising and falling like twin slabs of furred rock. "Is nothing. Kerrish know razorback not want to attack. He late to sleep, getting ready for cold season, warm in his hole. We are in his territory, and he must defend. Harna warn him. Tell him he cannot win fight."

As if in reply, Taatchi lifted her flattened head and hooted into the sky.

"Ya'ousa's homeland of Skourass has many such animals," he explained. "We call him *razorback, the angry pig*. He always quick to rage. Dangerous. He not ask questions! He can kill with those hasty tusks of his. Hah! Even kerrish jump up tree when he come. Then we kerrish respect him even more." Ya'ousa chuckled.

Vareena raised her eyebrows. "Thank you again."

Scowl pushed past her, walking towards the lichen-covered stone. He cleared away the congealed vegetation and muck, using his poniard with precision.

She had not seen the blade in full sunlight. A wicked thing of grey twisted metal. The dagger appeared warped, bent as if by tremendous heat. She shuddered.

Blackbeak revealed a series of complicated filigrees underneath the yellowed lichen, the iron scraping and scratching.

When he was done, Vareena pushed him aside and fingered the eroded grooves. *The code I learned as a child, but no secret to the ancients who created this signpost.*

"Well?" said Ya'ousa, unable to contain himself.

A crack in the clouds, and sunlight framed Vareena in gold. "Give me a few minutes to make sense of this."

Ya'ousa turned away, frustration showing in the creasing of his snout.

Blackbeak put a calming hand on the kerrish's shoulder. "Do not hope too much. These stones are old and Vareena—very young."

"Shush!" said Vareena. "If you can't say anything positive, don't speak at all."

"Come," said Ya'ousa, walking Scowl over to where the

Burrstone stood. "Let me tell you about Margolyn's greatest gift. About our harna."

Blackbeak rubbed his half-hand down Burrstone's tightly packed black hair. Unlike any other creature, the harna did not shrink in fear or revulsion at his presence or touch. Instead, she hummed with content.

"Harna come from the forest, from Margolyn. Do not worry, Scowl. They untouched by shadow. They exist before the arrival of kerrish and will exist long after our departure. Ya'ousa could spend many days in story of harna, many months on our entwined history. Is their joy to ride. We cannot force them. So was falsehood in part, to say, Ya'ousa give harna as gift, for they only lend themselves. They will be yours for all life if you want, but still only *lent.* You understand?"

Scowl took a deep breath, letting it escape from his ruined nose with a familiar rasp. "I can sense delving, Ya'ousa," he said as if admitting a deep, dark secret. "I can sniff out its illness wherever it may lie. I am made for such things. That is my purpose and yet, if there is an opposite feeling to such ugly rancour, to such woeful evil, it is invested in these creatures."

The kerrish's snout parted, the skin pulling back to reveal an array of yellowed teeth. "Yes, Ya'ousa understands," he said. "We kerrish would be nothing without harna. Nothing."

Taatchi crooned. One big foot kicked at the wet snow, showering them both in slush.

Blackbeak shook ice from his mane-like flock of black hair. "Ya'ousa, you say you are a Jantiff in Cland Totu?"

Ya'ousa's chest expanded like a furry balloon. A raised paw thumped against his magnificent weavery and a roughly hewn badge. A circle of wood rudely painted with reds and blacks. "This Ya'ousa's Mark. Mark of the Totu Cland."

"From what I know of the Margolyn, and its Clands, it is not common for kerrish to travel alone, especially those of rank. You are far away from home my friend."

The huge bullhead searched the empty sky. "We kerrish sometimes too proud, Scowl. Clandsfighters sometimes too hard." He looked down at his distorted, ruined limbs. "We are an afflicted race, are like twisted tree in forest—it lives, but we know the wood inside is rotten."

"You have not answered."

The man-animal scowled. "Ya'ousa travels alone on a noble errand. That is all you need to know." He turned away. The furry back hiding the quick show of emotion incongruous with anything Scowl had heard about the Clands.

Vareena's noble tones broke into the silence. "—We are to the northwest of Palim and directly south of the lith-stone marked on your map. Well, at least, that's what I think."

"Man-girl has solved puzzle of ancient stones?" Ya'ousa blurted with a joyous growl.

"Took me a bit of working out, but yes."

"How long to travel there?"

"We must carry on northward for at least a week, till we find your lith-stone. Then a short day's walk northeast to the mine.

Ya'ousa pointed a claw at her. "On harna or foot?"

"Of course, Purl. I forgot we were riding. I've no idea how fast and far these harna can travel. We will be crossing *The Grikes*. I'm sure the broken land will be just as treacherous for harna as ourselves."

"Man-girl may reason that, but Ya'ousa know better. Harna travel faster and farther than you think. If you have no goal, harna like you—slow, aimless. Give harna purpose and she like dart on wind!"

Four days later, they arrived at the lith of their destination, facing north above a long, winding ravine atop a tall, craggy hill. The land had become a bleaker place, pocked and chiselled as if some preternatural hand had twisted immense swathes of rock into weather-beaten pedestals. Once gentle rivers and streams had created a riven landscape of deep meandering valleys, sunken holes and convoluted watery caverns.

"Mining Country," whispered Scowl.

Ya'ousa shivered.

The lith-stone had somehow resisted all that the Gyre had thrown at it. It stood high and proud, buttressed underneath was a similar squat building of black slabs. Here grew more exotic, yellowy lichen—the glyphs highlighted as if by gold.

The journey had passed with little incident. Vareena had attempted to explain how the stones worked. They existed in repeating patterns that, once understood, would spread out like an array in front of your eyes. The knowledge was an idle fancy of her youth and, like such things learned in childhood, it had stuck in her mind.

Scowl gave up trying to understand this impossible feat of memory. Ya'ousa had been more than intrigued. During the three nights of encampment, he swallowed all that Vareena could teach him on the subject.

The kerrish thirst for learning was well known. It worried humankind who feared such deformed creatures and envied their riding beasts. There was flesh to their concern: the kerrish organised themselves into socio-military groupings. The Clands. A dangerous force if united in war. They were tolerated by Cairn and the Usery, a protection that many despised.

"Something wrong here," blurted Ya'ousa. "Lith-stone unbroken, Gyre has not eroded. Is unnatural."

"Yes," answered Scowl. "Delving."

Vareena's head jerked towards her two companions. She did not share their sense of doom. Instead, she thrilled with a growing excitement. *The lith-stone is a beautiful thing, magnificent.* "We must follow the ravine north-eastwards."

The kerrish raised a fur-covered arm and pointed in that direction with a rough claw. "Look!"

Low on the horizon rose oily smoke.

"Mines," said Blackbeak.

The kerrish lowered his arm and pondered. "Ya'ousa thinks we must leave harna hidden. He does not like it here. Harna feel it too. We take them to safe place. Then we go."

Scowl nodded, and Burrstone grunted her approval.

Ya'ousa produced a small pouch of red powder and another

of blue, white, yellow and black. He then searched for five flat stones. Using a trickle of water from his leathern flask, he mixed these powders into a collection of bright paints.

Vareena and Scowl looked on with a certain understanding. Taatchi was painted, as was the fourth harna. Purl and Burrstone carried only the badge of the Totu Cland.

"Here. You must mark your harna. It is way of kerrish, of harna-lore. You must put your sign upon them."

"But what'll I paint?" said Vareena.

"Think of home," answered Ya'ousa. "Think of your life. You will find your mark."

"My home is Keep Krall. I'm not sure I'll ever return there. It has bad memories for me," she said. "But long before I entered its walls, my father gave me a ring. It bore the seal of Krall. A hunting bird, a flying predator of blue-black wings, bright eyes and a noble, if not dangerous, aspect. That will be my mark, Ya'ousa." Whilst she spoke, Vareena painted the magnificent bird upon Purl's flanks. The curious harna looked on, twisting his flattened head and nodding as if in approval.

"Man-girl paint well," grunted Ya'ousa.

"Before I discovered the sword, I was a master with the brush and the needle." Vareena's free hand patted the hilt of Scowlsbane. "Of course, I must include this," she added with a smile, grabbing at the white paint, daubing quickly, but with precision, "to remind me of the nemesis of delving's gift."

"The white sword and the blackened bird," said Scowl, and upon his lips those words contained a hint of darkness.

"Is good," said Ya'ousa as Purl crooned in delight. "And you, Scowl-man? What is your mark?"

Blackbeak stood transfixed. He could not think of anything he belonged to. No order and no creed—nothing in his past from which to create a symbol.

Vareena saw his concern, and without thinking, grabbed his half-hand and plunged it into the red paint and onto the black flank of Burrstone. The mark, half a palm with stunted fingers and thumb somehow fitted. "Now you have a new name: *The half-hand.*"

Scowl said nothing, only stooping to clean the crimson from his fingers. If he approved, Vareena could not tell.

The three adventurers found a secluded corral where bits of green poked through snow, and left their harna to graze.

"They wait here for us," said Ya'ousa.

"And—and what if we don't return," asked Vareena, suddenly worried she would never see Purl again.

"Harna go home. Back to forest. Back to Margolyn." He patted Taatchi.

The kerrish's expressions and moods were hard to read, but Vareena was sure he shared her apprehension.

A short while later, they entered the valley on foot. Vareena fingered her lump of gold, her pace quickening, anxious for her companions to hurry.

"We will arrive soon enough, girl," said Scowl.

Vareena did not hear him.

vi. Delvers

THE SCOWL stared at the oily water gurgling over a rocky stream bed, letting his fingers play in the stunted flow—evidence of a fenneral quarry close by. Mining of all types disturbed him. Removal of stone caused no permanent harm to the land but the smokes and slicks reminded him of ages past when gold, silvers and irons were the reef exploited by diggers and tunnelers.

He sighed. IronScythe was also the work of delving. She was an unavoidable evil—to destroy the wicked, you sometimes needed a weapon of equal malevolence. *Will I ever be free of her?* The question often came to his mind. She had been lost to him time and time again, but the cruel iron always found a way back to his hand.

"You in pain, Scowl-man?" asked Ya'ousa standing at his shoulder. Vareena walked a hundred or so feet ahead out of earshot.

Blackbeak stood to his full height. “Of a sort.” A laugh like a hiss, escaped his lips, his hand coming to rest on the long hilt of his blade.

“Ya’ousa is aware of how such banes are not all evil, nor have heinous purpose. But Ya’ousa has seen IronScythe at work. She worries him. How did you come by such a sword?”

“That is a question for another time. For now, she is your ally. Be thankful. You do not want to become her enemy.”

“You threaten Ya’ousa?”

“No, my friend. I speak fact—that is all. To carry such a bane is a burden indeed.”

The kerrish pondered those words for a second or two. “You wish for something more?”

“What I wish for is irrelevant. I am bound to the She-blade’s iron. Without her, I am nothing. With her, I can at least have half a life.”

“Then Ya’ousa understand.”

“Do you?”

“Kerrish live only half-life too. We not long-lived like man. Kerrish span short. We suffer disease and infirmity and live in fear of what we call the *long-death*. This is why kerrish fight one another. Why Clands always fighting. Better to die quick.”

“I have heard of this,” said Scowl. “To gain in rank, you must slay your superior in combat. You are Jantiff. Many you have killed to get to where you are, and even more who challenged you for your status.”

“Scowl speaks truth. Kerrish take life day by day. None trust to live to sunset. No feelings for kerrish. No true friendship, just words. No love.”

“From what I can tell, there is little hope in your race—other than to die in combat. And yet you and your brethren are far from your forest home. You have abandoned your Cland, despite how proudly you wear the Totu badge. I have also heard of others—outcasts from Margolyn roaming the lands.”

“Ya’ousa no outcast! Margolyn is his home. Always.”

“But why then did you leave?”

"Harna."

Scowl pondered his answer for a second. "Go on."

"Time with harna changes kerrish," he began. "Ya'ousa not like any other of his race. His span is nearly two passings of the Gyre. Ya'ousa is older than any other kerrish who has ever lived."

Blackbeak's misshapen face showed shock. "Two passings of the Gyre—you're no older than a teenager. Even Vareena is your elder."

"'Tis true."

"I knew you were short-lived, but this is a revelation."

"Yet Ya'ousa is old. Is *oldest.* That is why they let him leave. And over his many seasons, Taatchi of the forest has been with him, has shown him new way to be. Ya'ousa believe harna try to heal him, to heal all kerrish—to fix us."

"I don't understand."

"Taatchi helped Ya'ousa to—" the voice faltered, turning into a low growl "—Taatchi helped Ya'ousa not be afraid."

"From what I know of the Clands, they are fearless."

"No, Scowl, they frightened of everything except death. Death is their only friend. Their only certainty. The kerrish are afraid to live." The kerrish thumped a heavy paw into Scowl's back, a growling laugh erupting from his furred maw. "No. Harna have changed Ya'ousa. He mended. Harna will also mend Scowl-man."

"That I very much doubt," said Blackbeak. "Come. There is delving in these hills. I can feel its ugly call."

They caught up with Vareena, and stole silently up the steep-sided valley, travelling through winding gullies worn smooth by the regular passing of feet until they reached a wide bowl. The rocks here were cracked, a vast area of opencast mining. At its centre stood a high-walled compound from which came the sound of water and the voices of men.

At a signal from Ya'ousa, they clambered up the valley wall and lay prone, looking down into the quarry and its compound. An ice-laden waterfall splashed into a large artificial pool. An eddying mist hugged the ground through which walked ghost-like figures.

"About thirty to forty men," said Scowl

"Thirty-eight," grunted the kerrish.

Blackbeak twitched his head. "And more we cannot see, I'd guess."

"Many swords shine. They not made for tunnelling or digging. Weapon-men."

"You are right, my friend."

"Something wrong here, Scowl-man. Man has fenneral mines in our northern land, but not like this. See high compound wall?"

"You reckon that's to keep people in?" said Vareena.

"Not people. Kerrish slaves."

Wet fenneral rested in glistening heaps in the centre of the compound. "Two mine entrances," said Scowl. "They dig underground."

"It looks like a normal stone mine to me," said Vareena. "Fires used to heat the rock and a pool of water released in sudden deluge to quickly cool it, causing fractures and—"

A man ran out of the smaller mine entrance, shouting. More men followed him. Yells and screams stabbed up to their hiding place. A flurry of panic filled the compound below.

Two dust-covered animals also emerged from the mine—slow, encumbered by rocks attached to ropes tied to their feet.

The earth shook, followed a second later by a deafening boom. Black smoke, flames, and a hail of debris erupted from the tunnel, engulfing the two animals.

"Nhulya!" Ya'ousa shouted, jumping to his feet, his voice swallowed by the echoes of the explosion ricocheting around the rocky quarry. It took all Scowl's strength to pull the kerrish back down.

Long moments passed as the dust settled. The two animal captives stirred, stumbling amongst the rubble. Ya'ousa breathed a sigh of relief. "She alive," he rasped. "Nhulya is alive."

Vareena looked on with entranced eyes. She had expected Ya'ousa's brethren to resemble him, to show some kinship in form and shape. Only two things were the same—their obvious animalistic origins and an over-powering deformity. One creature had a distortion down the right side of its body, as if an artist, unhappy at his painting, had tipped water down half its length and the colours had run into each other. Its good side was muscled and sure. Dust-covered brown fur framed a long-snout from which canine teeth protruded and a pink tongue lolled. A withered arm was strapped to its side, a leg bent and twisted. "Marks of delving passed down to punish the innocent," said Vareena in a whisper.

"Watch your words, girl, have you learnt nothing?" chided Scowl.

But Ya'ousa was not listening, his full attention was on the scene below.

Scowl pointed his misshapen face at Vareena. "The Bacchust Isle taught me things you cannot begin to comprehend. Yet no learning can match the confrontation of evil. The feel of it down your spine, the insidious cold crawling around in your sensibilities. You know of what I speak. You were with me in the lair of the golem. Such evil comes with rancour. A smell like old sweat on a summer's day. Yes, the origin of the kerrish is shrouded in perversity, but delving and dark majiks do not taint their souls. They rose above their beginnings. Became something else. Something good and noble."

The cloud of smoke settled to reveal the second kerrish. Grey with black dust-stained patches, a thick tail trailed behind a squat body. A man dressed in the manner of Raza and those who frequented the tavern in Fisk, went up to them and started shouting.

Ya'ousa grumbled to himself in his own language—a fearful sound.

Scowl sniffed the air. "They are using powders. No wonder they keep their mine secret."

Vareena took a deep breath. "Powders?"

"Yes, evil things, fulminating tinctures used for display and exhibition, turned to volcano-flame by desire for metal. This is no fenneral mine, despite the show. I can smell their delving."

"Ya'ousa feared as much. Since Nhulya disappeared, he has

heard rumour of such thing, but could not believe it. Is Scowl sure?"

From one of the low buildings, a round figure emerged. He was covered head to foot in yellow.

"By the Smokes!"

"That's—that's gold," whispered Vareena. There was something almost delicious about the display.

Scowl unsheathed IronScythe in a single convulsive movement, as if the presence of gold alone was enough to set her free.

Vareena was familiar with the She-blade. A shadowy, blurred thing. Yet she couldn't face her in the full glare of sunlight. Contained in the iron was the same metal that glinted in the sun before them, a thin limning of gold. The heinous arts of delving rested in IronScythe. She seemed too much for one person to control. There was no envy, no greed for such a weapon.

"Is gold dangerous to you?" asked Vareena.

Scowl's head shook side to side. "No, Vareena. The threat of gold comes from Chicanery. You must never touch, nor go near such metal."

"You can't tell me what I can and can't do. You're not my master."

Blackbeak's eyes remained fixed upon the glinting golden god that lumbered towards the kerrish captives. "If it is your destiny to take up the majiks, you cannot have anything to do with such metal. It will corrupt you, change you—it will burn a black mark across your soul. But there is another danger. The Great Age of Darkness was the result of the delving of the land. Its metals should remain buried."

The kerrish thrust his bull-head towards Vareena. "Man-girl possess majiks?"

"It has been foretold, Ya'ousa. She will become She-savant. Although she must conquer her arrogance before that can become a reality."

Vareena turned away. *What does he know about my destiny? Scowl is jealous.* She squeezed at the nugget of gold in her weaves.

It's as precious and as necessary to me as Scowl's iron is to him.

Below them, the gold-arrayed figure stopped in front of the two man-animals. In one deft stroke, a golden weapon flashed and removed the head of the grey, squat-looking kerrish. It raised a second time.

"Nhulya!" bellowed Ya'ousa, jumping up and brandishing his club of fenneral. His animalistic voice echoing from the sharp walls.

The golden figure turned towards the powerful sound. The other men looked up also.

Before Scowl could stop him, Ya'ousa bounded down the side of the hollow. He moved with incredible speed, jumping and skipping in a sideways gait making the best of his deformity. He leapt from rock to rock, swinging his club of fenneral in front of him. It was a feat of physical power and precision incongruous with what appeared to be his major weakness. Ya'ousa reached the compound wall and leapt, landing badly atop the rough barricade. He wobbled for a second and fell. The men ran forward, and the kerrish was lost amidst many bodies.

"We have to help him!"

"We cannot," Scowl rasped. "Ya'ousa did what he had to do to try and save his mate. He does not expect us to sacrifice ourselves also."

Vareena's emerald eyes flashed with anger and confusion. "But we can't do nothing!"

Scowl's head shook. "It is not my way to sit idly by, but not even IronScythe can win-out against so many. She will not willingly let herself fall into the dominion of delving and gold."

Fists rained down upon the kerrish. A sword-hilt to the head, and Ya'ousa dropped for the last time. Nhulya, struggled to get to him, but she too fell under the force of many blows. At the direction of the figure dressed in gold, two rough looking men dragged the kerrish away, a thick line of blood curled in the dust behind Ya'ousa's limp frame.

"Thank the Gyre!" Vareena whispered. "They did not kill him. We can try a rescue." She turned her eyes towards Scowl.

"Can't we—?"

A sound like a sigh escaped Blackbeak's lips. "This is a gold mine, Vareena. It must be destroyed. If we can save Ya'ousa while doing that, then yes. We will try."

"But how? We are just two, and they are many. Do you have a plan?"

Scowl ignored her urgent questions. "Some of those men have the look of Arakian mercenaries from south of the Ingram Sea," he said with a scowl.

"Arakia? Is that important."

"My travels once took me close to that land. It is a stain polluting the South. I have heard many rumours that delving still lurks there, but iron drew me north, to the Unbidden Isles and Oldiva. But when her attention again turns to the South, they will come to feel the cold edge of her blade." Sweat dripped from his brow. Scowl's face had taken a haunted look.

"Are you all right?"

"'Tis the presence of so much delving metals. Of this little golden god. We must beware. *You* must beware."

A shadow passed over Vareena's face. "What'll we do now?"

"We wait till dark, and try to find a way inside."

"Dark? Use your eyes. There's no way in, other than through the front gates. We've not the legs of Ya'ousa."

"Time and iron will show us the way."

Vareena drew breath to reply, but the compound's massive gates were suddenly thrown open. Many men poured out, running towards their hiding place.

They scrambled backwards out of sight and dropped down into the ravine, running. The gully became alive with men. Vareena and Scowl had little cover among the rocks. She took the lead, moving with strange purpose. A rock formation ahead caught her attention. It seemed familiar. She ran towards it, finding a tight gap. She squeezed through, followed by Scowl, and emerged into a small hollow dominated by a giant bramble.

Scowl's uneven iron-blue eyes furrowed. "You've led us to a dead end."

"No, look." She pushed the bramble aside to reveal a boulder-strewn hole.

The sounds of men echoed from behind the gap.

"Quickly!" Vareena jumped into the hole, swiftly followed by Scowl. They landed a few feet down in the dark. A second later, two men pushed themselves into the hollow above. They muttered for a few moments, and left.

"Here." Scowl handed Vareena a dried stranding taken from his pack. With a whisper from his misshapen lips, it burst into life.

They stood in a man-made cave. Roughly circular with twin ruts in the floor. Dripping walls lent the tunnel a fetid air. The end had partially collapsed, creating the hole they had escaped into.

"We are in an old mine," said Scowl. "We must be careful."

Vareena shivered, but not from the cold. She was filled with excitement. "I think this tunnel will take us to their mine.

"How can you be so sure?"

"I don't know. Just a feeling. I have led us well so far, have I not?"

Scowl bent his misshapen features to the darkness ahead and sniffed. He was reminded of Fulminara's prophesy. Yet the caves of Vareena's doom were many leagues and seasons away. "Are you sure?"

The torch reflected in her eyes, flickering across the glassy black of her huge, excited pupils. She seemed powerful, arcane. "Let me lead you, Blackbeak. I'll find a way."

vii. Call of the Caves

BLACKBEAK SNIFFED at the fusty mine air and extinguished Vareena's stranding with the thumb and forefinger of his stunted half-hand. "Gas."

Vareena was surprised by a low-level light that seemed to emanate from the walls.

"Bad gas down here. We cannot use a torch, nor breathe too deeply." He pointed to the tunnel walls. "I have seen this light-bearing lichen before. It grows in foul air. We must be careful."

They had descended into the abandoned mine workings for

over two hours. Vareena led them with a sense of purpose. If this worried Scowl, he did not show it. He followed one step behind, silent except for the wet rasp of his breath.

Occasional sounds leaked from the surrounding rocks. Creaks and moans like the far off groans of trapped men. Vareena knew of the shades that inhabited dark, damp places. Of the direful voices that tried to trap the curious and the foolish. "Do you believe in ghosts?" she asked.

"Don't waste your breath on such silly questions."

"You do not believe in the shades of dead men. Of all those killed working in this mine? Trapped here. Forced to roam these tunnels forever?"

"They bother me not. Only the real world is worth any thought or curiosity."

"You are not frightened that they may try to lure us into traps and dangers?"

"You breathe too deeply of the gas, Vareena. Miners also hold the same superstitions. No dead hand can harm that which is living. Fear them not. What is dead is passed, what is passed has left forever."

She found strength in his matter-of-fact dismissal, but the groans did not go away, if anything, they became more human, more woeful.

At the next juncture, Vareena felt the breath of cleaner air coming from above. And slowly, they ascended, leaving the under-mine behind. Her pace quickened and soon, the faraway thud and scrape of digging, of mining and the real world, replaced the groans of ghosts and shades.

"I'm impressed," said Scowl. "Although I'm intrigued by how you managed to guide us so well?"

"I don't know. Maybe it's something to do with Fulminara's prophesy. Maybe it's my—it sounds odd to say this, but it could be my majiks again, helping us, helping Ya'ousa."

"I hope it is just that, and not the lure of gold. You must keep away from it. The metal can harm you irreversibly."

"But does not gold sit in your She-blade?"

"IronScythe is designed to combat delving. She cannot affect you, be sure of that."

"But what if I know gold can do me no harm."

"You cannot have such knowledge."

She reached into her weaves and pulled out the ingot of gold Raza had used to impress her. "It fell from his hand when I killed him. I couldn't leave it behind."

A flash of horror crossed Blackbeak's misshapen features, replaced by fierce anger. "You little fool!" he barked. "Now I see what has pushed you upon this journey, what has pulled you into this mine of delvers. You needed no lith-stone to guide you here. Rid yourself of it, now! Before it is too late."

"You're not my master. You can't tell me what to do!"

"Do not dare to disobey the will of iron, Vareena. You do not know the danger you are in."

"You can't lecture me. Your precious weapon is also made of forbidden metals, of iron and gold. Will you not also throw her away?" she spat. "Or does the *Hooded Scourge* live by different rules?"

"You speak of my iron? You are not fit to be in her presence." He unsheathed the She-blade and raised her with threat.

Vareena took a step back. "You don't scare me. I know when and where I will die."

"Have you not listened to all I have told you since we met? Iron is the nemesis of delving of *delvers.* Of those who seek power from dark majiks. You risk her fury!"

"You threaten me?"

"Not I, but IronScythe."

"But you control her?"

"No, Vareena, I but carry out her will. You must throw away the yellow metal or feel her wrath." He pointed his blade at Vareena's face.

She stood firm. "Have you forgotten Fulminara so quickly? Her words. You cannot kill me, Scowl."

"No?" He swung IronScythe around his head, the blade keening and worrying in the dark, wafting Vareena's lank hair.

She was defiant, unafraid. "Iron is not my master and never will be."

He stepped forward, knocking her to the ground. "That is gold speaking. And you are foolish to trust the Carline."

"Am I?" she said, raising herself upon her elbows. "If I had not helped you, you both would be lost. Fulminara's reward was given in good faith. Deep down, you know that."

Scowl's head twisted from side to side, a desperate look in his eyes. "IronScythe's power lies beyond the fate of any one person, Vareena. She can break prophesy and destroy oracles. No one is safe from her. Do you not yet understand?" He raised the She-blade above his head.

Vareena baulked. "Don't!"

The sword came down, plunging deep into the rock floor only inches from her head. He let go of the blade and fell back into the gloom.

Long moments passed as she lay under that dark metal, her heart beating in a flurry. When she again found her feet, what met her eyes filled her with dismay. Scowl lay upon the tunnel floor. A twisted ruin of a man. *Without his blade he is nothing. The She-blade wanted my blood. Yet he stopped her.* Guilt overtook her then. Distraught, she looked at the nugget of gold in her hand and for the first time found evil in its appearance. Like some dreadful golden watching eye. She threw it down the tunnel as far as she could and went to tend to her friend.

"I'm sorry, Scowl," she said, staring at his warped physique. An awful malaise inhabited his limbs, some constricting force twisting his legs and arms, hands and feet. He shook and quivered as if in apoplexy. *More animal than man. The creature I first saw in King-Emperor Jhaz'Elrad's Reeving Chamber.* "Forgive me."

Blackbeak did not answer, weakened without the touch of his iron.

Guiding his one good hand to the hilt of IronScythe, Vareena gave him back his dignity.

At the touch of the grey metal, Blackbeak breathed deeply, taking strength and power from the iron. His limbs relaxed and straightened. But it was long minutes before he was strong enough to speak.

"Gold," he rasped. "Gold does this. We are both its victims." He stood up, wrenching IronScythe free from the rock floor, showering the pair of them in rocks and debris.

Vareena jumped away from the rubble, her eyes staring at the wavering tip of the now free blade. IronScythe trembled for a few minutes, hanging in the air close to her face.

Warning me.

Finally, Blackbeak sheathed the blade. "You have been lucky. It is not many that IronScythe has spared. She lives for punishment, for vengeance. Sometimes even the innocent are not safe.

"I did not realise, Scowl. Truly."

"Gold is the curse of Chicanery. It is through this metal, and through irons and tins, that the majiks flow. A sacred part of the earth. Once removed, it can push any savant, regardless of his or her good character, into insanity and hate. You must be careful, Vareena. This is a gold mine. You stand amongst its reef."

"I've felt different ever since I took the nugget from Raza. I heard your warnings, but—"

Blackbeak grabbed at her weaves with his stunted half-hand. He pulled her close to him, face to face. "You forced yourself upon my company when I did not want it. You ignored my advice at every opportunity. After we rescue Ya'ousa and I destroy this mine, I want you gone. Do you hear me? IronScythe perverts those around her. All fall to her blade—if you stay with me, she will one day take your life. And I will not be able to prevent it."

"It's a chance I'm willing to take." Vareena leaned in and kissed his exposed cheek. It was unplanned, and yet it felt natural.

Scowl reacted like he had been stung, pushing her away. "Come, there are more important matters ahead of us. Let us concentrate upon our task and nothing else."

Vareena followed him. "What did you mean earlier, by 'destroy this mine'?"

Scowl said nothing, but Vareena didn't hold out much hope for the delvers and their pits. *As for Scowl?—He cannot get rid of me so easily.*

viii. God of gold

THEY HOLED up inside a smaller ventilation tunnel close to the now-abandoned lesser mine's entrance. The thin, cruel speech of the southern men echoed around them. They hissed and whispered in a peculiar cant that expressed moods and understandings in staccato repetition and long drawls. It rose to an echoing crescendo with the rough shout of many gruff voices and sank to a menacing jeer that crawled around their hiding place.

Even Scowl seemed bowed under its cadence, his warped face occasionally grimacing.

Vareena thought she might go mad with its sound. "Why do they do it?"

"You ask me this? You have already felt the pull of gold upon your mind."

"But—"

"Listen Vareena. Chicanery, like any other Crafting, has its shining lights and its disappointments. Some savants can evocate with the power of ten lesser users combined, while others only gently caress their majiks. And there are many who will never have the ability to take up the azure-robes, but within whom the majiks still flow—even if that flow is but a trickle."

"You mean—?"

"Yes, it seems that this Jessop is drawn to gold by his own majiks, however small the flame burns within his breast. And for some the pull of gold is irresistible. It gives the owner natural authority, charisma. It gains them acolytes and blind followers. Henchmen. With gold, Jessop can experience real power."

"You're saying Jessop is a savant?"

"A part of Chicanery? No. He is no more dangerous than the next man. You know the type—a philanderer, a man of easy words and easier pleasures. The weak-minded are drawn to him like flies to ordure. He is apt to inspire loyalty in his followers. A big fish in a small, murky pond. But with gold in his hands? It is like a magnifying glass, making him more than he is. It would seem that this Jessop represents the force behind this mine, and behind the use of kerrish slaves. It is likely that he and his men are getting rich from gold-trade with the South."

"But he must know of the risks he is taking. He must realise what he's doing?"

"He is an addict, Vareena, as are the others. Gold is a drug many find hard to resist. But worry not, they will all be punished. Now be quiet. We must wait till nightfall."

The sounds of men digging and toiling stretched over the long hours until the short night finally fell and the men downed their tools. Scowl lit a torch. "Now we search," he said, his nose sniffing at the gloom.

"Search?"

"Yes, for the miners' delving dust, their powders."

"But what about the men? We cannot wander their mine at will, we will be discovered."

"You forget, Vareena. Miners, especially delvers, are superstitious. They leave their workings under darkness for fear of the dead. Of ghosts and shades. No, we will be quite safe."

"But should we not go find Ya'ousa? He is in danger."

"I have but one task now that I know these men are delvers—to destroy them and their mine."

"You can't forget the kerrish. The gifts he made to us, your vow to him. You can't."

"I have not forgotten, but if we are to rescue our comrade, we will need a diversion."

"But—"

"Silence! I seek to kill two crows with one fire-hot stone. If Ya'ousa still lives, what we now do will be his only chance."

Vareena sighed in resignation. "Come then, let us be quick."

They ran, navigating their way through the mine's many levels, softly padding through well-used, winding tunnels until they neared the other, larger entrance. Scowl extinguished his torch, for the tunnels flickered with candle light and strandings.

They revealed abstract paintings, weird carvings, and the bleach-white of whittled bones. Here and there were alcoves in which rested the rotting remains of food offerings and the occasional sacrifice. Scribbled parchments, blotted and stained with dry blood were pinned to the walls. The whole mine was a shrine to sickness and death.

Scowl stopped, his misshapen nose twitching. To their left was a small opening. He entered a dry, gloomy cave, pungent with the smell of sulphur and the bitter taint of urine. Here, covered with rough weave sheets, was a stack of roughly hewn barrels. "Good," he whispered in the dark.

"Have you found it?" asked Vareena, following him, carrying a lit stranding taken from the wall outside.

"Stay away," he barked. "One ember from that torch and both our futures end here."

She stepped back into the entrance.

Scowl broke open a small barrel with a quick thrust and twist of his poniard. A muslin bag rested inside. Unravelling the loose knot, he revealed the dark powders. "We shall use their delving ways against them."

"But what of Ya'ousa and his mate? Night is short. They may already be dead."

"Ya'ousa accepted his fate. He knew what he was doing," said Scowl. Stuffing the bag into his gird-belt. "Now extinguish that flame and help me."

"I'm not like you, Scowl. I cannot be so cold. I need to see if they are still alive."

"It will achieve nothing. You will endanger yourself."

"But I must. And besides, my end is far away in another time and another land, I will be safe."

"Such knowledge is already making you rash and over-confident, Vareena. You must watch those emotions for one day they may be your undoing. Fulminara only prophesied when and where you will die. Forty-three passings of the Gyre is long enough to suffer much injury, loss and pain. When your end comes, you may wish it had come sooner."

Vareena digested his words. "Only Scowl could turn such news to darkness and woe. I'll be careful. Now get on with your work."

A sound, like that of a hissing toad escaped his uneven lips. "Try and find where they are keeping Ya'ousa and Nhulya prisoner, but do not attempt to talk or get close to them. Understand?"

"I won't get caught. Will you be alright on your own?"

"Remember the gas?" he said, expertly rolling one of the barrels.

Vareena nodded.

"It mixes well with delving powders, and they have quite a store. Be careful, Vareena."

"I will." She left Scowl to his plans and stole towards the mine entrance.

A massive fire burned in the centre of the compound, roaring into the black of a starry, cloudless night. Golden motes, like a swarm of fireflies, flew into the sky. Many men surrounded the fire, dancing and gyrating, drunk on beer or some other substance.

A ceremony or a sacrifice?

A flash of gold and Vareena almost cried out. Standing directly behind the pyre, catching glints from the flame that burned orange and incarnadine, was Jessop.

Rings, bracelets, necklaces, and amulets; heavy pieces of flattened and worked gold covered his neck and arms. He wore a belt of gold upon which hung a great golden sword. The yellowed metal had been fashioned by reverent hands, scored and filigreed by skilled, although misguided, fingers. The hilt was a claw encircling a golden globe: a crude representation of the planet Arn.

The symbol of his authority. A beautiful thing, but IronScythe she is not, thought Vareena.

Thick flesh slid over the gold of many rings, making it difficult for Jessop to bend his fingers. Gold entwined his head like a crawling snake. It banded his calves, and pierced his ears, nose and belly. It adorned all visible parts of his body, dancing hypnotically in the light from the fire: a liquid demon of delving.

Vareena felt dizzy. *Scowl's words make sense now. I can feel Jessop's gold. It wants me to take it, to own it. I won't let myself get tempted again…* But she could not take her eyes away.

Sometime later, how long she knew not, a commotion outside a row of squat open buildings like cowsheds broke her reverie. Vareena shook her head, coming back to herself. A group of men stumbled towards the pyre, dragging the two kerrish captives between them. Both Ya'ousa and Nhulya stared ahead, ignoring the scene around them. *Scowl was right. They have made their peace with death. It does not scare them. But they may not have to die. Not if Scowl can pull off his plan.*

Blackbeak arrived at her side. "The fuses are lit, the mine will blow soon," he said. "How fares Ya'ousa and his mate?"

Vareena nodded towards the two bound kerrish, made to kneel before Jessop and the pyre.

"Superstitious fools." He spat. "The land is not appeased by such sacrifice. Bones can never replace the loss of gold. A burning will not free them of their crimes. But do not worry, we may still have time to save them." Iron-blue eyes roamed the compound. "There are fewer guards than earlier, but the gates are still watched. Come."

They crept out from the mine entrance, hugging the auburn-tinted shadows. On the other side of the fire, many men sat cross-legged in a roped off area.

"Prisoners," Vareena whispered. "They may aid us."

"No."

"How can you be so sure?"

"We can trust no one in this den of delving."

They stole further into the orange night, moving from rubble to building.

Jessop's rounded belly jutted fatly from beneath his chest-plate, emphasising his stubby legs. Red-faced and ill looking, his eyes yellowed and red around the edges, he wheezed and spluttered unhealthily. He smiled at the prisoners, revealing even more gold: a ring in his upper lip.

Scowl pointed towards the prisoners. "Look Vareena, they too have such a ring. A sign of Jessop's dominion. And his snare. The pull of yellow metal traps them; they would rather die than live away from its allure. We can trust no one to help us."

Vareena was reminded of the curious hole in Raza's lip. Fisk, and its little tavern, seemed a long way away from this perverse scene.

Ya'ousa and Nhulya were kicked to the ground. And, as if this was a sign, Jessop began to speak.

"We hass come long ways my frens, travelled far northes from our lands. We hass come great distances cross kingdoms an' seas for tha feel of hot gold upon our hanss. Toiled an' fought, dug an' delved."

The followers of gold moaned and groaned in recognition of these phrases. They drank heavily, as if the ale contained opiates.

But Vareena now realised what really befuddled their sensibilities: *gold*.

Jessop continued. "But tonight, let uss gives a little back tah tha land, for she's `ungry an' needs her bones returned. Bones!"

Vareena was almost mesmerised by the voice. There was something uncouth about the accent of Arakia. It had no tongue of its own, but spoke the common language with a twisting lilt that slanted words. A compliment in that land sounded like a sugary insult.

They scrambled closer to where Ya'ousa and Nhulya lay.

"An' nows—nows is tha time for tha payment tah be made!" Jessop lifted up his golden sword and muttered, half to himself, half to the crowd. *"Give her bones—Bones—Bones!"*

"Where is your diversion?" whispered Vareena.

Scowl glanced back to the mine entrance. "Curse the works of delving!" he hissed through uneven, clenched teeth.

The golden god's face turned to one of hate. He took a step toward the kerrish captives and spat at them. "You whose were created by delving, shall dies forrit!"

Scowl's powerful, yet nasal voice reverberated from the gloom.

"Jessop!" It was as if the land itself had found vent for its hatred.

Blackbeak entered the cauldron of flickering light and unsheathed IronScythe. He walked with slow purpose, raising the blade before him.

Frightened, thinking their master had summoned some dark creature of delving, the men pulled back from his path.

"Whose—whose are ya?" demanded Jessop.

"I am the avenger of darkness and delving. I have come to claim what is mine."

The light of the fire caught Scowl's blackened and ill-wrought nose, the smashed ruin of his face and the intense unblinking iron-blue eyes. It cast unnatural shadows upon his face—as if some preternatural heat had melted his features. His blade crawled and danced.

Jessop nearly fell over backwards at the sight, his befuddled followers wailing in a chorus of fear. The grip upon Ya'ousa and Nhulya was loosened. Vareena noticed they were tensed, ready.

"Gets back! I am gold!" shouted Jessop. "Duzzent let him fools ya! He's nah avenger of delving, he's an ugly friend of tha Kretch!"

The men murmured in confusion, but a few reached for their weapons.

Scowl chose his moment well. He held up IronScythe threateningly. "You think gold is power? I challenge you to put it in contest against the power of iron!"

The earth grumbled and shook, roaring from deep within its depths. A series of conflagrations exploded from the mine entrance, sending Jessop and his followers, scurrying away from Scowl and his dark weapon. Stone missiles riddled the air, smashing into rock, wood and flesh. Fire erupted from sudden cracks that opened in the ground, incinerating men where they sat and catching others as they ran. Human torches staggered and stumbled, screaming in terror and pain.

Ya'ousa and Nhulya jumped to their feet and, although tied with thick ropes, they used the sudden commotion to head-butt and bite their captors. Blackbeak and Vareena ran towards them, bringing twin blades of stone and iron down to slice their bonds. The dazed men were easy fare—IronScythe butchered them into so many cuts of meat.

"Run!" Scowl shouted.

The four of them sprinted towards the compound's massive gates looming before them in the deafening, exploding night.

"By the Gyre!" Vareena squealed. "I could not believe my eyes."

"My knowledge of powders is limited only to their use, Vareena," he gasped as they ran. "I had no idea if they would ignite the underground gas—although I hoped for that outcome."

Only two men guarded the gate. This time IronScythe was idle. Nhulya ripped into one while Ya'ousa crushed the other with massive paws. Neither missed a stride.

Then it was IronScythe's turn. She spun in the air and split asunder the great wooden beam that held the gates shut. Pushing with the might of four bodies, they escaped into the dark night.

Once outside they were met by the sound of excited hooting, low bellows and the thick rasping sounds of harna.

"Yak tek fejjik tullo pah buh gragwerren!" growled Ya'ousa angrily. Taatchi pushed his enormous head at him and the kerrish's angry words were soon replaced with those of greeting.

"Purl!" Vareena was pleased beyond belief to find her new friend waiting for her. She mounted easily, keen to leave this place behind. There was no saddle, but contact with Purls thick neck lent a warm feeling of security and reassurance. The earth continued to shake with underground explosions.

Nhulya crooned to her harna who was joyous at her side. Only Burrstone seemed quiet. Scowl stood by her, his half-hand stroking her sleek hair.

"Quickly, Scowl. Mount!" Vareena shouted.

Scowl shook his mop head. "You go ahead. There are things I must do. Wait for me by the lith. I shall return before sunrise. If not, remember me well and look after Burrstone."

Before Vareena could say anything to stop him, he strode through the breached gates and into the compound, Burrstone crooning sorrowfully at his back.

Vareena urged Purl to follow him, but Taatchi blocked her way. "Leave him be, Man-girl," grunted Ya'ousa.

"But he'll be killed."

"Ya'ousa think not."

"But—"

"Did you not hear Scowl speak out against gold?"

"What?"

"He challenged with iron. Such a challenge cannot be left unfulfilled."

Ya'ousa and Nhulya urged their harna forwards. And despite Vareena telling Purl to turn back, he followed them, leaving the gates, explosions and the collapsing compound far behind.

ix. Powders

THE SCOWL strode through the gates of the compound. Around him, the vast quarried hollow began to collapse in on itself. Soon there would be no evidence that a mine existed here at all.

He marched forwards, searching for the little god of gold. Confusion reigned as men struggled to escape the still exploding mine. Few noticed the tall, sable-weaved nemesis that stalked the compound, and if they did, they gave a wide berth.

A flash of yellow, and Scowl caught a glimpse of Jessop hiding behind one of the small buildings. He lifted his head and looked straight into Blackbeak's vengeful eyes. Jessop called out to his men in fear, but even his commanding voice was lost to the surrounding din of shouting, and the boom and ring of blasts deep inside the rock. Terror-stricken, the god of gold ran.

Scowl followed, his pace unchanging as he stalked his prey.

Jessop reached the compound wall and turned to face his pursuer.

"I have come to set my iron against your gold, Jessop," said Scowl. "Let's see how your blade fairs!" He swung IronScythe, but despite Jessop's shaking hand, he parried with his golden sword.

Scowl was momentarily taken aback. He swung again, and again Jessop blocked his strike.

Something about the gold would not allow IronScythe to pass.

A smile crossed the yellow-bathed features. "Sees? Youss cannot conquer gold. It alone destroys. Youss are no avenger. Irons is no match."

They engaged in a frenzy of attack and defence. Scowl and IronScythe twisted and turned, stabbed and slashed. Blackbeak tried every trick; every move he knew, but could not pass the golden wall that was Jessop's defensive blade. Yet all the power of Jessop's gold could not turn the combat to his advantage.

Blackbeak became aware of a ring of men watching them, drawn to the spectacle—and to the gold,

"Face it, ugly! Youss has lost. Jessop commands all. I say, kills him. Kills him now!"

Another blast from the mine entrance and flaming coals fell around them in a burning hail of fire.

Scowl's grasped for the muslin bag held in his gird-belt and threw the contents at Jessop. Powders clogged the gold, sticking to it with a weird adhesion.

An ember caught Jessop's shoulder and ignited him into living flame. Fire licked at his face, burning his hair and peeling away the skin so that it became one with the melting gold. He fell forward, screaming and shouting. Fat hands tried to stifle the flames. But it was no use. Thick drops of fat bubbled and frothed, guttering down the heated metal—leaving behind a blackened, smoky ruin of melted gold, twisted limbs and charred bone.

Scowl faced the shocked men. "The Land has had her sacrifice." As if in answer to this offering, the earth rumbled, a deep resonating growl that convulsed in paroxysm after paroxysm. Blackbeak was thrown to the ground. Deeper groans followed, the terrain cracked and fire belched.

The valley exploded in a deafening roar that buried it forever.

x. Arnhenge

THE HARNA crooned sorrowfully in the bright dawn, their haunting sounds reflecting the destruction around them.

A series of rumblings, lasting long into the night, had devastated the land for leagues. When they had reached the lith, it too lay in ruin.

Whatever force has kept this silent sentinel untouched for so long was unable to resist the might unleashed last night, thought Vareena.

If not for the dexterous speed of their harna, they would have been caught in the collapse. Ya'ousa had taken a heavy fall and Purl, too, was hit by a glancing rock, but their desperate gallop rushed them to the farthest reaches of catastrophe, and they had been saved.

"The Land reclaims its own," said Nhulya. Her voice thin and reedy, as if it struggled to pass through her animalistic mouth, but her words were warm and soothing. Her command of the common tongue made Ya'ousa sound like a child. Vareena nodded in understanding.

White mist hugged the ground, gently dissipating upon an early breeze. It was an eerie scene. The sun shone low on the plain, her disk pale and cold.

The landscape had changed forever, becoming a featureless, flattened, rock-strewn wasteland. A whole area of *The Grikes* had fallen in on itself in a landslide of boulders and stones.

There seemed little hope for Scowl. "Is he dead?" Vareena whispered to Ya'ousa. "Will he return?"

The kerrish breathed in deeply. "Air is fresh this morning, is clean. It speaks of new beginnings. Kerrish have many skills, many powers, yet knowledge of future is unknown to us."

"Then you cannot tell."

"That is not entirely true," said Nhulya. "In return for this shortcoming, the Gyre has given us a heightened ability in the now—in the moment."

Ya'ousa nodded enthusiastically. "Ya'ousa feel that Scowl is not dead."

"But then we must go and look for him."

The kerrish shook his head. "No. We wait."

"But—"

"You have listened to Ya'ousa, but have not *heard.*"

"I can't sit around if he needs our help!" Vareena raced over to Purl, and clambered upon his back. The harna made no response, except to croon sorrowfully. His peculiar face looked up apologetically at her and seemed to frown. "If you won't take me, then I'll go on foot!"

"Stop and listen! ...Land is broken. For leagues. Where would Man-girl look? No. We wait. If Scowl survive. He come here, to lith stone."

The words were unbending, but the Kerrish was right. *The Grikes have gone, collapsed in on themselves... but I can't do nothing.* Vareena dismounted and fell in a heap. Purl nudged against her. She pushed him away.

How much time passed before Burrstone trumpeted at her side, Vareena was not sure. She looked up in a daze.

Scowl's massive black harna raised herself upon sturdy back legs, her head bobbing. She grunted in pleasure; crooning into the thin air of the cold morning, and launched herself across the sharply jutting broken rocks.

Vareena jumped to her feet, searching the mists. A sudden breeze and there he was, standing tall and proud, IronScythe girded at his side. Scowl's weaves were bloodied and torn, but he was alive. Relief washed over her.

Burrstone was first to arrive, nearly knocking him off his feet as she pressed and pushed against him, bathing him in warm blasts of moist air from her widely expanded nostrils—groaning and whimpering and stomping next to him.

Vareena arrived next, jumping down from Purl's back.

Scowl appeared worn thin by the night's events and the slow journey over clint and grike.

Ya'ousa put his paw upon his shoulder and nodded—a sign of deep respect for kerrish. Nhulya too, dropped her head in his direction.

"What happened?" Vareena said.

Blackbeak fell to the ground in a faint.

Vareena was all action. While she tended to his wounds, Ya'ousa and Nhulya lit a fire and heated some water.

A day later, when Scowl had recovered sufficiently, they made ready to ride.

Vareena was keen to get moving, for she feared the sudden appearance of Bluster, the season of snows and hails, sleets and freezing rains. It was already months overdue. When the snows came proper, it would blizzard for month upon month, covering the land and suffocating the earth. Any unwary traveller could not hope to survive such a time. They needed the safety of a Keep or castle.

The kerrish appeared to be unaware of this danger, and even Purl, her harna, showed a calmness that was against all instinct to the danger that was about to come.

"Ya'ousa senses your worry," said the kerrish, mounting Taatchi. "He sees your fear. But Big-Snow is no threat to us."

"What do you mean?"

"You do not understand about harna. They enjoy snow—love it. On hard ground they are fast, upon snow, they travel lighter, move with greater speed. Blizzard may blind rider, but harna *see*—they not get lost. If you know where you want to go—harna take you there."

Something in his tone said that this was no idle statement, that the kerrish had a goal in mind. A journey. "I travel to Palimara with Scowl. Will you come with us?"

"Listen Vareena, Ya'ousa is old. Very old. He will never again return his home of Margolyn. He says: let him guide you. Let harna take you South to land of Bikar."

"Bikar? But that's—"

"Yes. Ya'ousa and Nhulya travel to Arnhenge for festival of Alycion. Ya'ousa want to spend his last days in ring of stone. To visit Arn's greatest monument."

"It's an impossible journey, thousands of leagues away, half the Northern Continent and more."

"Vareena is forgetting harna."

Purl rubbed his snout at her back, nudging her—like he too was pushing her forward upon this expedition.

"But I travel with Scowl, we are—"

Blackbeak raised his gloved half-hand. "Go with them, Vareena."

"But I'm travelling with you to Palimara. To raise an army to… to…" Her voice died.

"You need no Keep, nor revenge. We must part—you know that."

"But—"

The beak-face showed no emotion. "Destiny will find you wherever you are, Vareena. You must prepare yourself for what is to come." Scowl mounted Burrstone. "Goodbye my kerrish friends," he said, bowing to Ya'ousa and Nhulya. "Trust and friendship are never the easiest found, in you are both—with abundance."

"No." Vareena jumped on the back of Purl. "I'm coming with you."

"Goodbye Vareena."

Before Vareena could protest, the harna began to sing. Their multi-tonal voices uniting in a sad lament.

Scowl reined Burrstone. "Look after Vareena well," he said and, with a shout, galloped away.

"Come, Vareena," said Nhulya. "Arnhenge awaits us. Turn your sorrow into purpose. Ride with us. Let Ya'ousa be your guide, and let destiny fuel your actions. Vareena must decide, but follow Scowl-man she must not."

Vareena watched Burrstone gallop into the distance. She could sense Purl. If she so wished, he would follow Scowl. No command from Ya'ousa could prevent that. Yet she had made her decision. *I'm sure we will meet again, one day. I shall look forward to it, my friend, no matter how long it may take.* She allowed her eyes to roam over the land. To the southeast she could feel Cairn, the city of majiks, but was not yet ready to visit its vaulted spires.

"Then Arnhenge and the Alycion it is. Let us go, for I tire of this place."

At that, Ya'ousa let out a loud bellow and the three harna leapt away, leaving the ruined lith-stone and the collapsed mining lands of *The Grikes* far behind.

NINE

ESCAPING THE CRADLE

"SOMETHING WRONG?" Chira yawned, coming out of the artificially induced coma of the void and wiping sleep out of her eyes. She took in the first amity-linked images of local space and blinked. "Stephen? Are you there?"

After a long pause, the droning, metallic voice of *The Stephen Hawking*, replied, speaking directly into her mind. *I… I have lost the dice, Chira.*

Stephen was the living *Percept* of the ship that surrounded her. An eon's old intelligence that ran this ancient, yet serviceable, Delta Class Voidripper—a hollowed out, peanut-shaped asteroid fashioned in the back end of god-knew-when. Stephen had been in her family for generations, although no one had yet managed to come up with an explanation for his peculiar, yet soothing speech matrix. One thing was for sure though—the Percept's intellect was as awesome as it was all-encompassing.

"Lost the what?" Chira asked, yawning.

The dice.

Stephen's tones were somewhat subdued. Chira had experienced nothing like this before. If anything, he was usually rather arrogant. "Dice? What are you on about?" she said with the first hint of real fear in her ninety or so years.

They'd been performing a rare, if not straightforward rip to the Outer Gaiacologies, importing her nifty cargo of news items from the Core. Everyone thought these colonies were isolationist, but Chira had heard otherwise. Political change had brought about a hunger for what she had to offer—fifty years of data—gossip, politics, sports and science. This was going to be the big one, or so she hoped. She patched again into the ship's navicon. They were in a solar system of some kind, but if she were honest, the space between planets looked pretty much the same as space between stars.

"Where are we?"

You want to know our present location? Stephen drawled.

"Yes."

Silence

He never hesitated, especially when there was a good chance

of making her look small and human. "Stephen?"

Yes, Chira?

"What the hell is going on?"

I'm afraid this system isn't on any chart. We appear to be temporarily… lost.

"Lost!" Chira climbed out of void bunk and stood up, stretching her stiff limbs and rubbing at the dead skin that covered most of her naked body. She entered the shower, the water coming on automatically. "But you can get us back? Yeah?"

…I do not know.

Stephen's words chilled her to the bone, even under the hot, soapy spray. A Percept never admitted to not knowing something. Or if one ever had done so, she hadn't heard about it. "You've got to be kidding me."

No Chira, I am not kidding you. In response to this situation, I have started a level one navscan of the background starscape.

As dwarfed as she was by the sheer intelligence of the Percept, Chira knew enough about space travel—relativity and the motions of stellar bodies—to realise just what an immense task that was. He'd need to examine millions upon millions of stars, calculate their gravity and movement and then try to extrapolate their position in relation to them. Not impossible, but such a task would challenge even Stephen's vast intellect. She left the shower and dried herself off, wincing as her back muscles complained at the sudden effort. "But you must have some idea of our general position, yeah? If we rip from one place to another, doesn't that mean that we could have arrived somewhere in between?"

Ripping the void is not simply moving from A to B via C, Chira, as you well know.

"So we are really lost then?"

Temporarily. With time, I am sure to locate our position.

Chira slipped into a fresh jumpsuit and groaned. *Temporary* to an ancient entity such as *The Stephen Hawking* could be anything upwards of ten or twenty years. The ship was a hollowed-out, five-mile long asteroid, but with the amount of space taken by the Percept and the void engines, there was little room left for comfortable living. She could survive inside Stephen indefinitely, but the prospect wasn't appealing.

She took a deep breath. "Okay, so there's no spin to put on it."

Chira walked over to her console and sat down. The amitylink allowed her to see what Stephen saw, but she always preferred to be hands on whenever possible.

"First things first… what's this system like?"

Typical Type G binary system. Eight planets. A high number of asteroids between the orbits but nothing remarkable—oh.

"What is it?"

The fourth planet.

Chira saw the anomaly straight away. A blue-green planet, mostly veiled in thick cloud and similar in size to Ancient Earth. There was no information about the surface; Stephen's scans couldn't penetrate the upper atmosphere, not from this distance. This was just passing information—something resembling a tiny asteroship hung in geosynchronous orbit. Another voidripper like the *Stephen Hawking*. "Any life?"

I cannot tell. It is possible that others have ended up here in the same way we did. I will rip closer.

"What? You sure that's a good idea after what happened last time?"

My systems are all in the green, Chira.

She'd learnt a long time ago that it was pointless to argue with a Percept. "I'll brave the void if you will," she said, biting her lip.

Using the immense power of his advanced intellect, flashing threads of living gossamer materialised in front of Stephen's roughly hewn mass. Deep inside the asteroship, protected from the rigors of space by metres of rock and simple lead, Chira sat back in her chair and watched both though the amitylink and her screens. The gauzy clouds wafted forward, generating an array of iridescent hues, casting rainbow shadows over Stephen's pocked and scorched surface, catching glints from his many navigation arrays and manoeuvring boosters. A flash of white light and the fabric of space unravelled like a snag in black silk. A gentle thrust was all it took to slip into the void. One moment of screaming, terrible emptiness later, they emerged above the ugly, clouded planet.

Stephen launched his whiskers—a hundred tiny naviprobes. As soon as the amitylink was activated, he patched the navigation information to Chira and manoeuvred into a geosynchronous orbit above the cloudy planet.

"Wow!"

Yes. The gutted remains of an asteroship. It is ten times my own mass. A people transporter. They must have salvaged what they could and left it in orbit.

A heavy-looking platform hung in the upper atmosphere. Chira zeroed in on the object and was astounded. It sat above what appeared to be a thin tape that stretched down, disappearing into the atmosphere.

"What is that?"

It is what was once known as a Space Elevator.

"Huh? Why would the crew want to build an elevator *down* to a planet?"

I think, Chira, that the purpose of this device was to get off world, or to escape its gravity in the most economical fashion. There is evidence that they were attempting to convert the damaged voidship into an Asterohab.

"Off the planet? You mean they were living down there?"

Maybe they didn't have a choice.

"Even so, everyone knows planets are death traps."

That is true, began Stephen. *Planets are unstable platforms that are essential in the creation of life and quite terrible at sustaining it. Volcanic activity, meteorite impact, aberrant weather systems, tectonic events and a host of other uncontrollable environmental characteristics simply mean that planets are uninhabitable to any species interested in advancement.*

Stephen's all-knowing tone had returned. He was back in his element and enjoying it. Chira said nothing, although she knew her history—as did everyone in the Core.

Early humans soon realised that to survive, they had to leave the highly unstable cradle of life and move into more controllable environments. Why spend hundreds of thousands of years changing planetary atmospheres, attempting to influence vast weather systems, biospheres and the minutiae of life when any miscalculation could spell disaster?

No. Humans found that once they had solved the relatively simpler environmental control systems of the Asterohabs and Gaiacologies, such places offered a more secure and welcoming habitation.

That is why this construction, this elevator was created—the stranded crew and passengers were probably trying to escape some similar planetary disaster.

"I've never seen anything like it."

These elevators are an obsolete invention now. But the time of the ancients, they were one of the most important innovations in human history. Without them, the human race would have died out thousands of years ago.

"I never knew."

You must understand that your view of planets is relatively recent, Chira. To ancient humanity, planetary dwelling was entirely natural. Humans left Ancient Earth only after a constant series of natural disasters—even so, the creation of the first space elevator was greeted with derision and anger, as it was seen in those unenlightened times as an indulgent waste of resources.

The window of life was closing rapidly. Within two-hundred and fifty years of its construction, an ice age had overtaken most of the planet, quickened by the ancient's dirty technologies. Humans only survived because the elevators provided an economic way into space that led to mining and the first Asterohabs. Lifelines to a world that was rapidly changing for the worse.

The further movement towards the Gaiacologies was a slow one, but without the space elevator, humankind as we know it would be extinct.

"Do you think the crew is still alive down there… on the planet?"

Unlikely, the surface is too cold for human life. I am detecting dead forests and stagnant seas. There is a high density of metallic particles in the atmosphere, cadmium and other heavy metals interfering with my scans. Also dust, sulphur dioxide, aerosols and CO_2*. Still, we cannot rule out the possibility that someone survived.*

"It seems unlikely, but—"

Wait! I am detecting another Percept on the planet's surface. Its amitylink is incapacitated in some way.

"Can… can the Percept help us?"

What I have scanned of the elevator tells me it is functional. The primitive fusion generator driving the car is still working.

Chira sat up, worried. "It is?"

The tether is made of an advanced nano-graphene, akin to spider silk but much stronger—light, durable and flexible, and seems in good repair. Automatic systems protect it from the destructive atmosphere and micrometeorites. I sense that it has been unused for a long time. You must go to it, Chira. If the Percept is still fully alive and functional, it might hold valuable information to assist us.

"Go to the planet's surface?" Chira ran a finger through her long, red hair, twisting and pulling at it. A nervous habit from childhood. "Are you insane?"

Insanity is a human trait, Chira. You must conquer your fear and descend.

She knew better than to argue with Stephen. In all their dealings, he had never put her in harm's way. Their situation was serious. She simply had no choice. She stood up, still feeling stiff, and walked awkwardly the short way to the hatch, donning her survival skin and nervously closed the inner door behind her. She fastened her helmet and waited.

Stephen manoeuvred his massive bulk to within a few metres of the platform and Chira popped the hatch. Spacewalking was second nature, yet as she glided out, floating high above the doomed planet, she felt a sudden stab of fear. A short distance away, hung the enormous upper-platform of the improvised space elevator. In one corner sat a battered and abandoned Wing, its cargo doors open to space.

A simple transport for use between the elevator and the asteroship, said Stephen into her mind, his emotionless metallic tones somehow soothing and full of encouragement.

The survival skin propelled her forward. Chira crossed the few metres of empty space between *The Stephen Hawking* and the platform and came to rest by a primitive airlock.

You must go in.

Chira recycled the airlock and entered the small, dark elevator control room that was nothing more than a staging post. Her suit told her the room contained no atmospheric pressure and she saw the reason why at once. A large, square, double hatchway lay open in the floor, below which hung the immense chamber of the elevator car, itself open to space.

"Their hatch failed," she said, peering down into the car. Something touched her arm and Chira shrieked into her helmet.

What is it, Chira?

"Nothing," she replied a few moments later, regaining her composure. "Human remains." A desiccated body floated next her. A woman of indiscriminate age. Her face frozen into a silent, perpetual scream. A further two bodies, strapped into chairs, sat behind her in the gloom.

The control is hand operated, Stephen said to her dispassionately. *Automatic systems control the descent.*

Chira pushed the corpse aside and dropped through the hatch. Thankfully, the car was empty—she didn't fancy any more nasty surprises. She noticed a paper-thin plastic-looking tape, perhaps only three to four feet in width, upon on either side of which hung the enormous car. "It doesn't look very safe."

The nano-technology is well tested, Chira. If it did not work, you and I would not be here today. The design is robust, allowing for both ascent and descent.

Chira found the operating mechanism and hooked herself to the car. With a lurch, the elevator began to descend. At first, Chira could not detect any motion, but looking up, she saw Stephen and the elevator platform diminishing rapidly.

Down she plummeted, twin rollers clamped onto the magically thin strip. She had no sense of speed yet the planet grew below her feet. The car entered impenetrable clouds and the tape seemed to twist below her.

"It's out of control."

Relax, you are safe.

Time passed interminably. Finally, the car broke through the cloud cover and Chira looked down upon a darkened and depressing coastline. The sun, dimmed by black clouds, was high in the sky. The sound from the spinning rollers increased dramatically. The tape held firm. Air brakes fired and Chira's weight increased dramatically. Her tightfitting survival suit hardened around her. Protecting her from the impact that, when it came, was softer than she'd expected. The whine of the elevator was replaced with sounds of lapping water and a noisy wind. The elevator rested upon a small platform floating in the sea not far from a coastline. A beach of black sand stretched to the horizon, sitting in front of a dead, greyed forest covered in ash.

Chira steadied herself against the motion of the platform and the gravity that was slightly higher than she was used to and marvelled at the sky. Instead of the land curling up and over her head, like the asterohab she was brought up in—like all the other human habitats—the land simply disappeared into the distance. She had little time to marvel—a priority amitylinked alert pulsed red in her mind. She patched in automatically.

... Who is that? The voice was weak.

"I'm Chira of *the Stephen Hawking.*"

I am the Maria Goeppert-Mayer. *Is this a rescue?*

"No, we are lost. Can you help us? Or we you?"

Amber lights flashed in Chira's mind as she received a weak data-spike from the stricken Percept.

Search in the part of the sky I have sent you, The Maria Goeppert-Mayer said. *The rip that threw us here was catastrophic. I could only manage to limp into orbit before my parts were scavenged. We settled here on the fourth planet. It was quite an Eden. We called it Kattowitz—but it was no home.*

"Tell me, Maria, is there anyone alive down here?"

We could have made it if not for the last asteroid impact. It wiped out everything. We were so very close to escape. But now my job is done. It is my turn to join my comrades.

"Don't say that!"

I was old before the accident that nearly destroyed me, Chira. I am a sentinel only, a shadow of myself placed here to pass on what I know. I waited many decades, using that time wisely to scan the heavens for an escape route. I conserved my energy as best I could, saving my last reserves for this moment. For this conversation. Find your way back home and warn others of this place… my time has come. Goodbye Chira…

"Maria!" Chira shouted but there was no response. With tears streaming down her face, she activated the elevator and began the lonely ascent.

A long time later, she was back within the warm safety of *The Stephen Hawking.*

"Will you die one day also," she asked, not wanting to hear his answer.

Nothing lasts forever, Chira. Not people, planets, stars nor Percepts.

"I know, but—"

I could have spent decades searching the star-field. With the information from The Maria Goeppert-Mayer, *I have found a way home. The target stars are younger and are in the wrong position, relatively speaking of course. Extrapolation from their distance and relative motions, leads me to believe that I can navigate the void back to the Core.*

"I hope so. It's a shame that time ran out for Maria and the others."

Yes, planets are unforgiving places. They had a window for escape. Opportunity does not last forever. Now we must go.

In front of *The Stephen Hawking*, the fabric of space began to tear.

Chira lay back down in her bunk and patched a command to her central nervous system, which began to shut down for the extended void rip.

"Good luck Steve," she said through the amitylink.

The Stephen Hawking, who had ripped the void for over four and a half centuries, paused.

Luck is not in my vocabulary, he said, as Chira slipped gently into hyposleep.

You forget that I can understand the universe. That makes me something very special.

TEN:

THE JUPITER STONE

THE HOT, glorious summer of 1976. I was six, going on seven years old. The boys and tomboys that formed the Hillside Gang spent those long scorching months playing in Dooleys Wood, a dark and magical place full of weird intimidating birch and oak that crested a large steep hill behind the village.

Its outskirts were green and bright—great for adventures and games—but its dense centre was quiet, foreboding, damp and murky even on the hottest days. We made a den in a large, hollowed out oak about halfway into the trees and, from there, we'd plan forays into the wood's gloomy recesses and bring back treasures and prizes—pinecones and toadstools, dead birds and frog spawn.

The Hillside Gang was a mixture of village locals and those summering at *The Large House*.

Playing rough and roaming free was a new thing for me. Constantly shunted between relatives, I spent most of my time alone, usually cooped up and ignored. I suppose, by modern standards, I was mistreated. Maybe so, but as a result, I found the gang both exhilarating and terrifying.

At first, it was difficult for them to accept me. I was so very different from the others. Awkward, shy—not like now, where I've learned to fit in with ease, to hide that side of myself far away. But over time, I overcame my inhibitions and I became one of the gang.

The gang's leader was an older boy called George. He had a rough flock of unkempt, sun-bleached hair, smooth skin and no fear. He'd climb the tallest trees, put his hand in dark holes and catch snakes and birds and other animals.

I looked up to him—all of us did.

I so wanted to be his special friend and had many fantasies about us adventuring together. But despite all my efforts, George didn't like me. Whenever I suggested the gang do something, he'd always say "No way!" and treat me like I was stupid. And just like that, the others would join in with his mockery.

It hurt me, made me feel funny inside, *in that bad way.*

One day we were playing at war in the woods, the girls letting themselves be kidnapped and tied up, the boys running around with sticks like Tommy-Guns. George brought his famous marbles to show to us. He had a fantastic collection of balls and steelies of all sizes. His favourite marble was small, white and heavy with a red, swirly spot upon it. A real beauty.

His *Jupiter Stone.*

It fascinated me, and I knew then that I must have his marble for myself.

Not wanting to lose his precious bag of marbles, he hid them in the den while we played. And when there was the opportunity, I snuck back and found them. I took out the Jupiter Stone and carefully replaced the bag.

We played hard all day. When we got back to the den, I'd totally forgotten what I'd done. George went straight to his marble sack and poured out the glassy balls. It was as if he knew the Jupiter Stone was missing. He went berserk. I'd not seen him act like this before. He lined us all up and made us empty out our pockets.

My stomach hurt, twisted into a hard knot and my head was dizzy. Trembling, I took the Jupiter Stone out of my pocket and held it out.

"You!" he said with venom. "I knew it!"

He snatched it off me, knocked me over, put his rough hands around my throat and squeezed. As soon as I started to gasp for breath, he seemed to realise what he was doing. He stood up, angrily pocketed his marble and disappeared into the woods. The others were too upset with what happened to say anything. I was ashamed and ran home crying.

I spent the next few days moping around on my own, planning revenges, crying to myself, getting angry and shouting. Until, one morning, George came unexpectedly around to see me.

I was shocked and suspicious, but all he wanted was to see if I was all right, and to invite me back up to the den.

I was wary but, kids being kids, within a few days everything was back to normal again. It appeared that everyone had forgotten the Jupiter Stone incident. George didn't mention it, and inexplicably, his attitude towards me totally changed—maybe it was guilt, but he was suddenly very friendly.

I spent more and more time with him. I found out that he'd a bad home life, that his father regularly beat him. He started to confide in me and would often come and call and we'd go down the den together. I was so pleased with his friendship that I sometimes forgot how much I hated him.

No matter how good things were, that dreadful knot in my stomach wouldn't go away. I found it hard not to think about the Jupiter Stone incident and kept replaying the event over and over in my mind—and whenever George laughed, or smiled, or winked—all I saw was the face that tried to strangle me, that humiliated me.

Soon it became hard to sleep and eat. I'd lie awake in bed trembling. Sweaty and angry. Like I was ill. I tried everything to make it go away but the feeling only became worse. Deep down I knew what I must do. I'd known the moment George put his dirty hands around my neck.

George had to die.

I wasn't new to killing, although I'd pretended to myself that what had happened in London that cold spring morning a few years ago had been an accident. But I knew that wasn't the case. What I did was deliberate. And… *I enjoyed it.*

Why did I kill? Because some snotty older girl had treated me like an inferior in front of my then friends. Was horrible to me. Made fun of me and made me cry. And I felt that dreadful knot in my stomach for the first time.

The knot only went away when she fell under the truck. I say 'fell' but I stood on her foot and pushed her under the wheels of a passing lorry. She was dragged by her hair into its wheel arch where she was crushed, her smashed legs poking out at odd angles, her dead eyes staring. Everyone thought it a dreadful accident.

That night, in bed, I was truly happy.

And after what George had done to me, I knew I needed to kill again. The only problem? I was older and more aware of the risks involved. I decided to wait until the opportunity came along… as I knew it would do.

George came back one day after a game of hide and seek in Dooley's Wood telling everyone he'd seen a giant bear. He called it *Big Grizzly*.

I can remember believing him, although even at that young age, I knew that there were no bears in England. But it was fun to think of a danger that could attack us at any time.

George talked about that bear from dawn to dusk and the Hillside Gang would occasionally hunt it. George was a simple boy, although I didn't recognize that then. Maybe if I'd known, things would've gone better for him.

I was out the back of the Big House one morning when I found an old paper with a story about a group of boys who suffocated when a tunnel they were building fell in on them. An awful, terrifying horror… And that's when I had my idea for the perfect revenge.

"We should try and capture Big Grizzly," I told George the next morning. "We can build a secret bear pit and cover it with canes and leaves like in the Saturday morning movies."

George's eyes lit up at this idea. "We could leave some food around the pit and, when Big Grizzly comes along, he'll fall in and be trapped!" he'd said, putting his arm around my shoulders and giving me a long hug. He was always touching and hugging me.

It only made me hate him more.

We arranged to get up early the next morning to go off into the woods and secretly dig our pit. I was very particular that it should be deep with steep sides… *so that Big Grizzly couldn't climb out*.

We found a spade and a fork in the gardens of the Big House and off we went, deep into the forest. George started talking about his bear again. How Big Grizzly would howl when it fell in our hidden pit.

The forest soil was clay-like and heavy. My plan would only work if we could dig down deep enough. I talked that grizzly up so hard, that George was nearly wetting himself. It was difficult to contain my own glee at the secret knowledge that the fool was digging his grave.

Nevertheless, the job didn't go well. There were roots and stones, and occasional pitfalls and I'd not yet worked out how to bury him once it was finished.

We decided to come back the next day and made our way back home, passing some of the others from the gang who were intrigued by our muddy clothing. It was great to keep the secret with George—we both lied about what we had been doing, the others knowing we were up to something and not telling.

The knot in my stomach almost went away, but George took out the Jupiter Stone saying I could keep it as soon as we captured Big Grizzly. Just the sight of the marble made me seethe and his fate was sealed.

I woke up at dawn the next day and raced to the pit, loosening the soil around its edge and digging the soil away to create an overhang.

That's when I knew how I'd do it.

George arrived a bit out of sorts, his enthusiasm on the wane. I'd seen that happen with him many times. But he climbed into the pit and began to dig. I said that he should enlarge the overhang, so that if Big Grizzly was looking like he might escape, we could topple the bank onto him.

George liked this idea and set about the task with gusto. I asked him to let me look at the Jupiter Stone and, smiling, he passed it up to me.

Everything was now in place. My heart was racing—it was getting close to doing it… *to killing George.*

"What's that?" I said, my voice shaking with excitement.

"Uh?" George answered.

"Can't you hear it?"

"Hear what?"

"Something coming this way. Big. Heavy footsteps."

"I can't hear anything. What're you doing up there?" George was starting to lose patience with the pit idea.

"Put your ear to the ground, George," I said excitedly. "See if you can hear him."

George stood there for a few seconds looking at me. Then he smiled that cheeky smile of his and, laughing, put down his spade to lay outstretched in the hole.

"Can you hear it?" I laughed, thumping my fork into the soil at the top of the pit, and levering it with all my body weight.

"Yeah, I can hear it! He's come for us," he laughed, "It must be Big Grizz—"

The entire side of the pit collapsed, burying George in over six feet of thick, heavy earth. I fell into the hole also, shocked by the force of the collapse. Soil rained around me. I kept my head and, even though I was partially buried, I managed to clamber free. I finally escaped and stood a safe distance away.

"George?"

No reply.

I used the fork to cover my footsteps and waited. I stood there for many hours, only moving to have the occasional pee.

I'd done it. Killed him. The sense of relief and of personal power was intoxicating.

I planned my story meticulously. I'd go back home and say nothing. When the grown-ups realised George was missing, I'd direct them to the pit, saying that George wanted to make it deeper and that I'd come home.

And that's what happened. I was there as they dug him out, hiding in the dark of the heavy trees. I had to stop myself from laughing as they lifted him free, his flock of blonde hair muddied, his face black and lifeless.

I felt reborn.

It was difficult to pretend to be sad, but I had to. I even cried, but no one guessed they were tears of pure joy.

I waited until after his funeral and when no one was around, I peed on his grave.

You're wondering what happened to the Jupiter Stone?

It's in my pocket now.

I will carry it with me.

Always.

ELEVEN:

BLESSED ARE THE CHILDREN

THE COLD grey velvet carpet of the lunar surface stretches out before me. A terrifying vista that I've both longed and dreaded to see for most of my cloistered life. I stand, with the other children, lined up before the Holy-Dawn, waiting for Godmother Earth to rise from below the dusty horizon.

Waiting to be blessed.

Behind us, Gaia-Afra Makada and Sooth-Sister Marni, pray in silent witness—their once calming she-presence chilling me to the marrow. Despite my suit's in-built regulators, I shiver. The blackness of empty space is sucking the heat out of my body and with it, my resolve.

I must be strong!

I look up into the lunar sky—my sky—for the very first time. Elegant gossamer-winged constructions swing above me like the enormous dragonflies hovering in the hydroponics gardens deep below in the caverns of my once-entombed life. The light reflected from these orbital platforms illuminates the surface, driving the enormous solar generators that throb dull and hard beneath my powder-covered feet.

Of course, I have seen the surface many times, on screens within the Basilica, from the many sky-eyes that look down upon us from *Up-On-High.* But to see the cold expanse of Black Heaven with my own eyes… it panics and dizzies me.

The other children seem equally shaken—awestruck by the sheer enormity of all this open space. I wonder if they too are frightened, afraid that they will be sucked upwards and forever lost, shrouded by eternal darkness, our mission a failure before it even begins.

For we are the Revered, the Chosen.

It shows in our thin etiolated bodies that tower over the elders whose own sin made them squat and rounded, barely free of the heavy Earth they come from. That was the price they paid for being so close to Godmother Earth. The weight of their guilt drags them down, pulling them back to that same Earth, their lives foreshortened, punished.

I cannot help but feel superiority over them.

They are surely not what the Godmother intended at the dawn of Creation. Instead, our saintly brood, of which I count myself a member, moves with natural God-given grace whilst the elders blunder down the tunnels and caverns like the most foolish children.

No wonder Godmother Earth sent them all away, spitting them out of Her angry atmosphere like so much sour fruit. Occasionally, when the melancholia overtakes them, the elders tell us about blue skies, of the hot glory of sunlight against naked skin and of great pools of water stretching as far as the eye can see—a lost Eden teeming with life.

It is beyond all imagination.

We know nothing other than the caverns and the tunnels, and the deep all-consuming darkness of meditation and sleep. I have often wondered if the elder's teary-eyed stories could be truly possible. Yet over time, I have come to learn that these things were indeed the gift of Godmother Earth to Her then-children, a gift that after many warnings was taken away.

Of course, the elders foresaw this, although they were powerless to effect change. Pilloried, abused and discriminated against, they fought against the raging storm of self-destruction that filled minds with so much hate and lust. For the elders came from a generation of dissenters—gallant, heroic and principled men and women who resisted the evils of progress-at-any-cost. At first they tried reason but all too soon, as the Holy Scriptures tell us, they had no choice but to convert themselves into a Just-Army fighting on the side of Divine Righteousness.

Outlawed across continents, their beliefs and practices made illegal, the True Believers relentlessly toiled against the smokes and evils that sought to destroy All-Creation. This was a dark time for the Holy.

Many suffered and died.

We do not forget them—the elders take us daily to the sacred Chancery to recite stories from the Book of Sagas. It contains their sacrifices and punishments, vile persecution and contemptible murder.

It is, for all to see, a dreadful potted history of the slow sink of blessed civilisation into darkness and dissolution. We children do not often leave the Chancery dry-eyed.

When the end inevitably came, the elders showed no pride, no self-righteous anger. No. Their warnings had been given and ignored. And so, equipped and ready, they, the only survivors, fled to safety and a new life here on Godmother Earth's barren sister.

A story long told.

I stare ahead, broken from my reveries by Godmother Earth's aura brushing the crater rim—panic constrains my chest, the sound of my own breathing suddenly loud and heavy in my ears.

"Please do not let my sinful dread taint my soul!" I pray in the silence of my suit.

As ever, there is no answer. Godmother Earth does not speak—*She* does not need words. It is by Her actions that we recognize Her needs and moods. I try to be content that *She* understands my fear and will make my journey an easy one. For I and the other children will soon be starting the passage we have spent our lives preparing for.

We are to be the redemption of humanity—its only chance for survival.

And as the oldest—fifteen years as measured by Godmother Earth herself—I must not show any weakness in front of them.

Not now!

The children look up to me, they trust me. The doubts and fears they whispered to me at night are my own fears. And the gentle reassurance I gave in return, soothed my own sinful worries…

"What will it be like?"

"Beautiful. A place like no other."

"How long will it take?"

"A long journey, as are all journeys to Salvation."

"Why are there no more children?"

"The elders cannot make them. The gift was taken away by Godmother Earth."

"I'm scared, what if I fail?"

"We are all scared, yet we are the Chosen. We cannot fail."

"The elders… there is something in their eyes, it frightens me."

"Do not be troubled, little one. It is hope, plain and simple. That is all. They have prayed hard and long for us. They are as excited and as hopeful as we. We are their last chance for survival and would go with us if they could."

"I don't want to go, I can't!"

"We must. We are the only hope. We are the last hope of humankind."

"Where are we going?"

"We leave this place to go to a better place."

And we, amongst everyone in the community, cannot let the sin of fear contaminate us.

With slow grace, Gaia-Afra Makada, the eldest and most wise of our elder community, lifts her arms above her head to stand before us, proudly erect, her serene black face seen clearly through the golden mask of her visor. She is the tallest of the elders, yet even she is bowed before we children of the Moon.

A hiss in my ears and she speaks:

O Godmother, who willest to us that no man or woman is above the natural laws of mountain and skies and the Holy Birth-Seas of Thy once Encircling and life-giving Waters, we give Thee our obeisance on this most cherished day of days.

We, the off-spring of Thy warm earth-bound womb, whom You alone have spared—come to Thee this day with love, devotion, prudence and patience—and all things whatsoever Ye shall ask in Your name, shall be done unto Thou.

We, who are devoted to Thy labour, who
work conscientiously, putting the call of
duty above our many sins, to work with
thankfulness and joy, considering it simple
respect to employ and develop, by means
of the final assistance received from Thee,
our sacred Godmother, convey to Thee our
greatest of all gifts to gladly place within
Thy Holy trust.

O Righteous Spring from whence All
Creation splashed forth, we bring to
Thee that which is most precious to our
hearts: we bring to Thee our future.
Our Children. Spawned here by Thy
omniscient will upon Thy barren sister.

O Mother of truth, who art blessed
forever and ever, we say unto Thee with
clean heart: Thou have redeemed us. And
so, with humiliation and tribute, we
request Thee: Bless these timid souls who
travel today; bless those that are to do Thy
work, for truly Blessed art those who bear
no shame…

Blessed art the Children!

Amen.

Gaia-Afra Makada's voice tried to soothe, yet the exultation behind the words was plain to hear.

Beside me, the children tremble as do I.

With a quick motion, we sink to our knees, holding our heads up high to stare intently at the Watch-Stone, a perfectly carved circle sitting on the lunar horizon through which we will view the

Godmother Earth. My heart thuds frantically in my chest and, praying silently to myself, I began the Litany.

To learn about the Godmother, to spend days and nights in fasting meditation, to devote my whole being to this one certain icon of humanity, to come to this moment where I will look upon Godmother Earth with my own eyes and have my journey blessed by Her physical presence evokes emotions difficult to describe.

A dark curve breaks the ring of the Watch-Stone, and at this sign, Gaia-Afra Makada joins Sooth-Sister Marni to stand in reverent silence behind us.

How difficult our going would be for her I did not know. Of all the elders I am leaving behind, Marni is the one I will miss the most. Smooth-skinned, strict, but also gentle, she was mother to all the children, embodying the unremitting faith of our lives more than any other.

I love her.

It was she who taught me the Litanies, she who sat with my worries and fears, she who nursed me through the illnesses and tribulations of childhood.

Marni taught me of my destiny, preparing me for today, for this moment. She talked regularly about Pure Evil, and from her tongue it became a palpable thing—a force that could strangle you in your sleep.

Through her, I learnt the many evils of my body and the base malevolency of my flesh. The rituals and ceremonies to keep myself clean and free of sin were many and complex and it seemed that with every new day came a new sacrament.

But I knew that I must be regularly purged, regardless of my sores and blisters.

Marni's love was plain for all to see, and despite the sin of pride, I believe I am special to her—*more than the other children.*

Gaia-Afra Makada touches my shoulder and I bow my head. It is time, and I, as the oldest and the most pure, will take the first step of our long journey.

I will lead the children and all humankind to Salvation.

There have been so many false religions, so much wasted life and thought, so much effort and mind put into hate, persecution, intolerance and bogus gods. And yet, out of all the many belief systems, not one human has ever properly laid their eyes upon their divinity.

The gods of humanity exist only inside the minds of men, in their singular desires and follies, in their holier-than-thou self-righteousness and in their greed and in their hate.

But if they had looked with unfettered eyes they would have seen the Godmother in the dirt under their fingernails, would have felt Her breath as a breeze upon the air and Her grumbling in the shift and groan of the land under their feet—and they would have truly understood the nature of life and death, of simple atonement and surrender.

They would have known Her sadness and regret and feared Her terrible retribution.

Humans have always suffered such folly, living and dying in the name of whatever gods were popular at any given time, and wasted themselves and innocents in the pursuit of false belief.

It is their curse and their downfall.

Only we, the Children of the Moon, can truly understand. We can see through the thousands of years of religious confusion and horror. We now know there is only one way to atone for the sins of humankind. And that knowledge is love, is peace and true comprehension.

Most of all, it is hope.

Godmother Earth will listen to the last gasp of Her offspring for we are truly *the blessed.*

I raise my head with pride, all fear exorcised—ready for the final passage.

I feel only a rough tug upon my throat as the cold blade purifies me for my journey. Gasping for air already sucked out of my lungs, I fall amongst a cloud of reddened dust and steam, praying that the Godmother will hear my heartfelt plea.

Please, oh Earth Mother, oh Gaia, make my journey, my faith, my sacrifice, worthwhile…

TWELVE:

GAIA WITCHERY

The human race had come a long way since its fledgling steps back on the hatching ground called Earth.

They had conquered the cosmos, populating the surrounding moons, planets, star systems, and galaxies. Their potent genetics exploited every niche on land and underwater, in the skies and in space—in an infinite variety of form, size and purpose.

So far had humankind come that most had forgotten their humble beginnings of millennia ago. Yet some remembered, kept hold of their heritage, and celebrated its original shape…

Lost, quiet, and alone amid the blackness of space, the vast cigar-shaped habitat Gaia-Prime carried on just as she had done for the last few thousand years: silent, majestic and self-contained.

The hab orbited a gas giant in the Lalande system, gliding among the planet's waves of energy like a colossal whale feeding upon a bloom of plankton. A living museum to a long-lost past.

But Gaia-Prime was failing. An evil had found her. Some remnant of humanity, so twisted and changed as to be almost unrecognisable, had infected the corporeal organism of the hab and sought her destruction.

And the curators had long since forgotten their purpose…

i. The Fetishmen

A CRIMSON blur in the increasing dusk. The Yore and his fetishmen hurried up the jungle path, pulling their worn, red velvet robes together against a growing squall, their naked feet rhythmically padding, their chanting matching the cadence of their footsteps. A low, frightening dirge. Their stern faces were daubed with the bright blue of punishment, and each held a hefty wooden club engraved with the harsh angular runes of beating.

The Yore clutched at his emblem of office, a tightly wound whip, stained leathery brown by his own dried blood. A frantic wind, like an invisible giant hand, whipped at the sickly vegetation—angry, searching, and desperate. Even here, where the once verdant rainforest grew untamed, the Dying showed itself in etiolated branches and yellowed leaves.

The Yore knew the island was failing and the community relied on him and his fetishmen to beat away all evil.

How else will we survive? he thought. *Only penance can save us now. The Dying is the result of debauchery, corruption and... witchery.*

They emerged from the jungle onto a high jutting promontory—a rock knife thrust into a stark, worrying ocean. A hundred feet below, the sea surged, pebbles and shells chattering between each crash. Boundless waters surrounded them for league upon league. A churning, foam-covered blockade. Above, in the massive vaulted curve of the over-sky, lightning silently bloomed from behind distant black clouds, followed long seconds later by the sharp crack of thunder. The air was heavy with the threat of yet another storm.

The Yore glared at the vast curve of the world, warping above and around to form a huge, perfect cylinder. It encircled the dark, elongated night-sun to meet itself high overhead.

A crowd waited for them, their flaming torches dancing in the coarse wind. An emaciated, ill-looking group of people standing in a clearing hacked from the jungle many years ago. They surrounded a prone, overweight young woman crouched on her knees. Arms outstretched, her wrists tightly encircled by rope tied to twin posts.

The Yore walked forward on stalk-like legs, the crowd parting to reveal the prisoner dressed in nothing more than a loose crushed-leather smock.

The island starves, and she puts on weight… the girl is evil.

He regarded her with the solemnity of his office, yet he found it difficult to control the swell of his emotions.

I was bewitched by Tamina, as were many others, but I am no longer under her spell. She should not have dallied with me… I am The Yore!

Tamina raised her head, long blonde-streaked hair hiding her eyes, a fleshy smile appearing upon a beguiling face. Tears spilled in recognition.

"Yore help Tam?" Her voice was childlike, quizzical. "Tell the nasty men to let Tam go. It hurts!"

The Yore raised his whip. "I have helped you enough, Tamina." With a practiced flick of his wrist, the wicked leather lash uncurled.

Tamina pulled against the ropes and sagged. "Why Yore angry?"

A gust of wind whipped at her hair, revealing twin emerald eyes shining in the growing dark.

"Take your witch's gaze off me."

"But, Yor—"

"No one has eyes like yours, Tamina. They shine and entice with an unnatural hue—an obvious sign of evil, and these are evil days. The sun is erratic, the air colder, and our crops fail whilst sinister shapes wing increasingly in the skies. Curse these storms. We are besieged by them."

Black clouds, heavy and threatening, formed overhead. Lightning forked between sea and sky while the growing wind whipped mercilessly. Drops of rain landed heavily on the dense vegetation surrounding their feet. A thudding, forbidding drumbeat.

The crowd jeered and shouted, their expressions twisted into ugly masks of hatred.

The Yore's head twitched from side to side, teeth gritted in determination, his long silver hair whipped by the breeze.

They want blood... and I will give it to them.

"I cannot protect you any longer, Tamina. You reek of sin. Evil lives in your bones, thrives within your wanton flesh and... shines from those witch's eyes."

"They all hate Tam," she replied. "No one talks to Tam anymore. Except when Tam goes to them. At night. Tam gets so lonely when Yore is not with her."

"Loneliness? Is that what you call it?"

"Tam misses *her* so much."

"Your sister?" asked Yore, a sarcastic edge to his voice.

"She went away such a long time ago. My poor, poor Prim."

The Yore shook his head. "You had no sister, no siblings. This 'Prim' of yours is pure make-believe and mischief."

"Don't say that!" Tamina screamed. "Don't ever say that."

"The words you weave are evil. They twist and confuse."

A crack like a rifle shot—and the whip bit into Tamina. A red, bleeding welt raised itself upon her naked shoulder. Another crack, and another. Tamina shuddered, her mouth hanging open in spasms of silent pain. When sound did reach her lips, it escaped as a keening whine.

"We have all indulged you and your errant ways for too long, Tamina. Even I, the Yore, was seduced by your childlike manner—trapped, as it is, in the body of a temptress. I was deluded enough to think you cared for me, that I could change you. *I was a fool.* You not only betrayed me, but the whole island."

The Yore's red robes swayed in the rising breeze. The others huddled together for warmth, their faces eager, relishing the punishment to come.

"You are a witch and not as dim-witted as you pretend. It is *you* causing us so much woe. And..." The chief fetishman's eyes closed. "...witches must be punished." He made a gesture with his free hand.

The fetishmen approached, their clubs raised, their blue-painted faces agleam with righteousness.

"Beat her and blind her," the Yore barked. "Then… *throw her into the sea.*"

The drumming thud of raindrops increased to a raging torrent.

"No," Tamina yelped, finally able to speak, her pain turning her whines into a strangulated shout. "Tam love Yore!"

The Yore bowed his head, unable to watch and, in that moment, the storm smashed into the promontory. Twin bolts of lightning, exploding in flashes of white, searing light, shattered trees on the edge of the clearing. A powerful gust of wind lifted the fetishmen aloft, then hurled them to the ground. Others blew over as if they were made of paper not flesh and bone.

Tamina flung herself face down into the dense grass, her hands over her ears.

The Yore stared into the squall, straining through the pounding rain that sought to dash out his astounded eyes. An enormous bird plummeted toward him, like one of the many finches that visited his garden in the good times, but hundreds of times larger. Blue and red banded feathers and a bright yellow beak open as if in pain. The creature was pursued by odd leathery shapes of wet leather, gyrating within the storm. Twisting and turning as if they were a part of the swirls and eddies themselves. Shrieking like death given voice.

The enormous bird flung out a desperate wing and dived. Huge clawed feet sweeping past Yore's face to grab at the ropes that ensnared Tamina, grappling at them and pulling her aloft. Another shriek and the monsters of leather attacked, entangling the bird's wings. The ropes slipped through the creature's claws and Tamina fell back to the ground. One more crack of blinding lightning—and the bird and its pursuers were gone. Lost to the storm.

The islanders, fetishmen included, ran in panic toward the path away from the promontory. Tamina stumbled to her feet, freeing herself of the loose ropes.

She will not escape.

The Yore flicked his whip. The lash found Tamina's heel, tripping her. He ran over, grabbing her around the waist and dragging her to the precipice, ignoring the rain, the wind, and the deafening squall.

"No, Yore! No! Tam love you!" she screamed scrabbling at him.

"You do not know the meaning of the word!" Yore kicked her hard, twisted her around and threw her, screaming, into the abyss.

A long fall and then a thump. Tamina landed upon a thick, grass-covered treacherous ledge, arms and legs flailing over the drop. A powerful downdraft pinned her to the overhang long enough for her to scramble backwards. She hunched, perching dangerously, frightened, sobbing and drenched. Rain streamed in an ever-increasing deluge, battering the weak ferns and grasses clinging desperately to the exposed rock shelf, whilst angry seas crashed and thundered somewhere below.

"Yore!" she shouted against the squall. "Yore! Help Tam!"

Hours passed as she huddled there. Sodden. Too frightened to move. Her muscles cramping. Hoping above hope for a rescue that never came. A steady torrent brought mud to her ledge, seeking to dislodge her, the wind jamming her backward—the elements fighting one another for the prize of her soul. She hung on, her despairing tears hidden by the squall, her stricken face occasionally illuminated by flashes of lightning.

As dawn approached—the elongated sun flickering and glowing into slow, reddened life—Tamina became aware of a rumble beneath her feet. The sound grew in volume, drowning out the wind and the constant battering of rain. Terrifying her. With a deafening crack, her ledge and half the cliff side dropped in one huge landslip.

Tamina fell too. An unwilling passenger riding upon the falling promontory. The slide stopped with a jolt, rock and debris tumbling around her. The ledge cracking and crumbling.

A flash of lightning revealed a small cavern opened by the

collapse. Tamina scuttled into the sudden cave, throwing herself through the entrance.

…And that was how Tamina met the Lady in the Glass.

ii. Rider on the Storm

BAREFOOT, WEARING her single smock of mud-stained leather, her wrists red from the where the ropes had tied her, Tamina puttered along the ravaged shoreline—a high curved storm beach thrown up by last night's tempest. She had walked a long way from the collapsed promontory to arrive here. An isolated bay—her special place.

Gentle waves lapped with a soothing slap, their anger having abated. Thin lizards, the size of child's hands, danced between the flotsam and jetsam searching for shrimp pools and stranded fish, while bright red crabs hunted and scuttled.

The sun stretched into the distance, its glow sickly, diminished. Tam didn't remember much about her childhood, but she knew the light was different now. Colder. A pale reflection of itself and she shivered as she searched for her shack. But the weak huddle of branches and palm leaves was no more—lost to the squall. The seas had come far inland, destroying everything before them.

But Tamina was safe here, where the giant stone heads towered, staring silently toward the deep blue of never-ending ocean. These massive statues had easily resisted the ravaging squall. The islanders would not come to this place—frightened of the 'faces that stole souls,' as they called them.

Long, long faces, long, long ears, and silly big chins. Always frowning. Tam's only friends.

A stab of grief and she stumbled.

Yore tried to kill Tam.

Tears welled in her flashing eyes of deepest green.

Why?

"No one likes Tam!" she shouted, sitting down to rest against her favourite stone head. Smaller than the others, its features crude in comparison. Tamina often felt he was shunned by the other faces.

They never smiled.

"Tam will stay here with you. You can take care of Tam now."

He was just rock. She understood that. *But if he come alive? Tam would make the nasty islanders pay.* More tears filled her eyes. *Tam only wanted to love them. To be with them. To be with Yore.*

She lay back and let her weary gaze travel towards the Above Land. It was beyond her imagination, so immense, so beautiful. Tantalizing and unreachable. A vast continent straddled the sun, visible on either side of its hazy glare, covered in delicate clouds like tufts of white hair. The air swirled magically—an inviting gossamer veil flowing across coastlines and vast inner lands.

She wondered, as she had often done, about who lived there—of what kind of life those people led and, if they too, on days like these, would stare at her small island high above in the vast ocean on the roof of their sky. Her eyes followed the long sun stretching into the distance, finally ending in a mountain of white facing its faraway twin across the immeasurable expanse of the world. The white crept forward with every passing year. Yore told her it was *ice.* It scared him. Although she couldn't understand why.

Everything scares Yore. Even Tam's green eyes. Silly man. Silly stupid Yore!

Tamina was born with eyes of the purest evil—or so everyone told her. No amount of punishment from her long-dead mother could hide their hue.

Maybe Tam is a witch? Maybe Tam summons storms, speaks to winds, and tells the sun to shine less brightly?

Unbidden and serene, the calming face of the Lady came into her mind. Tamina had spent the latter part of the storm gazing into her weirdly serene face, bathed in an unnatural light that shone from the cave walls. A pale-skinned beauty, her hair a riot of shiny red curls, trapped within a block of smoothed glass.

Who was she? Where she come from?

Her expression was peculiar—beautiful and engaging, yet somehow disturbing. Her eyes were twin black holes and staring into them had made her shiver. Even so, Tamina could have stayed there forever, gazing into the face of the Lady in the Glass. It was hunger that finally forced her out of hiding and she'd gingerly made her way through what remained of the collapsed promontory to examine the storm-changed landscape. The sea had retreated to a distant splash of white foam, exposing a long beach. The avalanche of rock sat high above that. Elevated somehow. Slabs of broken stone tossed aside by some leviathan of the deep.

An annoyed chirrup brought Tamina back to her senses. She sat up from the pebble beach to find the lizards regarding her with their peculiar earnest faces upon heads that twitched impatiently.

"All right," she said in resignation, jumping to her feet and wincing at where Yore's whip had branded her. "Tam hungry too. Let's see what Tam finds."

After weaving a crude basket from a windblown palm leaf, she trotted back to the shoreline and waded ankle-deep into the sea. Behind her, more lizards gathered, dancing across the pebbles in anticipation, their chirruping rising to a crescendo.

Silly things.

Within seconds, silvery minnows began leaping into Tamina's basket. "So tinsy-tiny. Nice for breakf—".

A shout in the distance and Tamina froze. Angry voices carried on a cool breeze. Tamina ran back to the nearest stone head, throwing her basket aside, the host of hungry lizards hissing and fighting one another for the still-twitching fish.

More voices, coming from the far end of her secluded beach. Tamina spied a cluster of islanders, some of them dressed in the gaudy colours of the fetishmen, heading to the other side of the island.

Where they going? They searching for Tam? Why they always angry?

Used to sneaking and creeping around—mostly at night between the huts and houses of the islanders—Tamina stole carefully through the limp jungle ravaged by both the colder climate and last night's awful storm.

She crossed the spine of the island and dropped down to the opposite shoreline, making her way to a stinking pile of trunks close to where the islanders stood. Her breath caught in her throat. Lying on the storm-beach was a most magnificent creature. White and red feathers, wet and tangled, pepper-flecked wings and enormous claws.

A giant, beautiful bird!

Even with its muscular, red and blue-banded neck obviously broken, she could envisage how proud and strong this creature must have been in life.

The islanders crowded together, full of fear, the same tired talk of the Dying, storm-summoning and demons. And, as usual, they blamed Tamina.

What has Tam done to them? The poor bird is no demon.

A familiar commanding voice. "Silence!"

Yore.

The fetishman approached the stricken bird, his naked foot pushing hither and thither.

"An abomination," he said finally. "A fell beast brought to us on the back of an evil squall. The witch's familiar. I will send men to build a pyre." He turned to leave.

"Is that all?" cried an old woman.

"What else would you have me do? Tamina is gone. We all witnessed what she did on the promontory. The lightning. The strange winds and… *this monster.* If I had not seen those evil things with my own eyes…" The Yore's head twitched from side to side. Grizzled jaws clamped together, trying to contain his fury, his silver hair blowing in the breeze. "Even I, the Yore, once thought Tamina was innocent. A sign of witchery if there ever was one!"

"We have only your word that she perished," the old woman continued unabashed, naked hatred showing in the bulge of her jowls.

"The witch is gone," he snapped, his rage forming sharp jutting words. "I threw her into the sea myself. She is no more, or do you doubt the words of the Yore? …Her evil is drowned and broken, like this foul beast. We must instead concentrate our efforts on rescuing crops and finding our animals. Now, let us leave this vile place."

A thin man, weaselly and unshaven, with a pitted brown face and the sly stare of a hungry dog, stepped forward. "Can we be sure? You have seen how she is with animals. How they flock to her. If she can control beasts like this… who knows what she is capable of?"

Tamina shrunk in her hiding place. She had never tried to disguise her affinity with beasts and birds… and couldn't have if she'd wanted to. All creatures had a presence that glowed within her mind. Vicious dogs slunk at her side, feral cats jumped to her lap, and wild animals were drawn to her. The islanders had noticed this talent. It made them hate her even more.

"She is dead, I tell you," spat the Yore, although doubt crossed his face. "She must be."

"How do we know that you are not still bewitched?" the man continued, glancing around for support. "This beast tried to save her and paid with its life."

"She has ways about her," said another. "Ways to fool and cheat. We cannot be sure she is dead until we find her corpse."

The chief fetishman raised his ceremonial whip and waited for silence. "I am the Yore. You will listen to me and obey. Tamina is gone. As I said, I threw her into the sea myself. She can no longer disturb our crops… *nor our beds.*"

The man, who had been vociferous just moments ago, stared at the ground.

"We need no more distractions at this time. We must pull together until the sun becomes our friend and ally once again. But be assured. My fetishmen will not rest until we find her remains."

Voices rose around him.

"Enough! I will send men to come and destroy this thing shortly."

The islanders begrudgingly left the beach, yet the Yore lingered.

Tamina experienced an overwhelming desire to reveal herself to him, to put her arms around Yore's troubled shoulders. But she remembered the lash of his whip, and how he'd tried to kill her and did nothing. Soon, he strode angrily away.

She emerged when all was clear and examined the dead bird. Its sheer size astounded her. Huge enough for a man to ride—feathers as long as she was tall. The yellow beak lay open, the mammoth head tilted to one side.

Tamina stroked at the bushy, down-like hair surrounding the creature's bull neck and was surprised to find something hard among the feathers—a leather strap leading to a saddle hidden under the ruined wings.

"Oh my, oh my!" she whispered.

The bird had a rider. And Yore know this. He must know. Yore is so very, very clever. But where is the rider? Is he alive?

Tamina was startled by a barely audible groan. A whimper nearly lost in the clatter of the pebble-filled waves and the constant sea breeze. She strained her ears. Long moments passed, long enough to make her think she had imagined the sound… *and there it was again*. Less of a whimper, more of a gasp.

She ran into the ravaged jungle, green eyes searching the mostly destroyed foliage. With a shriek, she spied a man covered in mud entangled within a morass of leaves and seaweed, and sought to free him.

The rider! It must be! But if Yore finds him… No! Tam won't let that happen!

iii. Prim

THE CAVE of the Lady was at the far end of the island. Despite Yore telling her she was slow-witted, Tamina was not dim enough to take the unconscious man to her special beach of ancient and foreboding heads where her shack used to stand.

No one knows about the Cave of the Lady. Tam's new special place.

The rider was small in stature and surprisingly light, but he was still a difficult burden. After a long, hard struggle, Tamina finally laid the mud-covered man on the floor of the recently revealed cave. He was muscular with well-proportioned limbs, wearing a body-hugging leather suit.

Water seeped from the walls to form a trickling stream. Wetting her hands, Tamina washed the man down, revealing a shock of blond hair and a kind, smooth, sun-browned feminine face.

The leather suit was beautiful, mimicking the beautiful colours of the bird now lying dead on the beach. She turned the man over, cleaning quickly, revealing a long, black-stained gash from shoulder to hip. As if a giant claw had raked the flesh. The wound smelled odd and frightened her.

Tam must get him out of dirty clothes.

When she unstrapped the rider from his suit, it became apparent that this was no man at all.

A handsome woman! Oh my…

Her underweaves were crafted from a sheer material Tamina had never seen before. Soft and yielding to her fingertips. A cloudy green stone, flat like sea-smoothed shale, hung around her neck on an ornately woven leather band. The medallion was engraved with a majestic flying bird, similar to the one she'd seen dead on the beach. But she had little time for contemplation. Tamina cleaned the rider's wound as best she could, then took the fine leather suit outside to dry in the sun.

Other than the gash, the rider was unharmed. The injury was only skin-deep, yet…

She dying. Tam feels it. Something cold and frozen. Ice… like Yore said.

Death always showed itself to Tamina. A shadow. Darkening as the moment approached. And every animal and everybody had the same shade within them.

The rider will soon pass. Tam don't want her to die! She won't let it happen.

And despite the warnings of her past, Tamina's mind flashed

back to her childhood, to the dreadful time when everything changed. She had lived on an isolated farm with her mother and a small herd of gutes—hardy goat-like animals used for milk and meat. Tamina helped her mother to raise them, nurturing and loving them. When one of her favourites fell ill, she saw the shadow of death growing in the young animal and decided… *to make it go away*. Prim had come to her then. Her older sister who told her so many delightful things.

Wonderful, beautiful Prim.

Mother would laugh at Tamina, saying: *"If I'd had another brat like you, I'd know. Do not speak to me about your imaginary sister again."*

But Prim was real. The most real person she'd ever known.

Tamina recalled a face framed by raven-black hair, calm, pale-blue, haunting eyes, and a sense of security and peace. And Tamina would never forget their last conversation.

You Must Not Try And Save The Gute, Tam, Prim had said. *It Is Too Dangerous For You.*

"I want to try."

No, Tam. You Must Let The Creature Go.

"I don't want to, Prim, I don't. It's not fair!"

The Gute Is A Lowly Creature. You Do Not Understand What You Are Doing.

"We can't just let things die. I don't want to!"

All Things End Little One. Even I Will Not Live Forever.

"No!"

It Is Too Risky. You Cannot Do This.

"You can't stop me…"

Tamina possessed no knowledge of what she did to the wretched creature. She retained a lingering memory of the tiny animal sucking greedily at her life force… of Prim screaming at her to stop… and then blackness.

She awoke some weeks later from a coma. It took her months to learn to talk again, to walk. Her mother, angry and confused, had killed the now-healed gute and made Tamina promise to never, ever repeat what she had done.

It changed Tam forever…

Prim did not return, and Tamina had been haunted by a dreadful loneliness ever since.

Tam misses her so…

The rider, moaning in the quiet of the Lady's cave, broke her reverie. Tamina clamped her jaws together and placed both hands upon the wound, pressing down, pressing hard and, suddenly, she was filled with a desperate resolve.

Tam killed death before—why not again? And if Tam die? This girl can live in Tam's place. I hate it here.

Where Tamina's fingers touched the gash, there came an answering coldness and an urgent, intense need.

Tamina's strength trickled into the stricken woman, who murmured, gaining vigour from her touch. A dark thing lived inside the rider. Tamina visualised it as a writhing serpent that crawled through the rider's blood and heart, through her arteries and veins. A horrible, awful thing that tried to evade her probing. But she chased it down. Burning it away. She could almost hear it scream in her mind.

Tamina sat on a massive reservoir of vitality, but too quickly, it seemed, that reservoir was becoming depleted, the trickle of her energy turning into a steady flow that became a deluge. The rider was like the gute from all those years ago, sucking greedily at her and not wanting to let go.

Tam won't let the bad thing happen again… Tam won't.

Reaching out with her mind, she found the glow of other life—birds, insects, small animals and fish in the sea—and, desperate for survival, Tamina drank from them all. Made suddenly strong, she pushed the grasping woman away and fell into quick unconsciousness.

iv. Of Olden and Mavenry

A **SCREAM** woke Tamina.

"The Olden," explained the rider a few minutes later,

after she'd regained her composure. "Waking here, I was startled, afraid—and to find her face staring at me…"

The Rider had at first spoken in the strangest of tongues, but after a few sentences from Tamina, she recognized her language, although the stranger spoke it with a beguiling accent.

Tamina rubbed her temples, still dazed. "The Lady in the Glass is an *Olden?"* Her voice sounded crass by comparison to the stranger. Loud, ungainly. But it was more than just the difference in their voices—Tamina's senses were amplified. The colours in the gloomy cave seemed more vibrant and alive. And… *she felt different.* Less befuddled. Like a cloying fog had been lifted from her mind.

The rider's smooth brow creased, her eyebrows furrowing. "You have not been told of the Olden who keep vigil over the Gyre. The ancients from time long past?"

"The Gyre?" said Tamina, as if from a dream.

"Tis the name of our world and everything within, including you, and I, and… the Olden."

"I know nothing of the greater world, or of the Gyre," Tamina replied, the words coming easily to her lips, aware of many more words that she now had access to. Thousands of them. Tamina was somehow changed. Her healing had not only saved the rider, it had also remade who she was. She had also been healed.

"I have lived all my life here," Tamina continued. "On this windswept lonely island surrounded by the ever-present ocean. As for the Lady in the Glass—the Olden as you call her—this cavern did not reveal itself until the storm. Compared to you, I must seem naïve and unworldly."

"I think no such thing… What is your name?"

"Tamina," she whispered, fearing to make eye contact, hiding in the shadows and behind her long heavy locks. "And your name? Who are you that rides on the back of the wind?"

"I'm called Ennea. I once flew Mighty Almeera." Her eyes were open, but Ennea's attention was fixed upon an inner world.

"Your flying beast?"

Ennea stared past Tamina in an unfocused way—a frown

playing upon the smooth skin of her face. "Yes, that was his name before last night, before…" She put her head into her hands.

Tamina held Ennea close while the grief-stricken woman sobbed helplessly. When her wracking finally ceased, Tamina said, "You were injured. A long, black, wicked gash full of poison. It took all my strength to heal you. I have never seen anything like it."

"You *healed* such a wound?" Ennea replied, glancing up into Tamina's face.

Tamina turned away, convinced the magnificent woman had glimpsed the hue of her witchery.

"Look at me, Tamina. Show me your eyes."

"I'm ashamed of them."

"Ashamed?"

Ennea pushed aside Tamina's lank locks to reveal twin green eyes sparkling in the calming light of the Cave of the Lady.

"By the Gods… you are Maven!"

"What?"

Ennea flung herself to the cavern's floor, covering her head in supplication, trembling.

"*A Maven?* I don't understand."

"You have the mark of the Chosen—the gift of the Gyre."

"It is no gift," Tamina spat. "All here hate and despise me. I am nothing but an outcast. The other islanders want to kill me… Please get up."

Ennea gradually unfurled, a mixture of fear and respect mingling uneasily upon her even features. "You have not heard about the war? Of the evil that has engulfed the Gyre? Of Dark Mavenry and *who you are?*"

Tamina gave the woman a hard shake of her head. "No. But I have become aware of the shorter days, the colder weather, and of something loathsome on the breeze. The islanders are also aware of these changes. They call it the *Dying* and blame me for their misfortune. They are a foolish, superstitious people."

"That is your Mavenry," Ennea said with reverence. "Mavenry reveals things to you, gives you control and influence. Your needs and hungers are enlarged. Your desires intensified. But Mavens are rare and their powers dwindling. Our world is in danger, Tamina Maven, yet *She* is still trying to talk to us, to aid us against a dreadful threat."

"The world speaks to you?"

Ennea shook her head. "The Gyre hasn't spoken for over a millennium. The Mavens can feel Her presence. Her urging. Although it is becoming harder to discern Her needs. In truth, we are losing the war."

Did the Gyre speak to me as a child? As Prim? Could it be possible?

"Tell me, Ennea, how did you get here to this lost, lonely island?"

Ennea reacted as if this were a command, not a polite request, and stood to quick attention, proudly clasping the cloudy-green stone worn upon her breast and closing her eyes.

"I was on routine patrol, a few days out of my home city of Pillar," she began. "We had recently received reports of a Valkreed attack in one of the outer kingdoms—and there is nothing like a squadron of flying birds to put fear and panic to rest.

"The patrol passed with little incident. We were heading back to our makeshift eyrie after a long satisfying day on the wing, when Mighty Almeera gave a warning shriek. Alerted, we broke formation to take our fighting stations, but the skies were clear.

"I had never seen him so agitated.

"Before I could do anything to calm him, a powerful shaft of air hit Almeera from below, lofting us both high into the sky, leaving the patrol and the other riders behind. So strong was the wind that Mighty Almeera furled his wings for fear the updraft might wrench them from his body and we were pushed into the black space between the topmost clouds and the faraway night-sun."

Ennea stood rock still, only her lips gave away any emotion—trembling at the passing words.

"The sun that sits at the centre of our world appears like a long tube from the ground," she continued. "And as we approached, flung helplessly upwards at dreadful speed, it revealed itself as a thing of colossal dimensions and stunning beauty. A cylinder of purest jet. I was frightened for our lives, wondering what evil assailed us, yet I was unable to hide my awe at such a vision. We drew ever closer—and that is when I noticed the sun's blackened exterior was discoloured. Thousands and thousands of shadowy creatures festooned its cool surface, feeding there. Eating. I have seen many evils, Tamina, but these things… I possess no words to describe them." Ennea fell into silence as she relived the experience.

"Please continue," Tamina urged and, under this command, the curious bird-rider took a deep breath and finished her story.

"These creatures were similar to the Valkreed, but larger. *So much larger*. And where they converged? The sun was consumed, eroded. Whatever force pushed us forward wanted me to see this, Tamina. I'm sure of it."

Ennea opened her eyes, and Tamina glimpsed the horror she had seen lurking within them.

"An unimaginable time later, we left the sun, plummeting toward what is the roof of my world and entered the angry clouds and beating rain of a terrible squall. Mighty Almeera found his wings again, struggling within buffeting winds. Below us, overwhelmed by a swirling tempest, was the expanse we call the 'Never-Ending Ocean'. I have often stared at your sea, Tamina, at the storms silently passing across the vast breadth of my sky. To experience such a squall in person was a different matter. But there was another danger. *The Valkreed*."

"What is this Valkreed you speak of?"

Ennea took a deep breath. "Tis a creature unlike anything found in nature. All claws, teeth, and cowardice."

"That is no description."

"I'm sorry, Tamina Maven. They defy all words. I have seen them many times, but my eyes refuse to focus upon them. The Valkreed blur, they whirl, winking in and out of existence—their presence accompanied by unspeakable dread. They do not normally attack our birds, for the Valkreed are cowardly creatures, but this time, something forced them to pursue us. Some greater evil.

"I commanded Mighty Almeera to fight, but… he ignored my order. He flew ever downward, the Valkreed at his tail. And then I spotted… *an isle amidst an angry sea.* Your island, Tamina.

"Mighty Almeera flew with desperate purpose. Down he went, down he plummeted toward this small dot amid raging seas. I caught a glimpse of a promontory jutting into the crashing waters like a knife and a ring of flaming torches. Then the Valkreed attacked, raking Almeera with their dreadful claws, dashing him from the sky. His final act was to save me, twisting himself around as we crashed into rocks. The last sound that reached my ears was the snap of Mighty Almeera's neck… before I succumbed to my wounds."

Ennea's hand leapt from her amulet to grasp forlornly at the air.

"Mighty Almeera was my true friend. He would not sacrifice himself unnecessarily. The Gyre needed us to come here, Tamina, I'm sure of it. Now tell me, for I must understand… *how did you mend my wound?* The Valkreed are diseased. No power in Mavenry can heal an injury from such a beast. I should be dead."

Tamina's eyes widened in horror as the full memory of her healing came flooding back. *The animals!*

"What is it?" Ennea asked with confusion and fear.

Tamina ran to the cave entrance and climbed down to the beach. Hundreds of fish floated on the surface of the sea. Birds lay sprawled in twisted ruin. Instead of the steady chirrup of insects and the buzzing of flies, the air was quiet. "No!" she squealed, in full realization of the destruction her healing had wrought.

Ennea's lips parted to shout in warning, but it was too late. Bodies flew at the two women from all sides. Fetishmen!

Tamina tried to struggle, aware of Ennea putting up a good fight. Then a lump of wood caught a glancing blow across Tamina's temple and she pitched forward into blackness.

v. Gaia Prime

A **DISTANT** clamouring. Voices raised in anger. The banging of sticks, shouting and singing. Rage filled the air like a living thing. Tamina slowly came to, her head throbbing with the steady thud of her heart.

Earnest words in an exotic accent close to her ear: “You should have slept, my friend.”

“Ennea?” As the name passed Tamina’s lips, the foul vista of all those accusing animal corpses flooded across her mind. “No. *I killed them…*”

“It was not your fault, Tamina. Tis the darkness of these loathsome days. Mavery is become twisted beyond all recognition. Forget those dead lower souls, for we have more serious concerns. Your islanders are indeed a superstitious people.”

Tamina’s wrists and ankles burned. With sick confusion, she realized she could not move. She pushed open her eyes and tried to focus. As if this were a sign, the braying voices, dreadful singing, and shouting reached a deafening crescendo.

Sunlight threatened to sear the back of her skull. Her eyesight adjusted and the scene before her came into slow focus. She was tied, back to back, with Ennea, perched above a vast pile of bales, sticks, and a mass of feathers. The islanders—a mob of angry men, women and children—surrounded them on all sides. Through them strode the fetishmen, their faces painted with the blue of punishment, their ceremonial beating clubs snapping together as they chanted, sang and danced.

Where is the Yore? He can’t let something so barbaric, so awful happen. I have seen his gentle side…

Tamina’s thoughts stumbled to a stop. The Yore stood outside the raucous crowd. Silent, still, and holding a single flaming torch. His shock of silver hair and his grizzled beard were gone. Shaved. His whole head painted blue. The red flesh of his unblinking eyes glared into her.

Oh, Yore…

He strode forward on purposeful legs, the crowd parting, its voices suddenly stilled, and thrust the torch deep into the pyre like a dagger into her breast.

Tamina pitied him then. For his fear, for his many weaknesses, for the stupidity that had pushed him to this.

The fire took hold immediately, the flames leaping upward in the steady sea wind.

"We die," said Ennea. "Tis fitting that at my end, I should be with my Almeera..." A shaft of fire licked at her feet. She screamed, desperately twisting away from the growing conflagration.

"Dance the dance of death, witch!" a voice shouted. The other islanders joined in while the fetishmen took up their dirge.

Tamina's eyes once again found the Yore. Bowed as if by a dreadful weight, his back to the scene, to the burning. And standing next to him? A black-haired woman...

Prim? My sister? Now grown?

The woman smiled at her, and in that moment, everything made sense.

"Goodbye, my friend," said Ennea.

"No, we are safe," said Tamina, as if from far away.

A black cloud formed above the growing pyre. Lightning cracked into the headland and rain crashed down in a quick, gushing downpour. The forceful torrent extinguishing the flames.

"How did you do that?" Ennea gasped.

"I didn't."

"I don't understand."

"That voice you mentioned earlier, the voice that has been lost for so long..."

"Yes?"

"Gaia-Prime has been found again."

The air exploded above them with a deafening pop. Fifty enormous birds, their necks banded with reds, blues, and golds, their yellow beaks screeching in surprise, appeared as if from nowhere and descended toward the beach in a flurry of beating wings and nervous squawks. Each had a rider dressed in the same leathers as Ennea. The islanders scattered. The fetishmen dropped their clubs and ran.

A tall rider with a shock of blond hair dismounted. His eyes fell upon Ennea and climbed the sodden pyre to cut their bonds.

Tamina and Ennea clambered down and stood shakily before the amassed riders, the sun suddenly glowing with renewed vigour, bathing the beach in the warming rays Tamina had only known as a child.

"You did this?" Ennea asked, oblivious to the raw, red skin of her feet. "You summoned my brethren across the width of the world?"

Tamina gave the barest shake of her head. "Not I, although it was my wish to meet your friends." She smiled, and the green hue of her eyes shone bright for all to see.

"Behold, Tamina Maven!" shouted Ennea, bowing her head.

The riders and their birds also bowed in supplication.

A delicate hand fell upon Tamina's shoulder. She turned to gaze straight into the pale-blue haunting eyes of Prim. *Wonderful, beautiful Prim.*

We Have A Lot To Do, Little One, Prim said from behind a tired smile.

"I know. I am ready."

Gaia-Prime talked for long seconds and, with a mixture of rapture and growing determination, Tamina Maven learned what must be done.

EPILOGUE

STORMIN' AND BANGIN'

I OPEN my eyes and find that I am lyin' in the Blackash. Wet and sticky. But I don't mind because the Lady at last tolded me a story of hope. Of beautiful birds and strange, scary peoples. Of a girl who becomes somethin' special, somethin' wonderful. Somethin' amazin'.

And *She* was in the story.

The Lady in the Glass.

I'm so happy that she goes on from here to go live amongst the stars. Maybe she was there at *The Beginning* and will be there at the *Very End?* I hope so, but I don't knows about such fings.

Somewhere in the distance I hear the sky bangin'. It's always like this after I've spoken to the Lady. The sky becomes angry and loud. Black clouds comin' from nowhere. Flashin' and thumpin'. I gets up on creaky legs, hearin' the river, whooshin' and a splashin'. The angry waters, the fast waters are a comin'!

The Lady starts whisperin' and hissin'. Warnin' me. Tellin' me to run, run, run.

I says a goodbye and gives her my thanks—and runs. Runnin' through the risin', scary waters. Reachin' the bank and climin' up and up and up. Until I sit high above the angry river. My heart beatin' in my chest. Thumpin' and strummelin'. Hurtin'. Breathin' hard.

And then the rains come, thrashin' down. Angry rains. I have never seen such rains. Hurtin' my head and arms.

The river bubbles and roils. Risin' up to where I'm sitting, makin' me climb higher and higher, scarin' me. Cuttin' big chunks out of the land. The river eatin' the land. Chewin' at it. Bitin' and chompin'. I sit. Waitin' and watchin'. Worried for the Lady. Scared for her.

Finally, the angry stops. The waters slowin', the flashin' and the thunderin' goes away. And the sun shines again, makin' everythin' smell funny.

As the sun grows in the sky, the shimmerin' waters drain away. And sudden-like, I feel like Tamina, the girl in the Lady's story who also lived through an angry storm... I wish I had her big friendly heads as my friends. Scaring the angry peoples away.

Starin' with their big eyes. Haha. But I live heres alone. I'll always be alone. It's how I wants it. It's the best. Just me and the Lady.

The water slowly goes aways. Drainin'. And I waits. Lookin' for the Lady. Starin' at my special place. Hopin'. But she is gone. Taken by the storm. Taken by the angry waters.

The Lady in the Glass is no more.

Stolen.

Sobbin' and a cryin', I stumbles back to my shack and to *The Jesus* and *The Mary*. I stares at 'em. Screamin' and a shoutin' at 'em.

The Lady in the Glass is better than 'em. I knows it. That's why they hates her so much.

I rips 'em off the walls and throws 'em into the river.

Fucks 'em!

I lie on my bed, closing me eyes. Tired. I need to sleep, sleep, sleep… and tomorrow? Tomorrow, I leave here to follow the river. To go find her. I swears it. She has more stories to tell. And I will finds her and listen to her again. And if I dies?

So be it!

~END~

Reviews

If you loved reading *THE LADY IN THE GLASS* as much as I did writing it, can I ask you to please leave a review. This is not just for me and other readers, but for a whole host of other boring marketing reasons that I won't go into right now.

Suffice it so say, if you leave me a review on any of the e-book stores, or Goodreads or anywhere else, I'll be *well-chuffed,* and it will certainly increase the likelihood of further novels in this and other series.

Thanks in advance!

For information on further releases, please join my newsletter. Or you can pop over to my Mostly Readers Facebook Group. It's a friendly fun place to hang out.

And, of course, there is also my Twitter account @kjheritage with over 90K followers... *mostly*

Acknowledgements

Thanks for the red-pen, scribbling and 'telling me off in no uncertain terms' talents of my lovely editors:

Caroline Bean
Suzanne Buist
David Gatewood
Deanna Holmes
Blossom Young

Also by *K.J.Heritage*

Mystery and Crime

Dying Is Easy
The Peculiar Case of the Missing Mondrian

Science Fiction

Shattered Helix *(Vatic Book 1)*
Shattered Web *(Vatic Book 2)*
Blue Into The Rip
Quick-Kill & The Galactic Secret Service
The Lady In The Glass - 12 Tales Of Death & Dying

Sci-Fi Compilations

Once Upon A Time In Gravity City
Chronicle Worlds: Legacy Fleet
From The Indie Side

Fantasy

The Scowl

Non-Fiction

All About Copywriting: 55 Easy Edits To Improve Your Writing Forever
3000 Writing & Plot Prompts A-C: Supercharge Your Creativity & Improve Your Writing Forever!

Find all ebooks, paperbacks, hardbacks & audiobooks by *K.J.Heritage* at the following stores:

Amazon & Audible
Apple
KOBO
Barnes & Noble/Nook
Google
Smashwords & more

Links

Join K.J.Heritage's *Newsletter*

Get an inside track on all future releases, access to early reading copies (ARCs), sneak previews, and more.

http://kjheritage.com/join

Mastodon

@kjheritage@mastodon.social

Instagram

Photos of my wonderful Shollie rescue #RescueJack, piccies of my best mugs of tea, and various and shameless images of all my books. Oh and maybe yours truly on a good hair day!

https://www.instagram.com/k.j.heritage

Twitter:

90K+ followers

@kjheritage

TikTok

General silliness and book stuff. Search for #kjhtok

https://www.tiktok.com/@k.j.heritage

BookBub:

Not only can you check out the latest cool book deals, but you can also get an alert when I publish my next book

https://www.bookbub.com/authors/k-j-heritage

Goodreads:

Friend me here:

https://www.goodreads.com/kjheritage

K.J.Heritage Facebook Group: *Mostly Readers*

Fun chat and posts about reading… *mostly.*

https://www.facebook.com/groups/mostlyreaders

K.J.Heritage Facebook page

Follow/like and keep in touch with even more writery stuff!

https://www.facebook.com/theauthorkjheritage

Website:

http://kjheritage.com/

Email:

Want to get in touch? Well here's your chance

contact@kjheritage.com

About *K.J.Heritage*

"K.J.Heritage's uncanny sense of pacing and story puts him at the forefront of today's speculative fiction writers."
Samuel Peralta, Amazon bestselling author and creator of The Future Chronicles

K.J.Heritage writes books that he loves to read. From science fiction action and adventure mysteries to contemporary thrillers, comedy, and paranormal fantasy.

When he isn't penning third-person descriptions about himself, he's an international bestselling author writing the books he likes to read. From psychological thrillers and mystery sci-fi to crime, action & adventure, and epic fantasy. He should really stick to one genre, but he's not that kind of writer... or reader.

His first sci-fi short story, *Escaping The Cradle* was runner-up in the 2005 Clarke-Bradbury International Science Fiction Competition.

K.J.Heritage's short story *Churchill's Rock*, part of the 'Chronicle Worlds: Legacy Fleet' anthology, will be aboard the Astrobotic's Peregrine Lunar Lander set for launch on the United Launch Alliance's Vulcan Centaur rocket platform bound for the moon in June 2022.

He has also appeared in several anthologies with such self-publishing sci-fi luminaries as Hugh Howey, Michael Bunker and Samuel Peralta.

K.J.Heritage has done all the requisite 'writery' jobs such as driver's mate, factory gateman, barman, labourer, telesales operative, sales assistant, warehouseman, IT contractor, Student Union President, university IT helpdesk guy, British Rail signal software designer, premiership football website designer, gigging musician, company director, graphic designer, stand-up comedian, sound engineer, improv artist, magazine editor and web journo... Although he doesn't like to talk about it. *Mostly. Maybe a little bit.*

He was born in the UK in one of the more interesting previous centuries. Originally from Derbyshire, he now lives in the seaside town of Brighton. He is a tea drinker, avid Twitterer, and neurodiverse (ASD) human being.

For all media enquiries, event/booking information, signed copies, etc. please email: *contact@kjheritage.com*

All the very best,

K.J.Heritage

KJ Heritage has done all the requisite writers' jobs such as drivers mate, factory gateman, barman, labourer, telesales operative, sales assistant, warehouseman, IT contractor, Student Union President, university IT helpdesk guy, British Rail signal software designer, premiership football website designer, gigging musician, company director, graphic designer, stand-up comedian, sound engineer, improv artist, magazine editor and web journalist. Although he doesn't like to talk about it. Much. *Maybe a little bit.*

He was born in the UK in one of the more interesting previous centuries. Originally from Derbyshire, he now lives in the seaside town of Brighton. He is a tea drinker, avid Whovian, and neurodiverse (ASD) human being.

For all media enquiries, event/booking information, signed copies, etc. please email: *contact@kjheritage.com*

All the very best,

KJ Heritage

www.ingramcontent.com/pod-product-compliance
Lightning Source LLC
Chambersburg PA
CBHW010400310726
48979CB00017B/2792/J

* 9 7 8 1 9 1 5 9 2 7 0 9 5 *